ALEXANDRA BROWN

Ice Creams at CARRINGTON'S

HARPER

Harper
An imprint of HarperCollins*Publishers*
77–85 Fulham Palace Road,
Hammersmith, London W6 8JB

www.harpercollins.co.uk

A Paperback Original 2014
1

A catalogue record for this book
is available from the British Library

ISBN: 978-0-00-748827-8

Set in Birka by Palimpsest Book Production Limited,
Falkirk, Stirlingshire

Printed and bound in Great Britain by Clays Ltd, St Ives plc

Acknowledgements

Dear Reader

This is the fourth story in the Carrington's series and I really hope you enjoy it!

Firstly, a big, huge MASSIVE thank you to everyone who takes the time to chat to me via my website or on Twitter and Facebook; I couldn't do it without you. You mean the world to me. You spur me on and make it all worthwhile. Thank you so much xxx

Special thanks to my fantastic agent, Tim Bates, for putting up with me and for continuing to tell me what's normal. Many thanks also to my wonderful editor, Kate Bradley, for keeping me calm and making me laugh and for telling me I'm a drama queen, I wear it like a badge of honour. Many thanks to the amazing Harper team – Kimberley, Martha, Jaime and Liz – for their support, talent and expertise. And to Penny for perfect pruning.

Thanks as always to Kimberley Chambers, Miranda Dickinson, Elizabeth Haynes and Sasha Wagstaff – your generosity and friendship is so very much appreciated.

Lisa Hilton and Caroline Smailes – thank you my dear friends for always being there and for propping me up when I needed it most during the writing of this book!

A big thank you to Janine Quinn and Lisa Maguire for New York, Tim Smyth for Andorra, Liz Banner for Isabella's Italian, Louise Micu and Ann Faithfull for telling me about Winifred at Hanningtons and Naldo Morelli for all things ice cream, especially the truly scrumptious Morelli bubble gum flavour ice cream which I can highly recommend, it's very mm-mmm, as Georgie would say.

Jadzia Kopiel, for helping me to keep on keeping on – you're the wisest woman I know. My lovely, supportive father-in-law, Dr Brown, for helping with the medical details and for sharing the memories of his family's department store, Brown's in Newtonards. I hope I've captured a whiff of the memory. Yeeman To, for being a fantastic sales assistant and telling me all about it; your generosity is very much appreciated and any exaggerations or fabrications are totally down to me.

QT, for patiently waiting until I had finished this book before we could go to the cinema to see *Frozen*! You mean the whole world to me, sweetheart, you're the bravest, brightest, funniest little girl who makes all the right choices (well, most of the time ☺) and I love you with all my heart xoxoxo. Oh gawd, I'm going to cry, YET AGAIN. My lovely husband Paul, aka Cheeks, for holding the fort and never complaining – you are still my happy-ever-after.

And to my readers, book bloggers and dear friends online, you are all magnificent. I love chatting to you and feel honoured to be a part of your lives; it's truly awesome how the world is a far smaller place now that we have social media. So come join the party. I love seeing pictures of your handbags, kittens, puppies, Christmas trees, copies of my books, cupcakes (well, all of the cake, to be honest), chatting about *Revenge*, *Corrie*, *EastEnders*, *The Good Wife* and all of the films and TV shows that we love. I feel honoured when you get in touch to share personal things with me – to tell me how the Carrington's series has helped you through a difficult time in your life, or how you found the courage to come out after reading about Ciaran and Eddie; your own experience of bullying from hearing Georgie's story – your time in care as a child, too; or how you got that dream job, or that you just want to know what 'blimey' means. So find me on Twitter @alexbrownbooks, Facebook.com/alexandrabrownauthor or at www.alexandrabrown.co.uk and I promise to reply as quickly as I can.

Now, please sit back, relax and enjoy *Ice Creams at Carrington's*. I wrote this one for you!

Luck and love

Alex xxx

For my dad, Michael

1

It's Sunday morning in Mulberry-On-Sea and, if the dust-speckled shard of sunshine peeping through the chink in my bedroom curtains is anything to go by, then it's going to be one of those gloriously uplifting *start-of-summer* days. Bliss. And if this isn't reason enough to feel happy, then my boyfriend Tom, aka hottest man alive for sure, is leaning over the bed to kiss my cheek.

'Mm-mmm. Well, hellooooo, Mr Carrington.' I grin and run my fingers through his thick curly black hair, drawing in his delicious chocolatey scent and wishing he'd jump right back into bed, but he's already dressed – jeans and a soft grey T-shirt to nicely accentuate his velvety-brown eyes.

'I have to go,' he whispers, tracing a path to my ear with his lips.

'Stay a little longer. Go on . . . you know you want to,' I tease, doing my best to sound sultry and seductive.

'I'd love to, Georgie, I really would,' he says with a smile. 'But I want to squeeze in a swim and then sort out some stuff at home, plus I've got a ton of paperwork to plough through before the party later on.' Tom stands up to pat the leather laptop bag that's slung diagonally across his magnificently firm body.

'Hmm, well OK, if you must . . .' I stick my bottom lip out and pull a cross-eyed funny face to make him laugh.

'Pick you up at one o'clock, yes? And, seeing as we're making plans – can you keep the weekend after your birthday free?' He tilts his head to one side. I nod, and stretch out like a starfish.

'Oooh, why's that then?' *Mmm, curious, my birthday – the big* three zero *is coming up soon!* Friday 15 August, to be exact.

'If I tell you, then it won't be a surprise, will it?' Tom grins mischievously and my stomach does a somersault. God, he's gorgeous, and I hope this exquisite fluttery butterfly feeling never fades. I can see it now, I'll be an old woman and still infatuated with him. Oh yes, how wonderful would that be?

'Already missing you.' I blow a kiss as he goes to leave.

'Sweet Jesus, what are you *doing* to me, woman?' Tom turns back to the bed and gives me another kiss, his lips hot on mine, one hand in my hair, the other tantalisingly close to my knickers. I open my eyes to sneak a peek at his long dark lashes. I'll say it again . . . he is officially *gorgeous*! The perfect blend of chiselled features and delicious Mediterranean real tan – his mother is Italian. 'I just can't resist you. And when are you going to move in with me? All this coming and going just isn't practical any more.' He goes to tickle me just as Mr Cheeks, my supersoft black cat, leaps onto the bed and snuggles down beside me.

'Too slow.' Laughing, I roll away, almost squashing Mr Cheeks with my left thigh. 'Aw, poor thing, I'm so sorry.' I scoop the cat up and bury my face in his silky fur.

'Don't avoid the question. It really would make things easier; it doesn't seem sensible, all this toing and froing. And you can bring this little dude too, if you like.' Tom lifts Mr Cheeks from the bed and gives him a gentle hug before depositing him on the carpet, much to the cat's disgust. He likes nestling on the end of my bed; now he slinks off to the kitchen in a huff instead – I can always tell by the way his tail wafts extra-majestically, and I imagine he'd be giving us the finger right now, if he could . . .

'Soon. I promise.' Between you and me, I can't wait to live with Tom, but it needs to be about more than practicalities. I've been in that kind of relationship before – where I was the one who loved just that little bit more. Never again, this time around I'm not messing up. I'm determined to make it work and, if that means waiting longer to be sure, after we've chatted it all through, and I don't mean snatched minutes here and there before Tom has to go again, then so be it. I know he works hard, we both do, and he travels a lot too, meeting suppliers and sourcing new stock lines, so finding time to talk can be tricky, especially as when we are together we can't keep our hands off each other, but it'll be worth the wait, I'm convinced of it. Tom is my one, and I couldn't bear it if something went wrong between us, or if we somehow managed to ruin what we have right now, all because we rushed onto the next stage without planning it properly.

'Well I hope so. You know that I love you.' He smiles tenderly, pushing a stray tendril of hair away from my face.

'And I love you too.' I prop myself up on a pillow with one elbow.

'Most women would jump at the chance to move in with me!' He laughs at his own joke before deftly leaning back as I go to play-punch his arm.

'Cheeky! And I'm not most women, plus I actually

4

love my little shoebox flat,' I tease right back. 'It's cosy, and it's been my home for a very long time.' I scan the room. There's the triple wardrobe that fills the length of one wall – I remember lugging it all the way home on my own from Ikea, crammed into a rental van. It took me a whole weekend to put it together, but so worth it. And the glorious, enormous Art-Deco-style dressing table; I found it in the YMCA second-hand furniture shop and it only needed sanding down and repainting. I used a metallic bronze spray, which actually works really well now that the shine has faded, giving it a lovely shabby-chic look. It's authentic, and with the trillion necklaces looped over the sides of the triple mirror and all my lotions and potions lined up, I can just imagine its previous owner, a sophisticated flapper lady, titivating herself ahead of a tea dance, or something.

I like that – reminiscing, the feeling of nostalgia, a sense of history, and when I think about it, I've worked blooming hard to make this little shoebox flat my home for so long. First, stashing every penny I earned to buy it in the first place – a lot of extra hours and overtime was involved; and then keeping hold of it over the years – there were plenty of times when I very nearly couldn't pay the monthly mortgage. This flat holds many memories; it's my security, and that's important to me after spending time in foster care as a child. Mum died when I was thirteen – she had multiple sclerosis, which had worn her down so much that when she caught pneumonia she just couldn't fight any more. So I ended up in care because Dad was in prison for selling secrets from the trading floor of the bank where he worked to fund his gambling addiction, and my only other relative, Uncle Geoffrey, couldn't – or wouldn't – take me in. But that's all in the past now. I'm blissfully happy, financially secure and Dad and I are really close again – his new wife Nancy is lovely, so kind and warm and mumsy; I had missed having a mother figure in my life.

'Well, you don't have to sell it or anything, I know how much this place means to you. So just keep it – it can be your bolthole,' Tom suggests.

'Will I need one then?' I raise an eyebrow. My last boyfriend, Brett, cheated on me with a tall beautiful woman with super-big blonde hair and a sylph-like figure, in total contrast to my average height, curves and wispy brunette bob that requires a *lot* of maintenance (read: copious cans of Batiste Plumping Powder) to resemble anything near swingy. I tried hair extensions for a while, but had to have them removed after shaking my head a little too vigorously on a lunch date one time – a chunk above my left ear winged out and ended up floating in Tom's butternut squash soup. Eek!

'No. Only an idea . . . . it could be your girl pad,' Tom says casually.

'Did you really just say *girl pad*?' I stifle a snerk.

'Where are those knickers you used to wear? The ones with the cow motif all over them and the words "cheeky cow" emblazoned across the back?'

'Don't know.' I pull a pretend 'whatevs' face.

'Worn out, I bet.' He slides a hand under the duvet and pings my knicker elastic.

'Ha ha, you are so hilare! In fact, you crack me up *so much* I think I'm going to laugh myself into an actual hernia because you're just *too* funneee . . .' I shoo his hands away.

'Hmm, well, as much as I'm enjoying our banter, I really must go. Just think about it, please.' He kisses his left index finger and places it gently on my lips before turning to go.

'Will do. Promise,' I call after him.

'OK. Girl *paaaaad*,' he shouts as the front door closes.

And I really will think about it. But first I'm having half an hour in bed to luxuriate inside my new two hundred trillion, or whatever, thread count cotton sheets while I ponder on suitably sensible but witty one-liners to say to Tom's parents this afternoon – Isabella of the incredibly wealthy Italian Rossi dynasty, and Vaughan Carrington, direct descendent of Harry Carrington, the founder of Carrington's department store where I work as a personal stylist.

One rainy afternoon, Tom and I were cosied up watching old films, drinking hot chocolate and sharing our respective family stories, and he explained that his father, Vaughan, never showed an interest in Carrington's, so went 'off to see the world' instead. That's how he met Tom's mother, Isabella, on safari in Zanzibar. Meanwhile, the majority share in the store was left to Vaughan's sister, Camille, who later sold it to Tom, which is how he came to be the boss. Mr Carrington.

And this afternoon his parents are hosting a summer soirée on board their super-yacht! Yes, *super-yacht*. I know! Apparently, it has a cinema, a champagne bar and an actual helipad for, like, when they can't be bothered driving or taking a train in normal-people style, they can just be mechanically rotated from whichever exotic location they happen to be in, and boom! They've arrived. Not that I begrudge them, of course not, and I've only met them once before as they tend to spend most of their time travelling the globe, so perhaps I read it wrong. Or maybe I was having an oversensitive moment brought on by nerves from necking one too many jellybeantinis – I knew Tom and I shouldn't have met up in that cocktail bar beforehand. Big mistake. Huge. You see, I really want his parents to like me, of course I do, he's my one, my boyfriend, my happy-ever-after. But the slightly awks atmosphere when Tom's mother, Isabella, turned to me and said, 'So what do you do, my dear?' in her very breathy but regal-sounding Italian accent, told me it wasn't to be. Yet! Let's just say I'm working on it. Hence the proper preparation this time around. And definitely no jellybeantinis . . .

'I work part-time at Carrington's,' I had told her, brightly and proudly. And why not? I love my job managing the VIP customer shopping experience where I get to meet Arabian princesses, visiting dignitaries and the like. Since taking over, my role has evolved, and I'm more of a personal stylist now, with a number of well-heeled clients – actresses, celebrities, even royalty. But they're not all A-listers; some of my regulars are ordinary women who just want honest advice on what suits them best without having to rely on a well-meaning friend to fib – that an outfit looks good when it clearly doesn't. So they call for my advice on creating the perfect wardrobe. I even had one customer FaceTime me from a boutique in Dubai, wanting to make sure I approved of a pair of neon-green Choo heels she was about to purchase to match the pink shift dress I had selected to be part of her holiday wardrobe. I didn't. Instead, I couriered a pair of exquisite Miu Miu Mary Janes (exclusive to Carrington's), which I knew would match perfectly. She called me the very minute they arrived and begged for a pair in every colour to be sent right away, because she loved them that much with the shift dress, which she's now requested in every colour too. And that's how it works . . . my customers trust me, we have a rapport, and this means the world to me.

And the sales commission and other perks are phenomenal. Only last week I was asked to escort a selection of Carrington's exclusive couture gowns to a Premiership footballer's daughter celebrating her eighteenth birthday in Paris – they sent a private jet (yes I know, a proper YOLO moment) to collect me, the six dresses, matching accessories (high-end handbags and shoes), in addition to a selection of our finest jewellery collection, all because she wanted my personal advice on which of the exquisite ensembles would suit her best.

Maybe I should also have mentioned the weekly fashion and beauty column I write for *Closer* magazine, which takes up the rest of my time, where I get to write about international fashion shows, designer dresses at film premieres, and I've even interviewed celebrities for one of my special features: *What's In Your Wardrobe?* I go to their house, flick through their walk-in dressing rooms selecting outfits, and then explain how readers can source the same look by shopping on the high street, preferably in Carrington's.

The column came about on the back of me having been a reluctant reality TV star for a bit, when celebrity retail guru, Kelly Cooper, rocked up instore to film her last series – but that's another story that I really didn't want to go into when we were around Tom's parents' private dining table at the exclusive restaurant in London's Mayfair. My YouTube clips still surface from time to time – secret film footage of me twerking, really badly, on the shop floor to Beyoncé's 'Single Ladies' tune, and generally showing me in a far from flattering light. The less they know about my past the better, because it's just too much of a leap from what they're accustomed to. A whole different world. And one I'm sure they wouldn't select by choice for their only son and heir to be involved with. So I'm glad I kept it to myself. Of course Tom knows pretty much everything about me, but I just can't imagine his mother, Isabella, has ever thumbed through a sleb gossip magazine in her life. Oh no no no. I Googled her – this is a woman who speaks seven languages, was businesswoman of the year in her day and even has a Nobel prize for her pioneering work in global economics, for crying out loud. No wonder her expensively tightened face almost rearranged itself into a frown as the hideous realisation dawned – yep, that's right, that I work in the same Carrington's department store, the very one her son, aka Tom, aka my gorge, funny, sexy, kind to animals (he rescued Mr Cheeks right at the start), down-to-earth boyfriend actually owns! He's Tom Carrington, the boss, the managing director – and he's dating me, a mere employee. And a part-time one at that! Oh no.

To give her due, Isabella did try to mask her disappointment very well, but I spotted it nonetheless – the whitening of the knuckles as she gripped the stem of her champagne flute just that teeny bit tighter while flashing a fleeting sideways glance at her husband. But then it really can't be easy being the mother of – quite possibly – the hottest and most eligible man on earth.

I roll over. Oh *shiiiiiit*. Is that the time?

2

Flinging back the duvet, I bounce out of bed with an uncharacteristically exuberant flourish and immediately stub my toe on the side of an empty Prosecco bottle. Working through the pain, I squeeze my foot and think about last night as a more pleasurable distraction – Tom had just arrived back after a fortnight-long business trip, visiting practically every major city in the hunt for suitable premises in which to open a new store. Carrington's is expanding! So it was me, him and a large stuffed-crust Hawaiian followed by a bottle of bubbles and an evening of clothes-rippingly glorious sex involving practically every surface in my flat. Two weeks is a long time to be apart, and he'll be off again soon, no doubt, so you can see why we didn't waste a second of his R&R just chatting – oh no, there was so much more fun to be had. I still have the friction burns from the carpet on my backside and the stubble sting from his chin on my inner thighs as an exquisite souvenir. Tom may come over all gentlemanly and polite in company, but when we're alone it's a whole different thing. Pure filth! And I love it. Anyway, better get a move on, the soirée starts in exactly three hours.

I leg it down the hallway as my mobile buzzes with a text message from Tom, which I press to view while simultaneously kicking the bathroom door open with my good toe.

Sorry I had to dash. Really do need to get this paperwork done ☹ See you later. Mooooo! X

Ha-ha, in a *funneee boom-boom* way – he does work too hard, though, but then he's totally focused on building the Carrington's brand, and has already made some incredible changes since buying the majority share in the store from his aunt Camille – there's the pet spa, the gourmet food hall down in the basement, a new cocktail bar (installed specifically to attract the glamouratti instore from the new Mulberry Marina), the roof top ice-rink, the glitzy Cartier boutique and there's even a staff crèche now, so everyone's a winner, which reminds me, I must call Sam. She's my best friend and her adorable twin girls; Holly and Ivy (yes they were conceived at Christmas time) play in the crèche while Sam creates truly scrumptious comfort food and bakes delicious cakes in her café, Cupcakes At Carrington's, up on the fifth floor. Sam also owns the freehold for the Carrington's building, so she's invited to the party too. Her wonderful dad, Alfie Palmer, the charismatic and incredibly wealthy owner of Palmer Estates, one of the biggest estate agencies in the country, died last year, leaving his vast fortune to Sam. And we've known each other since boarding school days – before I got thrown out because Dad had gambled everything away and couldn't pay the fees. So I was billeted back home on the first train and then slapped around for talking posh in the local school playground by the following Monday morning.

I promised to call Sam for a pre-soirée briefing before arriving on board. And I never go back on a promise, even if I am tight for time.

'Hey you. How was last night?' Sam says after the first ring.

'Sizzling as always,' I smile. 'But how are you?' I quickly add, knowing how she's been feeling really jaded recently.

'Exhausted. Ivy was screeching at three o'clock this morning, which then set Holly off. And then my darling husband, Nathan, couldn't get back to sleep so started rattling on about a client that he's been having problems with . . . Like I'm interested in all his legal work stuff at four in the bloody morning!' She lets out a big puff of air.

'Oh dear,' I reply diplomatically.

'Never mind. I'm not complaining. Well, I guess I am a bit,' she quickly adds. 'But it's just what babies do. And lawyer husbands, I guess . . . So, tell me about the sex. Remind me, please, what it's like to have a whole night of bacchanalian bliss without the tandem wailing of year-old twins as an immediate passion killer, because I can't even remember my last time.' She does a feeble laugh. 'Don't get me wrong, I'd literally die for my girls, but it would be *sooooo* nice to have just one whole night off – to drink champagne, share a bath and have wild uninterrupted multiple orgasms courtesy of my own husband. Just like before. You know how much I love sex . . . does that make me a bad mother?'

'I don't think so. I'm not an expert – hell, I'm not even a parent, so what do I know about mummies and their orgasms, but aren't there places that use sleep deprivation as a preferred method of torture?'

'Ha! Yes, very good point. Nathan reckons we should get a nanny. A team of six, to work eight-hour shifts ensuring twenty-four-hour cover for each twin.' She heaves another weary sigh. 'He's practically dead on his feet at work each day – me too, I'm so exhausted, I feel like I'm wading through treacle most of the time. And I'm making mistakes – baked a whole batch of lemon drizzle cupcakes yesterday and totally forgot the crucial ingredient, the actual lemon juice!'

'Oh no!' Sam's lemon drizzle cupcakes are legendary; shoppers come from all over Mulberry-On-Sea to devour them. She's even had phone orders from people who've moved away but just can't live without them.

'Yep, we've tried the whole taking-it-in-turns thing to stagger out of bed, which never works as we both still end up wide awake in the middle of the night, and then start bickering over the duvet and whatever other trivial things our addled brains have suddenly elevated to paramount importance. But an actual nanny? I'm just not sure.'

'Why not?'

'Hmm, well, it just seems so grown up, somehow. And I'd feel a bit guilty, I guess. I've overheard the stay-at-home yummy mummies in the café bitching about the "*lazy women with help*" and, "*why did they bother having children if they were just going to give them to someone else to look after?*"'

'Oooh, harsh,' I tut.

'Indeed.'

'But that doesn't mean you have to be superwoman. Sam, you can't do it all – run the café, oversee Alfie's estate with all those meetings up in London, not to mention the management of the Carrington's freehold, and still find time to be Mary Poppins. For the sake of your orgasms you must say no!' I laugh to lighten the mood.

'Don't you mean *yes yes yes?*' Sam laughs too, not missing a beat.

'Ha!'

'Do you think Mary Poppins had orgasms?'

'Stop it! There's no place inside my head for that image.'

'Hmm, on second thoughts, you're right.' And Sam makes a *bleeeeugh* sound down the phone.

'Besides, you're already a fantastic mother just the way you are. You *really* are. So you must do whatever works best for you and ignore the opinions, because everyone has one, but they're just that . . . opinions!' I say gently, wondering where the old Sam went – she would never have been bothered by a bit of gossip; she's always been so self-assured and confident. Blimey, she's put me right on many occasions, but now it seems to be the other way around, which is OK – of course I'll champion her as best I can – but I'd much sooner see Sam happy. And by the sounds of it, this really doesn't seem to be the case.

'I know. And you're right, of course. But then my own mother couldn't be bothered with me, remember? So I don't ever want the girls to feel the way I did, and still do sometimes . . .' Her voice trails off.

'Oh Sam, that will never happen. You're not Christy . . .'

At boarding school, Sam and I had shared a bedroom, and she'd lie awake at night wondering about her mum, Christy, an interior designer who ran off to LA with a famous rock star client when Sam was only five years old. I used to try to comfort her by sharing sweets and whispering bedtime stories about princesses in castles, and even though Sam hasn't mentioned Christy for years until now, I think she still struggles to understand why she left. And even more so since becoming a mother herself, but then who can blame her? Christy literally did a moonlight flit. There at bedtime and gone by breakfast, and that's tough, especially when all you have is a bag of Haribo Strawbs and the vivid imagination of a nine-year-old friend to comfort you.

'True . . . but my brain is so addled from lack of sleep, it's affecting everything, and it's just *sooooo* not like me,' she replies.

'Of course it isn't, you've always been the most positive, upbeat person I know. Tell you what, why don't I babysit for a weekend or something? You and Nathan could stay in a hotel overnight, get some rest, chat, have loads of sex – do whatever you like, it would be just like the old days,' I say impulsively, instantly pushing away the panicky feeling that follows – I'm sure it can't be *that* hard to look after two tiny babies for an evening. *Heeeelp!*

'Would you really do that?' Sam perks up.

'Sure, that's what best friends are for. I'm just sorry I didn't think to offer before now.' I know Nancy will jump at the chance to lend a hand should I need it. She adores children and really *cannot* wait to be a grandmother; she even asked me one time if Tom and I had chatted about all that yet. I didn't have the heart to tell her we haven't – that our time together is spent mostly in bed, or across my kitchen table or in the shower, or the hallway, and my sofa has certainly seen a lot of action too – and that I'm just not interested in having babies, to be honest. No wild urge to procreate. That biological thing I hear so much about hasn't kicked in for me yet. Maybe it never will.

'Well, that would be brilliant. I'll chat to Nathan about it. It might put him off the nanny idea for a while longer.'

'Are you really that against it, then?'

'Hmm, I can't help wondering – what if she tries it on with him and they end up having a steamy affair? I know it's a cliché, but you hear about that kind of thing all the time, and the way I feel at the moment, I'm not entirely sure I'd have the energy to confront them, let alone slap her before chucking them both out,' she laughs wryly.

'Don't be daft. Nathan adores you, so that would never happen. Besides, you could get a manny . . .'

'A male nanny! Yes, now that's a good idea. Like a fit pool boy . . . But with childcare qualifications obviously,' Sam confirms, sounding a whole lot perkier, and more like her old self now.

'Yes, something like that.' I smile.

'You could help me with interviews?'

'Of course I could.'

'Wonder if I could get away with issuing a uniform – tiny running shorts, perhaps? Perfectly reasonable, seeing as they would definitely be doing lots of running around, the twins will make sure of it.' She sighs. 'Anyway, enough of this manny talk – more importantly, what are you wearing to the soirée? Indulge me with a few minutes of adult chat about frivolous things like dresses and shoes, instead of eco-friendly reusable nappies because, to be honest, I couldn't give a shit . . . oops, no pun intended,' we both snigger, 'what little Luella wears on her backside.'

'Who's Luella?'

'Oh, just another overheard conversation in the café – a group of eco-mummies were having a nappycino —'

'A *whaaaat*?' I yell, wondering if a bonkers barista somewhere has come up with yet another kind of hot beverage. Hmm, *skinny soya nappycino to go* – sure doesn't sound very appetising.

'Well, it's not an actual coffee.' *Oh that's a relief.* 'But from what I can gather, it's some kind of get-together to chat about nappies. I didn't join in or anything – was too busy working.'

'Of course you were,' I offer in solidarity.

'Anyway, it got me all edgy about my seemingly indulgent use of disposables, but I can't get my head around having buckets full of pooey nappies all over the place, waiting for the recycling van. Maybe I'm just not trying hard enough!' Sam laughs, but I'm sure I detect an edge in her voice. 'Sooo, your outfit? I bet it's gorge.'

'It is,' I confirm quickly, sensing she's keen to change the subject. 'I'm going with that new butterfly print silk maxi-dress that I bought in the Womenswear sale – beautiful, and such a bargain with my staff discount.'

'Lovely. And shoes?'

'I was thinking the silver strappy Laurent sandals.'

'Oh yes! Divine and very super-yacht yah-yah,' she says in an exaggerated plummy accent.

'How about you?'

'With a bit of luck, something baby-gunge free.'

'Don't be daft, you always look amazing.'

'Aw, thanks, and you always cheer me up.' A short silence follows. 'Oh for crying out loud – *Jeeeeeeesus*. I don't believe this . . . *Nathaaaaaaan*, where the hell are you?' My stomach tightens. *What on earth has happened?* Something catastrophic, by the sounds of it. I hold my breath. 'Gotta go – Ivy has just tipped raspberry yogurt over Holly's head.'

And the line goes dead. I sigh with relief.

Stowing my mobile on the bathroom shelf above the mirror, I flick the shower on and select my favourite body wash – Soap & Glory Sugar Crush. Sam has always wanted a big family full of children, and I'm thrilled that she has the twins, and she really does do a fantastic job all round, but I'm not sure I'm cut out for all that just yet.

As the warm water saturates my hair and cascades down my back, I can't help thinking how wonderful my life is right now, just the way it is – why change it? When I have a job that I adore – two, in fact, plus fab friends, money in the bank, and a cosy, secure home of my own. Dad is back in my life, with Nancy now too, and we're getting on really well – the three of us are close, loving and supportive, like a proper family should be, and I have a brilliant boyfriend who loves me, and I love him. (I make a mental note to make sure we find the time for us to talk about living together; perhaps he could move in with me? Now there's a thought . . . My flat may be small but it's much more of a proper home than his sterile new-build apartment.) And I honestly can't remember ever having all these wonderful things, together, at the same time . . . It's perfect. And I truly hope it stays this way forever because it's been a long time coming, but so very worth the wait.

3

Taking Tom's hand, I carefully step onto the narrow wooden gangway and through a twinkling fairy-light-studded voile tunnel, arriving in a Maplewood-panelled stateroom swathed in streams of silver satin with opulent mountains of fruit – grapes, plums, pineapples and pears – all piled high in pewter platters set on head-height pillars. There's even a ceiling curtain cascading from the enormous central chandelier. A string quartet is playing Mozart in one corner, and a group of waiters – who surely must be Ralph Lauren models, they're that fit – are loading up silver trays with canapés in the other.

The whole yacht looks like an Italian Renaissance painting. On one wall, there's even a giant mural of Botticelli's *The Birth Of Venus* – I know, because I read up when Tom and I first got together. He's a talented artist in his spare time, and I wanted to appear cultured and educated, show an interest in his passion for painting. And I can see where he gets it from now; I imagine he grew up surrounded by this stuff – a million miles away from the Take That poster I had pinned to the space beside my bed.

'*Ciao, mio bel figlio.* Tom, daaahling, you made it!' It's Isabella, looking resplendent in a floor-grazing lemon lace Givenchy gown. And blimey, she's even wearing a jewelled tiara on top of her immaculately coiffed jet-black hair. She loops her arm through Tom's and immediately steers him away from me. I smile as he glances over his shoulder to mouth 'sorry' when Isabella refuses to let him go. She's definitely not taking no for an answer; even when he tactfully tries to release his arm from her grasp, she grabs his hand instead and practically catapults him towards her guests. Poor Tom. He hates being cantered out like some kind of show pony.

'What's she come as? Queen of fucking everything!'

An arm circles my waist. I spin around – I'd recognise that outrageously acerbic voice anywhere.

Eddie!

Oh my God. We chat on the phone and Twitter all the time, but I haven't actually seen Eddie, physically, in ages, and now he's here, standing right in front of me and looking more like a superstar than ever. His dapper blond hair is now all messy quiff, and he's wearing an exquisitely tailored charcoal grey Tom Ford suit. And on closer inspection he's had a little lifting work around his sparkly blue-green eyes and his brows have definitely been manscaped. He looks fantastic. Flawless. And smells divine, too, of tropical summer holidays – coconut and citrus.

'What are you doing here?' I fling my arms around his neck and squeeze him tight. 'God I've missed you. I thought you were in LA.' Eddie is my other best friend and used to work at Carrington's as Tom's BA, or boy assistant – that was before he was 'discovered' on Kelly's TV show and practically became a superstar overnight. He has his own chat show with a Saturday night primetime slot, and a reality series called *Eddie: I Do It My Way*, and lives between his villa in the Hollywood hills and a penthouse apartment over-looking Mulberry Marina. And he's actually stayed at Simon Cowell's house in America, as Simon's personal guest! Doesn't get much starrier than that.

'Tom invited me – as a nice surprise for you,' Eddie says, as we pull apart.

'Aw, how lovely. He's so thoughtful,' I beam.

'Ooh, he is – the quintessential gentleman. Delish too. Not as beautiful as my Ciaran, mind you, but still, a very close second.' He nudges me.

'How is Ciaran? Is he here?' I scan the deck.

'No, he's looking after Pussy – you know what a diva that dog is, hates travelling and refuses to go in a crate, so Ciaran's flown straight back to LA with her on his lap after she created the most almighty fuss when Claire dared to go near her.' I laugh and shake my head. Pussy is Eddie's fluffy white bichon frise, and thoroughly spoilt, so it's hardly surprising. Claire is Eddie's manager, Peter André's too.

'Straight back? What do you mean?'

'Only a fleeting visit, petal. Filming starts on my second series tomorrow. We were in Ireland yesterday, at some windswept tiny town that time forgot . . .' He rolls his eyes. 'For Ciaran's cousin's wedding – Sinéad, Shona, Sorcha; something like that, anyway . . . I forget which one, he has that many . . . and I wasn't even drinking.' He waves a dismissive hand in the air and I smile, thinking, same old Eddie, as grandiose as ever, fame really hasn't changed him one bit; he must be the only person I know who can go to a wedding and then claim not even to know the bride's name the very next day. 'Yes, it was a last-minute decision – we weren't going to bother after the way his family shunned him when he finally leapt out of the closet. Anyone would think he'd tried to poke the Pope, the way they all carried on.' Eddie pauses to pull a face while I wonder if perhaps it was just that they were a bit shocked. I mean, Ciaran did actually come out at his own wedding, to a *woman*, after all. It was all annulled quite swiftly, but still, his mother is practically on first-name terms with the Pope, so I can't imagine it was easy for her. 'But you know how Ciaran is for all that family stuff, and then when his Catholic guilt kicked in, I just couldn't bear watching him perched on the proverbial spike doing all that hand-wringing, so we dashed to the airport and managed to get last-minute flights. Plus I needed to check on the apartment and then remembered Tom's invite, so I thought, why not pop in and see my most fabulous bestie in the whole wide world. So, *surprise surprise*!' Eddie bats a hand in the air. 'But I haven't got long, I have to check in for the return flight in like . . .' he pulls back a sleeve to glance at his watch, 'an hour!'

'Oooh, get you. Jet-setter.' I nudge him with my elbow.

'I know. Fabulous, isn't it? And see the group behind me . . .' I glance over his shoulder, and a guy shaped like an American fridge-freezer stuffed into a black suit, with a curly plastic wire hanging from his ear, is lurking ominously nearby. And there's a woman in leather skinnies and a floaty top who keeps checking her mobile phone and muttering something to a younger guy with an eager look on his face.

'I see them.'

'Meet my people!' Eddie laughs.

'You have people? Oh my God!' I ponder for a second before adding, 'Ed, do you actually *need* people?' My forehead creases with curiosity.

'Vital, darling! You can't make it in Hollywood without an entourage.'

'But what do they do?'

'Well, Ross is security, natch . . . and a total leather queen! You'd never guess, would you?' He makes big eyes, and I shake my head. 'And Carly is my PA – the boy is her assistant.'

'Wow! Your PA has a BA . . .' Blimey, how things have changed. It feels like only yesterday that Eddie was Tom's BA, bored and desperate to escape Mulberry-On-Sea for a mythical, seemingly unattainable world of stardom – or so it seemed back then. I shake my head, bemused but thrilled that Eddie is living his dream. I give him another hug.

'So, how are you, sugar?' he asks, letting me go – Eddie has never been big on prolonged displays of physical affection.

'I'm very well, thanks. Life is wonderful for me too.' I take two flutes of champagne from a passing waiter, who looks as if he's just stepped off the front page of *GQ* magazine, and hand one to Eddie.

'Ooh, peachy! And I'm so happy for you, Georgie. Just one pesky fly in the ointment though . . .' He raises an eyebrow.

'What do you mean?' I frown again.

'Her highness over there.' He flicks his eyes to the far end of the deck, where Isabella still has a vice-like grip on Tom's arm. 'Did she even acknowledge you from behind that surgically enhanced mask of hers?'

'I think her gaze may have hovered on me momentarily,' I smile magnanimously.

'Darling, it's called a bitchy resting face!' Eddie plucks a canapé from another waiter's tray and takes a big bite. I try not to smirk, just in case Isabella is watching, or Tom – he has no idea how Isabella makes me feel, and that's the way I'd like to keep it. At least until I feel more relaxed around her . . . And then there won't be an issue in any case – we'll be best friends and everyone will be happy, especially Tom. I hope! Yeayy. Well, that's the plan.

Sam arrives, looking exquisite in a crimson silk jumpsuit that flatters her tiny size six figure and perfectly frames her natural blonde corkscrew curls. She gives Eddie a hug before turning to me.

'You look beautiful – no baby gunge in sight,' I whisper

in her ear as she engulfs me in a big Cavalli-fragranced cuddle. 'How's Holly doing after Yogurt-gate?' I grin, hoping calm has now been restored.

Sam steps back to get a proper look at me.

'Love the maxi-dress. But where's Tom?' she replies, swiftly sidestepping the yogurt enquiry. Oh well, maybe she just wants to put it behind her and enjoy the rare afternoon off.

'Whisked away.' I motion with my head towards the other end of the deck, where Tom is now getting his arm pumped and his back slapped by an older beer-bellied guy wearing a straw boater, navy blazer and pleated mustard-coloured corduroy trousers.

'Ew, not up to your standards, honeypie.' Eddie pulls a face and hands the rest of the canapé to Sam. She hesitates before popping it into her mouth, and then pulling a face too, in between chewing and swallowing as fast as she can.

'Hmm, they should have come to Cupcakes At Carrington's – we would have laid on a lavish feast compared to this manufactured mush,' she manages, after rinsing her mouth with a generous swig of bubbles. 'I'm going to find out who their supplier is – always good to keep one step ahead of the competition. Although, it does surprise me . . .'

'What does?' Eddie asks.

'That they didn't come to Carrington's for the food! The store their son owns . . . Strange, isn't it?' And Sam heads off towards the catering area with a determined look on her face, leaving me to ponder on what she's just said, because it's true, it is strange. I wonder why they wouldn't want to support him. And it is supposed to be a family store, after all . . .

'Uh-oh. Here comes Her Majesty.' Eddie elbows me. 'Time for me to mingle.' Isabella is heading straight towards us, closely followed by an entourage made up of the beer-bellied guy, a couple of men I recognise from the Carrington's board and a woman with a static helmet hairdo, a sensible skirt suit and a very scary scowl.

'Hey, don't leave me to deal with her on my own.' Panic darts through me.

'Sorry, flower, I don't do divas, unless it's Pussy . . . or me! Tom will rescue you, I'm sure. Catch you later.' He kisses my cheek and then disappears too, leaving me all alone. I scan the deck, looking for Tom, but can't see him in the crowd. I brace myself and wonder what could *possibly* go wrong. Oh God.

Keen to keep a clear head, I surreptitiously place my flute on a nearby table. Calm with clarity, that's me. I inhale hard through my nose before exhaling as Isabella and her entourage form a semicircle around me. My resolve withers only slightly.

'Yes, that's her.' The beer-bellied guy pokes a finger at my chest, almost touching the fabric of my dress. Instinctively, I step back and rearrange my face into a smile. *How rude!*

'Err, have we met?'

'Only in my bedroom!' he sniggers, making his shoulders pump up and down like he's just told the funniest joke in the history of jokes, *ever*. And then quickly explains, 'On the television,' when the scowly woman gives him an extra-scowly look, if that's even possible . . . which, by the looks of it, certainly is. Ooooh, scaareeee.

'*Geooooorgie*,' Isabella says in an extra-breathy voice as she steps forward to stand proprietorially by my side. 'My dear, why did you lie?'

Whaaaat?

My heart immediately clamours inside my chest. *Loudly* – so loud I'm surprised someone hasn't grabbed the crash kit that's mounted neatly on the wall nearby. I rack my brain, desperate to fathom what she's going on about. *Lie?* Sweet Jesus, I may have been economical with the details of my past, but an actual outright lie to my boyfriend's mother who I've only met once before? I don't think so. Or perhaps the jellybeantinis mushed my memory? Hmm . . . I swallow hard and smile, keen to ride it out.

'Lie?' I manage to squeak, suddenly wishing the Maplewood deck below my sandals would part and plunge me into the deep dark sea below – cold and wet, but definitely preferable to standing here while they all stare at the *liar*! And suddenly a ridiculous tune pops into my head – *Liar liar, pants on fire*. Oh God. Where the *fuuuuuuck* is Tom?

'That's right, my dear. Why didn't you tell me you were famous?'

'Um, well, I'm not exactly famous, not really, that happened quite a while ago now,' I manage, practically shuddering with relief. Cringe. Maybe I should have mentioned Kelly's TV show after all, but you'd have thought Isabella would have known all about it in any case. Kelly is her friend from university days. Isabella manages a half-smile and then actually loops her arm through mine before doing a weird kind of cuddly thing into me. *Heeeelp*. She's being nice now, so why then do I still feel so edgy? I scan again ... where *is* Tom?

'Nonsense! Mr Dunwoody here says that you're the nation's sweetheart, and a columnist too; I'd say that's a little more than being just a part-time shop girl. *Sooo* modest. You really should have told me, my dear.' I open my mouth to speak, but Mr Dunwoody leaps in first.

'Please. I may be the Member of Parliament for Mulberry-On-Sea, but no need to stand on ceremony.' He puffs his beer-belly out a little further. 'You can call me Dougie,' he states, with an eager glint in his eye. *Oh goody.* After wiping a fleshy paw down the side of his cords, he offers it to me. Isabella drops my arm so I can shake Dougie's hand. 'And I was just saying that I need you.'

'You do?' I ask, raising one eyebrow while trying not to sound *too* sardonic.

'That's right. The town needs a high-profile person, someone in the public eye – I'd do it myself, but I'm not sure my constituents would thank me for it.' He chuckles while I resist the urge to smirk. 'No, my work is in Westminster! In London.' *Oh really. Like I didn't know that already.* I smile tightly. 'But you would be perfect.'

'Well I'm always happy to help if I can – what is it you'd like me to do?' I ask tentatively, making sure I keep the smile in place while silently praying it isn't something cringy or embarrassing: been there, done that, *and* on national television!

'Help organise the Mulberry-On-Sea summer regatta, of course.' It's the scowly woman. 'I'm Mr Dunwoody's personal secretary,' she says, fixing her beady eyes on me. *Hmm, so you don't have an actual name then . . .*

36

'Nice to meet you.' I smile, but she doesn't reciprocate.

One of the Carrington's directors explains instead. 'Georgie, Carrington's are going to be sponsoring the summer regatta, in conjunction with the town council, the Mulberry Marina management company and the local radio station, Mulberry FM. It will be organised collaboratively by a number of retailers and community workers, together with the sponsors. Dougie asked if you could be involved, seeing as you grew up here, and you're such a popular and well-known face in the town.'

'Um, sure . . . and thank you.' I feel flattered, and it sounds as if it might be fun.

'We hoped you might help organise it on our behalf, be the face of Carrington's? It's such a fantastic opportunity for the whole community – to bring the town together, to have some fun, and for all of us retailers and local suppliers to make a bit of money too. It will really put Mulberry on the map if we can pull this off.' He smiles and nods eagerly. 'So, what do you say? Are you up for it? And it really would help with our expansion programme – to open a new store; help us to show how "community-spirited" the Carrington's company is—'

'What a fantastic idea.' As if by magic, Tom appears

37

with his dad, Vaughan, following close behind – a tall, robust, bear of man, with a crumpled cream linen suit and a weather-beaten face. 'Georgie is an excellent organiser, a good team player, and she certainly knows how to look after people. She's an expert when it comes to customer service. And all our regular customers adore her,' Tom says, smiling proudly before taking my hand in his and giving it a big squeeze. Vaughan nods heartily in agreement. My heart melts, but the feeling quickly evaporates when I spot Isabella in my peripheral vision – she's pursing her lips and gazing majestically into the middle distance. What is her problem? One minute she's schmoozing me, the next she clearly hates me.

'Wow, well, after that glowing recommendation, how can I refuse?' I say, feeling thrilled. This could be really exciting – I'll get to do something new and I love Mulberry, I've lived here my whole life, so what a fantastic opportunity to show what this wonderful, pretty, seaside-postcard of a town is made of. 'When do I start?' I grin.

'Bravo!' shouts Dougie.

'Thank you. We really need Dunwoody on board if we're to open another store, he's heavily involved in planning and building regulations so could make it very difficult for us if he wanted to,' Tom whispers in my ear as he leans in to give me a hug.

'I wish you had mentioned it, though,' I smile and whisper back.

'Thought it would be a nice surprise, besides, we were kind of busy last night,' he laughs sexily, standing next to me now and swinging an arm around my shoulders.

'But Georgie, darling, you really shouldn't make a snap decision, or feel pressured into helping out – it's such a huge undertaking,' Isabella starts, placing a hand on my arm and surreptitiously pulling me away from Tom. 'Why don't you have a think about it first? If it's a little too much for you, then I could always get my events man, Sebastian, involved instead. See what a marvellous job he's done with today's spectacular soirée.' Isabella gestures around the overly opulent deck as if to prove her point. But I'm not sure Mozart and plates of weird-looking canapés will cut it with the residents of Mulberry. Mrs Godfrey, one of Carrington's regular customers, and a stalwart of the local WI, would definitely complain – 'far too fussy', I can hear her now. Oh no no no!

Ideas immediately buzz inside my head. I'm thinking ice cream in cones; donkey rides on the beach (if they're still allowed, I make a mental note to put it on my 'regatta things to do' list and find out). Yes, I'm going to need a massive 'to do' list – a bumper pad, in fact. And it's been years since I went on a donkey; the EU could have put a stop to it, for all I know, and what about a funfair? Everyone loves a carousel. And food! We could have stalls and marquees selling artisan breads – there's that great new bakery just opened on Bay Street, I bet they'd love to get involved. Exotic cheeses from the local farm shop over in West Mulberry, I know they'd be up for it, and they do assorted olives too. And maybe a special 'around the world' tasting experience – the customers loved it when a Japanese chef came instore one time to do a Teppanyaki cooking demonstration. It was amazing – razor-sharp blades slicing and dicing slivers of garlic-infused lamb and vegetable accompaniments before sizzling them on a hot griddle right there on the counter. And Sam could sell her delish cupcakes, macaroons and éclairs. We'd need a live band, of course, and even a mini-film festival, perhaps – something for everyone. I have loads of ideas already and my regular customers are going to love it. It's so exciting. Isabella pipes up again.

'Yes, Sebastian is far more accustomed to these things. You know, he was *very* involved in Elton's last black-and-white ball.' This prompts Dougie to let out a long whistle and do big 'I'm impressed' eyes.

'Well, I say we give Georgie a chance. I'm

convinced she'll bring her magic touch to the event,' Tom steps in.

'Superb,' Vaughan interjects, clearly bored by the conversation already. 'Now that's settled, I'm off to purloin more refreshments. Anyone for a top-up?' Vaughan waves his glass in the air and flashes me a cheery smile before wandering off in search of a waiter. Dougie and the directors follow suit while the scowly woman hovers awkwardly.

'I wonder, Mr Carrington, if you have a moment perhaps to give a quote for Mr Dunwoody's website. He's keen to provide a platform for local businesses; might be useful for you, considering your expansion plans,' she says tightly to Tom, who glances at me. I nod and smile, wondering why she's being so hostile. It's clear she doesn't share Dougie's enthusiasm for Carrington's.

'Sure, why not?' he says, before steering the woman towards a quieter part of the deck. I turn to Isabella.

'It's going to be so amazing,' I beam, my head still buzzing with all the ideas.

'I truly hope so, my dear.' Isabella leans into me and lowers her voice until it's almost inaudible. 'Especially after all the effort my son has made for the store. He has worked wonders with Carrington's, after all, not to mention his plans for expansion. It would be such a shame if you somehow managed to ruin it!'

And with that parting low blow, she sweeps away, leaving me to reunite my jaw with my face.

4

'*Shut uuup*, you are.' It's Wednesday morning. I'm at work in the VIP shopping suite and Eddie is calling on the staff wall phone from LA.

'Stop laughing. I really am. And it will be fun. If you hadn't abandoned me on board the yacht, then you would have heard all about it,' I say quietly, just in case a customer wanders in unannounced. Highly unlikely, as my assistant, Lauren, who used to work in the cash office but fancied doing something different when her little boy, Jack, started school, usually escorts them up, but you never know. And I'm guessing Lauren is already here, as the magazines have been fanned nicely on the gold marbled rococo coffee table, pink lilies placed on the matching side cabinet and the plum brocade cushions plumped and artfully arranged on the oversized chaise in the centre of the room.

'Yes, sorry, it was a bit mean of me,' Eddie apologises.

'And then disappearing without even saying goodbye.'

'Well, I tried to find you but the deck was heaving by then, and I was in serious danger of missing the flight. Carly was practically growling at me to get a move on.'

'Hmm . . . Well OK, I'll let you off. But only because she did look *super-scaareeee*!'

'So, what do you know about boats?' he sniffs.

'Nothing. But the regatta isn't about the boats.' Silence. 'Well, I guess it is a bit about the boats,' I quickly add. 'I'm guessing someone from the marina will be in charge of all the actual sailing stuff – the races, that kind of thing. My job is to make sure Mulberry puts on the show of its life, that Carrington's is represented well and we utilise the opportunity to attract more high-end customers instore. The first committee meeting is tomorrow.'

'Have you finished?'

'*Whaaaat?*'

'You sound like some soulless corporate brochure.'

'Oh, go away, don't be calling me from exotic locations just to wind me up, what do you want?' I pretend to be cross, but I'm well used to his teasing by now.

'Charming!' Eddie laughs. 'Listen, petal, I didn't get a chance at the yacht party to tell you I'm going to be back in Mulberry for the summer and thought it might be nice if we all do something together – the three of us: you, me and Sam. Can we pencil something in?'

'Of course – we can hang out like we always have for years and years; it'll be just like old times. Can't wait. We can watch TV and eat cake, but since when did we need to "pencil something in"?' I laugh – this summer is going to be brilliant. Even the weather is getting involved; the sun is still shining and I managed without a jacket this morning. A bit chilly, but once the clouds had cleared it was gloriously warm.

'Since Carly lectured me on forward planning, that's when! You know, she even had the cheek to reel me off a list on what makes an efficient PA. Like I never existed before I became famous. Honestly, she really thinks she's the boss of me. Anyway, how's that delicious boyfriend of yours? I didn't even get a chance to talk to him at the soirée.'

'Ah, Tom is brilliant as always.'

'Although he's hardly a boy now, is he? Oh no, *all* man. I clocked those beautifully built biceps.'

'You know, he's asked me to move in with him.'

'*Awesome*. Next you'll be getting married, sugar. Oh,

45

promise I can be your best man. Sam will be brides-maid, of course, but I'm in charge of your hair and makeup. And shoes! Oh yes, the shoes. How many pairs do you think you'll need for the day?' He pauses to let out a long sigh.

'Err, one?' I say, playing along with his fantasy wedding.

'Don't be daft. Three pairs at least!' He sounds outraged. 'And you'll need a proper planner. Me, of course.'

'Steady on. Haven't you got a career being famous and fabulous to keep you busy?'

'I'm deadly serious. Darling, you need to plan ahead, especially if you want a venue that's anywhere near wonderful. You don't want to have to settle for some draughty village hall in boring old Mulberry-On-Sea, all because you didn't bother to get organised already. What would Queen Isabella say?' He makes a tut-tutting sound.

'Stop it. Anyway, Mulberry isn't boring.'

'Well, it is compared to Vegas, or . . . how about Necker? Oh my God, you could get married on Necker Island and we could film it as part of my show. I bet Her Madge could swing that for you – she'll want the best for her son, and Tom's bound to have the money stashed in his trust fund or whatever—'

'Please, Eddie. When I get married, it will be here in Mulberry, with Dad giving me away and Nancy helping out with the arrangements: small and intimate and magical. You know how I hate being in the spotlight, especially when it comes to TV cameras.'

'Spoilsport. I've always fancied myself as a bridal stylist. It'll be just like dress up, but with an actual real audience. And I could be your very own David Tutera.'

'*Who?*'

'Oh, you won't know him – he's the dreamy host of *My Fair Wedding* – it's a TV show on over here,' he says in an extra-blasé voice.

'Then I'll bear you in mind should I ever need a wedding stylist,' I laugh.

'Well, what are you waiting for? Men like Tom don't come along twice in a lifetime.'

'True. But don't you think you might be getting a little bit carried away? We haven't even talked about any of that.'

'Well do. *Talk*. Try it; you might like it, instead of just having sex all the time. You must be the only couple I know who still have that all going on. Everyone else settles into twice-weekly sessions after a while – if they're unlucky: sex is so overrated!' I laugh, thinking: typical Eddie. 'Not twice-nightly!'

47

'Ha-ha! But we're not like normal couples who can see each other whenever they like. You know how busy Tom is building the Carrington's brand. I'm lucky if I get to see him twice in any one week! Besides, it's just living together . . .'

'But we all know what that *really* means,' he states authoritatively.

'We do?'

'Of course. It's man-speak for "I might want to marry you. Just not right now, but in a year or so when I'm really sure you're not some kind of *crazeee* control freak who won't let me leave wet towels on the bathroom floor, etc., etc." It's down to you to convert the offer of living together into your very own happy-ever-after. Go on, get that rock on your finger, darling – you know you want to.'

'Eddie! Must you be so clichéd about everything? These days couples do actually discuss important things like marriage, you know – and I'm not some feeble female eagerly waiting for a man to sweep me off my feet. I make decisions.'

'True. But you just said yourself that you don't have time to discuss things. And there's nothing wrong with helping things along a little, if it's what you really want.' Silence follows. 'It is what you want, isn't it?'

'It is! Oh God, yes, it sooooo is,' I say, suddenly

realising that it actually really is – I think I've focused so much on the physical aspect of our relationship until now – enjoyed it, no, scrap that, *adored* it – that I've somehow forgotten about the emotional side. Tom and I have both neglected it. Well, that needs to be fixed, right away, or just as soon as we next see each other.

'Brilliant. Then get a venue booked. Or, if you can't decide, then at least put a selection on retainer . . . it's the norm over here. My executive producer has had the Terrace Room at the New York Plaza booked since her Sweet Sixteen. It's the only way, she said.'

'Oh, Ed, there's someone here.' I can hear voices in the little anteroom outside. I pop my head around the door and see Lauren taking care of our guests. They're enjoying a welcome glass of buck's fizz, and so I reckon I'm OK for ten minutes or so. Give them a chance to relax – there's nothing worse for a customer than feeling rushed.

'OK, honeypie. But think about it. A year! Mark my words! I'll even put a wager on it.'

'What do you mean?'

'That Tom will propose within a year of you living together.'

'You're on,' I say, impulsively.

'Well, now you're talking – let's go for it: a hundred

quid says he proposes within six months of you officially living together. You can go for between six months and a year, seeing as you're being Miss Evasive today, but if it's within the first six months, then you pay me a hundred, and if it's after six months but less than a year . . . then, well . . . you still pay me a hundred.' He laughs.

'But,' I start, feeling totally confused, then quickly realise it's pointless: Eddie has made up his mind. And besides, from what I can gather, if Tom doesn't propose within either timescale, then I stand to win £200. Hmmm, but on second thoughts – at what cost? And I suddenly feel really disappointed. Damn you, Eddie, I now want Tom to propose to me more than anything . . . I realise that I actually don't want the £200. And to think I was blissfully and obliviously happy before we started this conversation.

'No buts! Right, I'm off to film a scene in a swim-up suite at a luxury hotel, with Carly tapping her watch every five seconds no doubt,' he puffs, pretending to be put out.

'Stop it!'

'Oh, you're just jel! But you're welcome here any time, you know that,' he laughs.

'I'm not jel *at all*!' I feign swagger, because secretly I am a bit jealous. Yes, I love my job, I love Tom, I love

Mulberry-On-Sea, but it would be so nice to travel too, to see more of the world. I've spent my whole life here in Mulberry and it can be stifling at times. Of course I've been to other places – Spain, Sam surprised me once with a weekend away for my birthday, and there was Lake Como for her wedding. Oh, and I've been to London loads of times, it's only an hour away on the train and great for nights out and exclusive West End shopping. Mum and Dad used to take me there too as a child to shop and see the sights. We'd make a day of it, first visiting an old-fashioned, posh little department store – it only had three floors but Mum loved it, and it sold my boarding school uniform (which I had to have before I got turfed out, of course), plus it made a change from Carrington's. But it closed down years ago. Then on to Big Ben, Trafalgar Square to feed the pigeons, Buckingham Palace and not forgetting the museums, a boat trip along the Thames, followed by fish and chips smothered with salt and vinegar straight from the paper, sitting on a bench beside the Cutty Sark. Ah, I cherish those memories of me, Mum and Dad, all happy together – this was years before Dad got into trouble and everything changed.

There was the private jet trip to Paris as well, but that doesn't really count as I only got to see the road through the taxi window from the airport to the hotel, and then back again. Eddie and Ciaran's wedding in Vegas was pretty spectacular, but I'm not sure the big glitzy bubble that is Vegas really counts as 'travelling', not when there's an actual escalator to perambulate you to the other side of the street. Mind you, I did manage to sit in a gondola and be serenaded along a pretend Venice waterway while I was there . . . hmm, on second thoughts, nope, not as good as the real thing. I'd love a proper Venetian experience. I promptly make myself a promise to travel more – take Eddie up on his offer and visit him in California, perhaps. Now that would be very exciting indeed. I'll be thirty in August, so I don't want to be heading for forty and to have never really travelled. And I reckon Tom could do with a holiday too. We could go to Venice for real, I could treat him just as soon as the summer regatta is over. It would certainly give us a proper opportunity to talk and move our relationship on in preparation for living together.

'Be good. Laters,' Eddie says to end the call.

I smooth down my duck-egg blue fit and flare dress. A signature piece – because when Carrington's staff wear Carrington's clothes, our customers *see it, want it, buy it!* True fact! And there's a duplicate dress just like this one currently being displayed on a podium in the main Carrington's window, which directly fronts the high street with its white colonnaded walkway of olde-worlde streetlamps and pretty hanging baskets bursting with sunny bright orange nasturtiums. It's the most prominent spot in the store and right next to Women's Accessories, which is where I used to work before I took over up here.

And I loved that job too – selling high-end handbags all day long: who wouldn't? I may not have been able to afford to own one back then, even with my staff discount, but it didn't mean I couldn't appreciate an exquisite piece of arm candy when I saw it. And there isn't anything I don't know about handbags – they're my passion – and it's even better now that I'm up here, as my customers always want the perfect bag to complement their new outfit. You know, I even met Anya Hindmarch one time. I'm a big fan of her designs.

My counter was next to the floor-to-ceiling window display, giving me a panoramic view of the bandstand opposite. During quiet times, I used to love watching all the people milling up and down outside, or relaxing in a deckchair enjoying a musical performance on the bandstand opposite. On a clear early morning, when the town was still empty, I could see as far as the peppermint-green railings down by the harbour and out to the glistening sea beyond.

Mulberry-On-Sea is the perfect location to host a summer regatta. I bet people will come from miles around; we may even get tourists travelling down from London, not forgetting the visiting glamouratti berthing in the marina for a few days. I can't wait to get involved, and show Isabella what a good job I can do – there's no way I'd ever let Tom down – or Carrington's, for that matter.

Smiling, I bouf up my hair in the mirror as I pass by and head towards the anteroom to greet my customers – mother and daughter, by the looks of it, and they've just finished their drinks, so perfect timing to bring them through.

'Ohmigod, I want that dress,' the teenage girl yells to her mother the very minute they emerge through the chrome swing doors, simultaneously giving me an up-and-down look. See, works every time.

See it. Want it. Buy it.

'Shall I whizz down to Womenswear – what do you reckon? A size twelve?' Lauren whispers, as the girl and her mother get comfortable on the chaise.

'No need, but thank you. The dress is already in the changing room – one in every size, so we have all options covered.'

'Now why doesn't that surprise me? Because those that *try it*—'

'*Buy it!*' I join in. 'You know it.' Lauren laughs and shakes her head. 'I'll make a start on the refreshments in that case.' She gives my arm a squeeze before placing a cake stand on a table and piling it high with miniature lemon drizzle cupcakes and pretty pastel-coloured fondant fancies from Sam's café.

Two hours later and the mother/daughter duo have each selected whole new summer wardrobes – floaty sundresses, strappy sandals, maxi-dresses, linen trousers, cruise wear and party gear: they've got the lot. All they need now are accessories, so I'm in the rickety old and incredibly slow staff lift on my way downstairs while they enjoy complimentary beauty treatments for the next hour or so in the specially installed pedichairs that line one wall of the VIP shopping suite. Sally and her team from the instore spa will look after them while Lauren makes a start on cocooning their mountain of merch in a puff of our signature powderblue tissue, parcelling it all up with navy satin ribbons and popping it into big striped Carrington's carrier bags. The concierge will then send someone up with a stock trolley to transport the bags to their car in the designated VIP parking area in the Carrington's car park adjacent to the store. We provide the complete shopping experience.

After pulling back the metal concertina cage door, I make my way along the narrow, winding staff corridor; it's like a time warp with its original 1920s faded floral wallpaper. I have to step around a couple of stock trollies piled high with flattened cardboard boxes, to push through the double security doors that lead out to the shop floor.

And wow!

The display team has done a brilliant job with this year's summer interior – the shop floor has been transformed into a nostalgic, halcyon, vintage beach scene. I love it! There is real sand mixed with gold glitter scattered on the display podiums, and each one has its own theme – mini-mannequins in floral retro-style swimwear courtesy of the Cath Kidston concession, fluffy towel bales from Homeware, a candy-striped deckchair decorated with a pair of Fifties sunglasses and a tartan blanket. A glorious red Decca record player and an old-fashioned picnic hamper complete with post-war utility-style plates, cutlery and a Thermos flask are strategically placed next to a modern funky range of Orla Kiely outdoor living items – flowery patterned radios, melamine plates and divinely scented candles.

There is even a row of Neapolitan-ice-cream-coloured wooden beach huts lining one of the cherry-wood panelled walls. Strawberry. Vanilla. Chocolate. I peep inside the vanilla beach hut and immediately feel transported – there's a speaker in the ceiling through which

I can hear the sound of the seaside on a busy summer's day. The swooshing of waves back and forward over pebbles, seagulls caw-cawing overhead and the sound of children laughing as they play in the sun. What a genius idea. It's just like being on an actual beach. And I swear I just got a whiff of sun cream – almond and coconut. It's so evocative of long lazy hazy summer days on holiday. It makes me want to race upstairs to the special pop-up beachwear shop in Womenswear to find the perfect bikini with matching sarong, big floppy sunhat, beach tote, flip-flops and shades, which I guess is the whole point. Ducking out, I dip into the strawberry beach hut and I'm at a fairground now, I can hear the music from the carousel and a sweet sticky aroma fills the air. Mm-mmm. Sugar doughnuts. Candy floss. It reminds me of going to Mulberry funfair in the school holidays, and I absolutely love it! This is summer right here. Brilliant.

Grinning from ear to ear, I head over to Women's Accessories and spot Annie behind my old counter.

'Hello stranger! What are you doing here?' I ask, giving her a hug. Last I heard of Annie she had left to get married, the whole works – a big-fat-gypsy-type wedding. Annie is a Traveller who lives in a caravan on the permanent site up near Mulberry Common, and when she first came to work here, she was the only girl in her family to ever have a paid job.

'Couldn't keep away.' She twiddles her nose stud and smiles wryly.

'And the wedding?' I ask, spotting her bare ring finger.

'Oh, he turned into a complete knobber – started mouthing off about how after the wedding my place would be at home cooking and scrubbing up after him, so I dumped him. I'm nobody's chalice.'

'Chattel.'

'Whatevs. If that's another word for slave, then that too,' Annie says, placing her left hand on her hip, and making me smile. I've really missed her. 'So, I got on the phone to HR and got my old job back. Well, your old job, to be exact.' She rolls her eyes. 'Anyway, I'm the supervisor now. My first day, too, and it's going really well. I've already shifted two Marc Jacobs top handles and a Juicy Couture crossbody bag. And I remembered all the little tricks you taught me, like surreptitiously sweeping the cheaper bag along to the end of the counter so as to focus the customer's attention on the more expensive piece of merch.' Standing tall, she puffs out her impressive cleavage while flicking her frosted hair extensions back over her shoulder.

'Good for you.' I wink, remembering when Mrs Grace, Carrington's oldest employee, taught me that trick on my first day as a Saturday girl all those years ago – Mrs Grace rocked Women's Accessories for fifty years before handing the mantle to me. She's retired from Carrington's now, after landing a book deal for a good five-figure sum to write her autobiography on the back of being in the reality TV show. It's going to be a trilogy, starting right from the beginning and detailing the history of Carrington's – the underground maze of tunnels that practically run the length and breadth of Mulberry town. There's even one that goes all the way to the old music hall at the other end of Lovelace Walk, a few streets away. Rumour has it that the original Mr H. Carrington, aka Dirty Harry (Tom's grandfather on Vaughan's side), had the tunnels built especially as a discreet way to 'visit' showgirls, then pay them in kind by inviting them back for secret late-night shopping sprees. Sort of like a free trolley dash in return for sex, I suppose. Mrs Grace told me all about it one time over a cream horn and a steamy hot chocolate in Sam's café. The books are going to cover the war years, too, when the underground tunnels were opened up to the residents of Mulberry-On-Sea to use as bunkers during the Blitz. Which gives me an idea – we could do a tour as part of the regatta! Apparently it's going to be a two-day event over the August bank holiday weekend (I got an email ahead of the first committee meeting tomorrow), so plenty of time for people to see 'behind the scenes' of the iconic Carrington's building. I'll add the idea to my list and be sure to bring it up tomorrow. Mrs Grace might even come out of retirement to be the tour guide. I bet she'd love that.

'And I've positioned the long mirror right here, see,' Annie points an index finger, '*becaaaaaause* . . .'

'Those who try it, buy it,' we both sing in unison, grinning.

Annie puts on a serious work face. 'Sooo, what can I help you with? I take it you're after some designer bags for your VIPs?'

'Sure am. I need top handle day bags, evening – a clutch or two, some totes and a couple of those big stripy beach bags over there.' I point towards the special 'summer fun' shelf that Annie has artfully created. A pile of bonkbusters, presumably for reading by the pool, are stacked at one end, and she's even snaffled some of the glittery gold sand and sprinkled it in between the bags on display.

'Blimey. Sounds as if they're splashing the cash then . . . Anyone famous?'

'I don't think so – didn't recognise them. A

mother-and-daughter day, treating themselves,' I say, as an image of me as a child, shopping with Mum, pops into my head.

'Ah, that's lovely. Right then, jump behind my counter in case a customer comes—'

'Oh, you don't have to pick out the bags for me,' I say quickly.

'Babes, it's no trouble. Besides, I want to – this is my kingdom now,' she pauses to gesture around the floor. 'And I really want to make this work. I want to be amazing at something. Just like you.' She gives me a quick hug.

'And you already are.' I squeeze her back, thinking how much she reminds me of myself when I first started out in Women's Accessories, full of ideas and enthusiasm. 'But thank you, honey.'

'No worries, leave it to me and I'll sort out a nice selection for you, starting with the exquisite Cambridge satchel in fluoro lime, yes? New in, and totes amaze-balls!' She gasps, fluttering her eyelids and waving a palm in the air as if experiencing her very own bag nirvana.

Once she's come to, Annie races around the shop floor picking out the best bags, while I stand behind my old counter reminiscing – I must have only been a little girl when I first came to Carrington's with

Mum; we would shop and eat fairy cakes in the old-fashioned tearoom and be happy together. Of course, this was years before Sam took over and turned it into a cosy café where the cakes are now éclairs and miniature pastel-coloured macaroons, and a good old-fashioned Victoria sponge is a magnificent six-tiered tower of rainbow-coloured layers decorated with blueberries and fresh lemon-infused cream frosting. Those Saturdays and school holidays were probably the best times of my life, although meeting Tom is right up there too. And I so wish Tom could have met Mum; I think she would definitely have approved, especially with him being the majority shareholder – Mum was always a little in awe of anyone out of the ordinary. It was my thirteenth birthday not long before she died, and the nurses in the hospital organised a little party. They even invited someone from the local football team to turn up and give me a teddy bear – Mum went all fan-girl. And she would have loved the VIP suite, feeling special for a day, pampered . . . Such a shame she's gone, and I would have loved treating her to a selection of gorgeous new outfits.

I used to miss her so much, I still do sometimes, but having Dad back in my life has made a massive difference, especially as we've reached the stage now where we can talk about Mum together and remember the happy times. I make a mental note to call Dad later, see how he is and suggest a trip to Mum's grave as we haven't been since Christmas. I'd like to take some flowers – maybe Nancy will come too. Last time she made a beautiful Christmassy arrangement of pinecones, miniature ferns and cinnamon sticks, set around a gorgeous red poinsettia plant, for me to put next to Mum's headstone. Nancy's kindness and generosity made me well up with emotion. She's such a kind, warm woman – and she really knows what it feels like to lose someone so close; her daughter, Natalie, died in a motorbike accident years ago, so she wears her necklace, with a gold letter N on, to keep her close always. I run an index finger over the silver locket that Nancy gave me as a Christmas present. It's on a chain around my neck, which I never take off. Inside is a picture of Mum (Nancy got it from Dad) when she was young and vibrant; hair fanned around her smiling face and cornflower-blue bright eyes. In the other side is a picture of me, with a brunette bob and the same blue eyes, a similar image to the one Mum would have seen of me just before she died. I love that Nancy did this; it's as if Mum's memory of me is crystallised for ever and ever.

'Here!' Annie says, catching her breath and breaking my reverie. She holds out her arms to show off the bags that are looped all the way from her wrists up to her armpits. 'Take your pick.'

'Can I have all of them?' I ask, scanning the floor for a stock trolley. Reading my mind, Annie nods towards the little alcove behind the counter.

'Yep – you will bring back any unsold merch, though, won't you?'

'Of course. But I plan on flogging the lot,' I beam, wheeling out the trolley.

'Good. And remember to scan each piece they purch,' Annie instructs, wagging an index finger in my face as we carefully load the bags so as not to damage the leather.

'Yes, Annie. I know,' I say in a singsong voice over my shoulder as I head back towards the lift with my stash.

'Just checking,' she calls out after me. 'I don't do shrinkage in my section. I can account for *all* of the merch . . . just so's you know.' She laughs.

Cheeky! I laugh too. I'm so proud of Annie – she started at Carrington's straight from school, just like I did. I gave her a chance, trained her, just like Mrs Grace trained me. And now she is indeed ruling her kingdom. Well, good for her. . . . I hope she loves it as much as I did.

I wheel the trolley into the staff lift and reach the third floor when it shudders to a halt.

'Hello, lovey. How are you?' It's Betty, our mumsy switchboard supervisor. She steps into the lift. Her glasses, which are swinging on a chain around her neck, narrowly miss getting caught in the metalwork as she leans across to close the cage door.

'Very well, thank you. And how are you?'

'Not so bad now the sweats are easing off,' she replies, wiping her top lip with a cotton hanky while I nod sympathetically. 'Ooh, and I heard about the regatta,' she swiftly adds, changing topic.

'You did?'

'Yes. My friend, Joyce, works at the council, so she knows everything that goes on here in Mulberry.' Blimey, news sure does travel fast. 'You know, I organised a village fete many years ago, so if you need a hand with anything . . . you just let me know.'

'Oh thanks Betty, I shall definitely bear that in mind,' I smile politely, not wanting to offend her, but really hoping the regatta will be a much bigger event than a village fete – more like a festival. And you never know – if we pull it off, then perhaps it could become an annual thing, with camping too, or special all-inclusive packages at the exclusive Mulberry Grand Hotel. It could be huge, like Glastonbury, only without the mud!

'Yes, do. Hashtag Team Carrington's!' she says,

cheerfully. 'Isn't that what they say on the Twitters?' Betty looks at me for confirmation and I nod. 'My Luke is on there all the time. I reckon he's addicted – that, or he's got himself a girl at last. Good thing, too, she can take him off my hands. He really should have left home by now – thirty-five is no age to be still sleeping in a box room with me doing his ironing and washing up after him. He has it too good, that's what my husband says. Georgie, do yourself a favour, lovey, and bypass the whole kid thing. I love my Luke, but he's so damn lazy. I suppose it serves me right in a way, I've spoilt him.' She stashes the hanky inside the sleeve of her hand-knitted cardy. 'And that MP's assistant certainly needs taking down a peg or two. Apparently she's got herself on the regatta committee, and Joyce was telling me that she's forever calling the council to lodge complaints – she's just a secretary, for crying out loud. Not a flaming Secretary of State, the way she carries on. You know, she was instrumental in campaigning against the new marina, so it's a bit rich that she now wants to muscle in on the regatta, the one to be held at the very marina that she tried to block!'

'Really?' I ask, shocked. The new marina has made a massive difference to Carrington's turnover, and to the whole of Mulberry, in fact, it's helped attract loads more customers to the area, especially those with money to spend after mooring their yachts. Who knows where Carrington's would be without the marina. Not so long ago, before the reality TV show instore, there was a very real possibility of Carrington's spiralling into a terminal decline, but things are on the up now. Carrington's is in the pink!

'Yes, that's right. But then she's never been a fan of the store. Well, not since she was asked to leave, that is . . .'

'Oh?'

'She used to work here . . . Years ago! She was secretary for a time to your Tom's predecessor, old Walter, aka the Heff, as in Hugh Heffner, on account of his numerous dalliances with women half his age,' she huffs. 'Anyway, she and Walter were caught at it in the boardroom, which was all hushed up at the time, but then Walter's wife, Camille, your Tom's aunty . . .' Betty looks for confirmation that she's got the Carrington family tree correct. I nod. 'Well, Camille found out and insisted she be sacked. So watch your back with her . . . I reckon she'd love nothing more than to exact a bit of revenge by ruining things for Carrington's if she can.'

Oh great. So not only do I have Isabella waiting for me to mess up, but also now it seems the scowly-woman-with-no-name could be out to sabotage things.

Well, in that case, I'll just have to make sure I pull out all the stops because I'm determined to make this the best regatta Mulberry has ever seen. There's no way I'm letting the scowly-woman-with-no-name ruin it, and I'm definitely, *definitely* not showing Tom up in front of his mother, or jeopardising his chances to open another store. It means the world to him to demonstrate his business acumen. He really wants to take Carrington's to the next level, grow the business, and I don't want anything to spoil that, especially if we really are to have a proper future together. Isabella would be my mother-in-law, which means as her daughter-in-law I would want to be the best one she ever did have. I love Tom, I adore him, so I'd want Isabella to adore me, for us to get on brilliantly, have shopping days and spa weekends together, that kind of thing – be the daughter she never had. I could even call her mum, if she liked. Not that she'd ever replace Mum, but you know what I mean. It could be lovely. Mmm, I mull it all over. I'd be a part of something magical, a proper family, an Italian dynasty – Tom has loads of aunts, uncles and cousins. And family friends, too, who he's known for years. I've never really had that – when Dad went to prison, everyone faded away, apart from Sam and her dad Alfie.

Georgie Carrington! Mrs Georgina Carrington.

Oooh, it has a nice ring to it, or would I keep my own name? Lots of women do, so how about Georgina Hart-Carrington? Hmm, or perhaps Tom could change his name – some men do. Mr Tom Hart . . . anyway, whatever happens, I have to say the thought of actually being Tom's wife is a pretty spectacular prospect, something wonderful to look forward to. I just need to show Isabella what a brilliant match I am for her son because, let's face it, having a mother-in-law who has 'issues' with you is bound to ruin things in the long term. And it's not like I could ever talk to Tom about it, I'm not even sure I'd want to put him in that position, stuck in the middle, and from what I've seen so far, they're very close – they chat on the phone practically every day. I couldn't expect him to choose between us, or anything silly like that. No, the sooner Isabella gets to know me properly and see what I'm capable of, the better. And where better to start than by organising a magnificent regatta, which in turn will show my support, not only to the Carrington business, but to the Carrington family too.

5

I make it to the town hall with just five minutes to spare after getting caught up on a Skype call with the editor from the magazine – she wanted to chat a bit more about my new idea for a *What's In Your Handbag* piece for next week. It's Nicole Scherzinger and it's going to be *shamazing* for sure. Her people were very generous in supplying a list detailing the contents of her designer bag.

'If you're here for the regatta meeting then you'd better get a move on.' There's an enormous desk just inside the door with two security men in black uniforms lounging behind it. The older one with the bushy grey hair and the lovely *Corrie* accent stands up. 'You're the last one, duck,' he says with a smile. 'Second on the right.' I head in the direction of his pointing finger.

'Thank you,' I breathe, pulling my scarf off as I go – it's like a sauna in here. I find the room and push through the double doors.

'Ahh, here she is, the famous Georgie Hart from Carrington's department store.' Oh God, it's the scowly-woman-with-no-name standing on a stage with a pen poised. She snaps up a clipboard and gives it a big firm tick before treating me to an extra-special scowl.

'Hello,' I mouth, giving her my best eyes-and-teeth grin, figuring it best to kill her with kindness – Mum swore by it, and that old adage that you 'catch more flies with honey than vinegar'. She pretends not to have noticed, so I scan the room instead. There must be at least twenty people in here, sitting on plastic chairs in rows, and they're all staring at me.

'Um, hi. Hello.' I do a feeble little wave but nobody reciprocates, so for some ridiculous reason, I quickly add, 'Sorry I'm late.' I glance over at the wall clock opposite and there are still five minutes to go before the meeting officially starts, so why on earth am I apologising? But they all look so serious.

I spot an empty seat, right in the front row and opposite the stage. I dive into it, grateful to be out of the spotlight, but conscious of the scowly woman's beady eye boring down into me.

'Right, so where were we?' she huffs, rustling her papers excessively, as if to labour the point of my perceived lateness.

71

'You were saying how important punctuality is, given that we don't have an awful lot of time left to organise the event. Every second counts!' someone behind me pipes up.

'Yes, that's right, and if you could all pay attention too. We really do have our work cut out if we're to pull this off within just a few months. To be honest, it's more or less going to be impossible, but then, what could we do?' The scowly woman sighs and shakes her head, clearly exasperated. 'We only got the go-ahead last week – one of the biggest sponsors did keep us waiting *rather* a long time . . .' She harrumphs a bit more before shooting me another look.

'Carrington's,' someone mutters. Oh, this just gets better. So I'm the reason the pressure is on. I make a mental note to talk to Tom later to find out exactly what's been going on.

'Right, let's get on with it. We've done the introduc-tions – Georgie, I'm Meredith, Mr Dunwoody's personal secretary, as you already know. You'll have to catch up with everyone else later.' Cue another sniffy look, this time accompanied by a pointy finger. *Hmm, so who made her the boss of us?* 'So, quick recap, we know Mulberry Yacht Club is in charge of all the sailing events and races; they'll be organising the entry forms, legalities and brochures too, detailing the programme of events. Now, as a quick aside – if any of you would like to place a business advert in the brochure, then please speak to Bob, the harbour master.' Meredith points to a rosy-cheeked guy in a chunky-knit Aran sweater who leaps up and waves both hands above his head like he's air traffic control marshalling a jumbo jet into landing. *Steady on!* 'But in your own time, please!' She coughs. 'This leaves us to sort out the stalls and fun events, which will take place around the marina's perimeter and on either side of Wayfarer Way, the main road from the town centre, taking in the market square and leading on to the marina.'

'But what about the new industrial estate?' a guy behind me heckles.

'What about it?' Meredith says, officiously.

'Seems all the action is in town, so none of the regatta visitors are going to bother with us and I'm only here to see about drumming up more business,' the guy huffs, before muttering something about his new indoor amusement arcade that's 'right next door to Asda so you'd think it'd be heaving', but is ridiculously quiet. He stands up, causing his chair to make a hideous scraping sound across the floor, before shoving his hands in his pockets and lumbering off.

'So, any more ideas?' Meredith dismisses, seemingly

unfazed as the arcade guy lets the door slam behind him. A few people stick up their hands, but Meredith just keeps on talking. 'The various youth groups – Brownies, Guides, Scouts, Sea Cadets, etc., are already busy organising floats for the carnival procession, which will parade through town ahead of the official opening of the regatta. And in addition to this marvellous event, we've come up with . . .' She pauses to refer to her clipboard, 'Yes, that's right – beer tent, tombola, welly throwing, lucky dip, wet sponge throwing at the mayor, guess the name of the teddy bear . . .'

Oh, God help us.

'Donkey rides?' someone at the back shouts out.

OK, a bit better. I make a mental note to cross that idea off my list.

'Don't forget the mini-music festival.' This is much more like it. I glance along my row to see who is speaking – it's a guy with a Bob Marley T-shirt and a big boffin beard.

'Hmm, a bit ambitious . . .' Meredith shakes her head and actually sucks in air, like a plumber denouncing the state of a broken washing machine – I half expect her to launch into a long, boring explanation of what actually constitutes 'ambitious' too! But luckily, Bob Marley jumps in instead.

'Not at all. The radio station has all the equipment and we've already got confirmation from a few local bands. But what we really need is a big name to headline . . .' *Ah, I bet he's from Mulberry FM. How exciting.*

'Well, let's not get too hasty, I'm not sure everyone wants—' Meredith starts, before she's interrupted by the woman sitting next to me, wearing a leopard-print bomber jacket and denim skinnies, who has the biggest treacle-coloured beehive I've ever seen.

'Oooh, I don't know, I reckon people love a good knees-up, and we're always rammed on band night,' she says in a cracking cockney accent.

'That may be the case in the . . .' Meredith pauses again to check her notes.

'The Hook, Line and Sinker,' the beehive woman prompts. 'It's a new pub, and we're right at the entrance to the marina. Oooh, I've got an idea!' A short silence follows.

'Do enlighten us, dear, we're not exactly time rich,' Meredith says in a monotone voice as she glances at the wall clock.

'Weeeell,' the woman starts, sounding really excited. 'We'd be perfect to host the mini-music festival. Our beer garden backs out directly onto the beach, and we could rope off a section and install a stage.' *Fab, this is much more like it.* 'Music and beer on tap, what's not to love?' She claps her hands together, seemingly pleased with the plan.

'Yes, err, Beryl is it?' Meredith purses her lips.

'Cheryl, love. But you can call me Cher, everyone does. I'm the landlady.'

'Hmm, well, OK, err . . . Cher. But it's not as simple as just roping off a bit of the beach. You do need to have a proper public performance licence, not to mention that there are all kinds of health and safety laws to adhere to – it really could get quite tricky to manage,' Meredith continues, tilting her head to one side, and talking as if she's placating a toddler.

'No problem, I have that all in place,' Cher beams, twiddling a finger around the inside of her massive gold hoop earring.

'And any rubber-stamping will be made a priority, of course.' A guy in a suit sitting at the end of my row jumps in. 'Plus I'd like to take this opportunity to assure you all that parking will be free across all of the town's car parks for the duration of the regatta, and we'll be liaising with the police, St John Ambulance, etc., and setting up the usual services – mobility scooter hire, children's security wristbands, etc. And I'm personally in charge of sorting out the Red Arrows – they always go down a treat.' He pauses. 'Well, err, not literally of course, because that would be catastrophic. No, a crash landing really wouldn't do . . . eek!' He pulls a face and shrugs apologetically before sitting back down.

'That's Matt from the council – he's all right though,' Cher whispers, leaning into me. I smile – she seems really nice. Glancing along the row, I catch Matt's eye and he gives me a welcoming nod. Perhaps this will still be fun, after all.

'Just need a proper pop star now,' the Mulberry FM guy says.

'I might be able to help with that,' I suggest, eager to do my bit.

'Oh?' Meredith quips.

'He's not really a mainstream pop star, though.' Silence follows. I'm sensing they're not impressed, but hold on, there's more. 'Yes, the person I have in mind is a Mulberry local too. He's a country singer and mega-famous. I'm sure he'll help out if he can,' I add, sensing a bit of excitement in the room now – people behind me are whispering and fidgeting.

'Is it Dan Kilby by any chance?' the Mulberry FM guy asks hopefully, and the whispering gets louder.

'Yes, that's him, do you know him too?' I ask, leaning forward.

'No, not personally. I'm Jared, by the way,' he smiles.

'Nice to meet you, Jared,' I grin back.

77

'I've tried to get him into the station a few times for a live on-air interview, but never quite managed to bring it all together. He's definitely a crowd-puller, though; everyone loves him. It would be awesome, and real kudos for Mulberry, and Carrington's too, if you really could pull it off and get him to agree to a live set.'

'I'd better make the call right away then – probably best to give him as much notice as possible.' I pull a pad and pen from my bag – once I had finished with my clients in the VIP suite earlier today, I popped downstairs to Stationery and bought four A4 notepads, a box file, a gorgeous soft brown leather pencil case, a bumper pack of multicoloured Post-it notes and a selection of different-coloured pens. I love stationery – who doesn't? Plus, I thought it best to be properly organised in any case. Taking a red pen from my pencil case, I add 'Call Dan' to my 'Immediate things to do' list, and then do a squiggle around it with a turquoise mini-highlighter – I've got a combination of colour codes for all my tasks, ranging from green to red, depending on urgency and level of importance to Carrington's.

'The budget is limited, though – we can only cover travel and refreshments, I'm afraid,' Matt says, making a sorry face.

'But the radio station would be happy to cover modest additional expenses for someone as high profile as Dan,' Jared adds.

'And I reckon I could get budget from the Carrington's board – they really are keen for this to be a huge success,' I say, knowing how important it is for Carrington's to foster good relationships within the community. I'm sure I can get Tom to organise a bit of extra money if necessary. I make a mental note to call Dan first thing tomorrow morning. If I can get him involved, then that will get me off to a flying start, not only with the rest of the committee, but with Isabella too. She's bound to be impressed by my A-list connection – I bet her fancy-pants party planner, Sebastian, doesn't know Dan Kilby personally. Oh no!

'Hold on. How do you even know Mr Kilby?' Meredith says in an incredulous voice.

'Well, he and I, err . . .' I pause, wondering just how much I should divulge – things were shaky between Tom and me at the time. It was right at the start, we hadn't been seeing each other properly for very long, and then Tom disappeared to Paris. I thought he had dumped me and was getting engaged to an old flame – and then with my two-and-two-makes-five thing thrown into the mix . . . well, luckily it all turned out to be a massive misunderstanding, but that's a whole other story. Anyway, Kelly the retail guru set it up – a showmance, if you like. 'Dan was involved in the TV show too,' I finish lamely, not really wanting to talk about my convoluted love life in this very public forum. I had enough of being in the media spotlight when I was a reluctant reality TV star, with my 'highlights' plastered all over YouTube every week.

'Oh, that's right. I remember the episode – loved it! You were dressed up proper classy, and that Dan is a real dish,' Cher says, swivelling in her seat so the people in the back rows can hear her too. I hold my breath, wishing I'd kept my mouth shut now; and I can already see Meredith pursing her lips disapprovingly. 'He snogged you on the bandstand, a proper Hollywood film kiss it was too. *Sooo* romantic.' I open my mouth, but before I can explain that the kiss was just for show (Dan had spotted a pap lurking nearby with a long-lens camera), Cher continues, 'You must pop into the pub one night and have a drink on me.'

'Oooh, yes please, I'd love to,' I smile, feeling relieved to be chatting about something else. Not that anything ever happened between Dan and me. He's a really lovely guy, hot and cool in a cowboy-kind-of-way. All leather jeans, checked shirt and guitar slung casually over his shoulder. Very Gunnar Scott in *Nashville*. We just had a bit of fun; it was never going to be anything more. I was already in love with Tom by then . . . even if we weren't properly together.

'That's sorted then—' Cher starts, before Meredith coughs impatiently.

'Err, excuse me, *ladies*! We do have a very tight schedule to get through, so if you can organise drinking sessions in your own time, please.' Meredith does a sarcastic smile. I inhale sharply and let out a long breath, as if to clear my head, thinking, what is her problem? She clearly hates Carrington's, and me, but what I want to know is, why? She got sacked years ago and has obviously moved on into a good job, so why is she still so bitter? 'So, before we wrap up, are there any more ideas?'

'Yes, I have a few.' After grabbing another notepad from my bag, I flick open the cover. 'I made a list,' I explain, waving the pad around like a looper and wondering if I should quickly power up my iPad mini – I've made a Pinterest board too, titled 'Carrington's Regatta', and found loads of brilliant nautical-slash-festival-slash-summer-slash-ice cream-slash-carousel-slash-cake-themed pictures to really get us in the mood. I could pass the iPad around so everyone can see . . . But on clocking Meredith's glazed look, I push the iPad back inside my bag and will my cheeks to stop flaming. I get on with just reading out the ideas instead. I'll save Pinterest for another time – doesn't hurt to have a 'double debut', as it were.

'OK, here goes.' I clear my throat and Cher nudges me gently with encouragement. 'We could have food stalls selling a variety of delicious delights.' I pause to see if I'm on the right lines, but nobody says a word. I'm just about to carry on when someone pipes up, 'As long as the fancy stuff is well away from my burger vans.' It's a man with a bandana around his head.

'Err . . .' I start.

'Yes, don't worry. We'll draw up a map of who goes where,' Meredith huffs impatiently, and then motions for me to continue.

'And a selection of cakes from Cupcakes At Carrington's. My best friend Sam owns the café and her cakes are legendary – people travel from all over for them, so they're bound to be a huge hit.' Silence follows. Perhaps I've got it wrong, and they'd prefer more of a 'village fete' event after all – guess the weight of the homemade cake, that kind of thing, to go with the welly throwing. Only, I'm not sure my customers will get excited by that, and I have to do my best for Carrington's. It's the reason I'm here, after all, plus I can't imagine Isabella being impressed by a small-town fete, not when she's used to commissioning Botticelli murals just for an afternoon soirée. Tom told me later that the yacht is usually adorned in framed water-colours, but Isabella fancied a change, so a team of interior designers were flown in from Milan to carry out the temporary transformation. Botticelli has since been whitewashed over and the framed prints put back in place. So, no no no! We must up our game.

'I had afternoon tea in the Carrington's café,' someone eventually says. 'And it was actually very nice.' *Fab.* I beam. 'A bit on the pricey side, though!' Hmm, and my smile fades.

'But worth it if the cakes are as good as Georgie says,' Cher chips in, and I want to hug her.

'Exactly. And we can have lots of cake stalls dotted around town to suit all budgets,' I say, 'and there are loads of cafés and cake places in Mulberry, so everyone will have a chance to get involved if they want to.'

'It's a good idea, but don't canopies cost a fortune to hire? Being a start-up, we just don't have the money, and it'll be sweltering without any shade.' Ahh, it's the woman from the new bakery. I smile and she smiles back.

'Carrington's can help – provide canopies, or how about a number of food marquees big enough for several stallholders to share? I'm sure the visitors and tourists on the day will welcome the shade, too, while they peruse all the delicious food on offer,' I grin, remembering the email I got earlier from the board saying that they've already done a deal with a local marquee hire company for this exact reason. So everyone wins – the hire company, the local food suppliers and Carrington's – which in return for covering the hire cost will have the store logo on a select few canopies (having it on all of them would just be ridiculous and defeat the purpose of this being a whole community endeavour – something Carrington's is keen to be seen to be supporting). And it wasn't that long ago that Carrington's was struggling and very nearly went under. If it hadn't been for the loyalty of the local community – coming in store to buy school uniforms, a special birthday present, treating themselves to afternoon tea in Sam's café or a pedicure in the spa, then we most definitely wouldn't have made it. It all adds up. It's thanks to them that we're now in a position to support others who might still be struggling in this economical climate.

'I'm definitely in,' the woman from the bakery beams, and a few other people all smile and nod in agreement.

'Fab. And I thought perhaps a mini-film festival,' I move on. Meredith sniffs with disapproval – I take a deep breath; I can sort of understand why she might be a bit down on Carrington's, but it's not my fault she got caught out, *in flagrante* as it were, with the Heff. 'And old-fashioned pop-up ice-cream vendors.'

'Ooh, that sounds lovely. I can picture it now, all candy-striped awnings and swirly Mr Whippy cones with sprinkles on top,' Cher says, nudging me again.

'Yes, that would be brilliant, and we could even have a special limited-edition Mulberry Regatta ice-cream flavour made – you know, like . . .' I pause to catch my breath. 'Of course, this is just off the top of my head – cinnamon, mulberries and cream for example,' I say, feeling excited now, and if I'm not mistaken, a little buzz reverberates around the room. 'And I was thinking a fleet of ice-cream vans would be good – the old-fashioned ones that chime tunes like "Greensleeves".' Cher nods and, feeling more relaxed, I add, 'You know, my mum used to say the chime meant they'd run out of lollies . . .'

'Mine too!' Cher laughs. 'Not for our regatta though, eh? We'll make sure of it.' She winks at me conspiratorially. Grinning, I carry on.

'We could have them dotted all around Mulberry, and lining the route to the marina perhaps, like a welcoming party so people can buy an ice cream plus pick up a programme,' I say, getting into the swing of things now.

'Yes, good idea.' It's Matt from the council. 'And that would save us having to draft in students from Mulberry College to stand around trying to flog the programmes. That's what we usually do for our other major event – the switching on of the Christmas lights – but it's not ideal as last time one of the environmental health officers found a big pile of programmes dumped in the bushes up on Mulberry Common.' A tutting sound reverberates around the room, but at least they're all getting involved now. I keep going.

'And in line with the retro theme, I thought a carousel would be cool, like the ones you get at the funfair. And, last but not least, a guided tour of Carrington's underground tunnels.' An ultra-ominous silence follows this time. Oh God, I've lost them now.

'Well, that's quite a list. Is anyone interested in working with Georgie?' Meredith asks the room, and I'm sure I spot a glint in her eye.

'I would, love, but I reckon I'll have my hands full with the music festival,' Cher says, apologetically.

'Me too. Sorry Georgie,' Jared chips in.

'And I'd like to do the donkey rides,' someone else adds, and then, in turn, they each allocate themselves to the various ideas, all except mine.

'Oh dear, looks like you're on your own in that case,' Meredith says. I gulp. *Whaaaat?* Surely she doesn't think I can do everything by myself? I swivel around, desperate for volunteers.

'We'll do the film festival.' A man in full combat gear stands up. 'My staff will assume responsibility for this one,' he adds, practically clicking his heels to attention.

'Oh that would be fab, thanks so much.' Relieved, I grin at the guy, and he nods as if to formally seal the deal.

'Well, I guess it makes sense, seeing as you own the television shop,' Meredith says quickly, desperate to claw back control.

'That's right. Mulberry Sound and Vision. We sell everything from home cinema systems to car audio equipment, and we have a specialist covert and surveillance department on the first floor,' commando man corrects, and there's definitely a hint of frostiness in his voice. Ha! So he's got the cut of Meredith then. Good, maybe he can hunt her down when he's next out on manoeuvres – or whatever it is he does dressed up in that gear. He even has a pouch on his belt, which I'm guessing real soldiers use for storing grenades – his has a mobile phone inside.

'Yes, yes of course,' Meredith mutters. 'So, that's settled then. Everyone know what they've taken responsibility for?' She does a cursory glance around the room before snapping her clipboard shut. 'Good, because I for one am parched. See you all next time – details will be emailed out. And do come with project plans – supplier names, costs and itineraries, that kind of thing, so we can go through them and get everything approved with the various authorities.'

Matt jumps up and turns to face us all. 'Before you all go – I've invited representatives from the emergency services, health and safety, traffic control, etc., to join our next meeting, so if you have any queries you'll have a chance to ask questions or get clarification. And then we can all get cracking on making Mulberry's first regatta a resounding success.'

'Right you are – no time to waste. Cheerio!' And with that, Meredith leaves the stage, pulls on her plum-coloured fleece and marches from the room with her clipboard tucked firmly under her arm.

Blimey, so it looks like I'm organising the Carrington's tunnel tour, the ice-cream vans, and the food stalls then! Well, I'm going to need some help if I'm to pull this off – the regatta will be here in no time at all. I wonder if some of the other staff would like to help out – we could be hashtag Team Carrington's, as Betty would say. She'll help out, of course, and I reckon Annie will be interested, especially when she hears that Dan Kilby is headlining, and he's bound to say yes, I just know he will. I could put a notice up in the staff room, asking for volunteers. I'll head it up with #TeamCarringtons Needs You – it sounds more professional, and it has to be worth a go. But, hold on, what about the carousel? Oh my God, where on earth does one get a carousel? I quickly pull out a pad, write 'CAROUSEL' in big red capital letters, and underline it four times, before rummaging around inside my bag for the turquoise highlighter.

6

The fresh zest of orange mingled with warm sweet honey greets me as I push open the door to Sam's café, on the fifth floor of Carrington's. It's my day off, so I thought I'd pop in to see how she is before meeting up with Tom later for lunch.

'Hey, this is a nice surprise, how are you?' Sam pops her head out from inside the kitchen. After wiping her hands on a navy-striped apron, she lifts the hatch in the counter and dashes through to give me a huge hug.

'I'm fine thanks, getting busy with the regatta plans – but, more importantly, how are you?'

'Knackered, for a change.' She shrugs. 'But come on, let's get a booth; I could do with a break and a bit of a gossip. I've got half an hour before I have to collect the girls from the crèche and then take them to a play date before their baby ballet class later on . . . it's a full-time job in itself trying to keep up with their hectic social life.'

'Lovely.' I wonder now if I should have volunteered Sam for a stall at the regatta; seems she has enough on her plate without more work from me. What on earth was I thinking? Sam beckons Stacey, one of the waitresses, over.

'Would you mind bringing us two hot chocolates slathered in squirty cream and marshmallows, and a plate piled high with cakes please, Stace?'

'Coming right up,' she says, cheerfully.

'Thank you, I really need a sugar hit,' Sam groans, and Stacey turns to me.

'I've been telling her all week to take it easy, but will she listen? Can you please talk some sense in to your friend?' Stacey shakes her head and gives Sam's shoulder a quick squeeze, before picking up a pair of giant silver tongs and heading over to a glass display cabinet which is full of creamy peaked cakes all lined up in rows. Sam rolls her eyes before looping her arm through mine.

'I sure will,' I call after Stacey. I knew it! What was I thinking? I'll just tell the regatta committee that Sam has another huge event to cater for, a wedding or something – perfectly plausible with it being summer-time, the wedding season, after all.

Sam and I make our way over to the best booth in the corner at the far end of the café – perfect for chatting and keeping an eye out to see who is coming or going. We flop down into the reclaimed crimson red velvet train seats; they're arranged in booths of four around low tables, with frilly shaded lamps that radiate a golden glow to create an authentic steam-train-carriage atmosphere. It's just like being aboard the Orient Express, circa 1920, and very in keeping with the elegant Art Deco style of the Carrington's building.

'So, tell me all about the regatta plans.' Sam leans forward eagerly.

'Oh, there's nothing very much to report,' I say, fiddling with my bag to avoid eye contact. 'Early days and all that. At the meeting last week we just divvied up the events; I imagine the real work begins after the next meeting when our project plans have been approved.' Stacey arrives with the cake mountain and two plates. Grateful for the distraction, I hand a plate to Sam and busy myself with sorting out the napkins and forks.

'Rubbish. Georgie, you've always been a bad fibber and I know when you're keeping something from me. What is it?' Sam scrutinises me as she helps herself to a particularly plump red velvet cupcake with glittery frosting, and so mountainous it completely coats her cheeks when she bites into it.

'Nothing.'

'Look, if they don't want my cakes, then I shan't be offended . . .' Sam puts her plate on the table and licks her fingers. 'It's not like I'm desperate for more work or anything.' She shrugs and grabs a napkin to wipe her face. 'And, you know, I found out who catered for Isabella's soirée.'

'Who?' I ask, suddenly desperate to know right away.

'Only that chef from the Mulberry Grand Hotel who does the private functions. He comes to your house – or yacht in this case – and does all the cooking on the premises, which just makes it even more weird. Why use him, when they could have stayed instore, as it were? And I have it on good authority – one of my regulars went to a dinner party that he catered for, so I know my food eats so much better than his.' Sam pushes her bottom lip out as I try not to smile at her 'chef speak'. It always amuses me when she describes how food 'eats', conjuring up all kinds of weird and wonderful images in my head . . . Anyway, I know she's right; Sam is a fantastic cook. When she left school, Alfie paid for her to spend a year at an exclusive culinary school in Paris. Her twice-baked goat's cheese soufflé is always astounding. 'Not very loyal, is it?' Sam shakes her head, making her corkscrew curls jig furiously.

'It is a bit strange – I could ask Tom, see if he knows anything about it?' I offer, before taking a vanilla slice, or *millefeuille*, as Sam calls them.

'No, honey, it's fine, I don't want to make a deal about it. I'm just curious, that's all. So have the regatta people gone with the Mulberry Grand chef too – is this what you're hiding? They don't want me—'

'Oh, but they do,' I say quickly, and then instantly wish I could push the words right back into my mouth.

'Brilliant! I'll start planning a menu right away. We could do nautical themed cupcakes with little chocolate anchors – even boats, perhaps! How long is the regatta on for? I'll need to make sure we don't run out, and that there's a good rotation with the selection; we don't want the same cakes for the duration. People like variety and, let's face it, some might stay for the whole event.' Sam beams enthusiastically, really getting into the swing of things.

'Two days, but are you sure?' I ask, tentatively.

'Definitely, why wouldn't I be?'

'Well, you know . . . will you have enough time?'

'Of course, and especially when the new night nanny, or manny, starts. And I've decided to recruit a manager too, to help run the café, do the admin side of things, which I hate. It all takes up so much time, the stock ordering, not to mention the accounts, VAT returns and all that. I never used to mind, but I guess my priorities have changed, and you're right, I can't do it all, not with attending the board meetings at Palmer Estates as well – trips up to London end up taking out a whole day. And Nathan is overjoyed that I've finally seen sense, as it will free me up to do what I love best – be with the twins and bake, instead of being dead on my feet all day long in the café and then just irritable when I pick the girls up. It's no fun for anyone.' Sam sits back; the look of relief on her face is almost palpable.

'Good for you. Let's have a toast.' We chink mugs, a little too enthusiastically, as hot chocolate splashes onto the table.

'Oops.' Sam wipes it away with a napkin.

'To you. My magnificent friend, Samantha, who knows when to ask for help!' I say, cheerily. It'll be good to have the old Sam back, full of energy and optimism.

'Thanks, honey, and you know what they say . . . happy mum makes happy baby, or *babies*, in my case. God, I literally can-*not* wait, I'm that exhausted. Are you still up for helping with the interviews? I've contacted a few agencies already and Nathan will help out, too. We'll be like a panel, he's even put together a list of questions we can ask.' She smiles.

'Sure. Just let me know when and where, and I'll be there . . . with my very best serious interview face on. Can I bring a clipboard?' We both laugh.

My mobile pings, announcing the arrival of an email. I ignore it.

'Oh don't do that on my account,' Sam says, gesturing for me to check my phone. 'It might be important regatta business.'

'Thanks. If you're sure you don't mind . . .' I click on my inbox. Ah, it's a message from Dad, in his usual shouty caps. It's titled MEET DAISY. Ooh, he's really getting the hang of communicating in the modern age now – he's even managed to attach a picture! That advanced silver surfers' course on how to 'fully engage in modern technological times' is obviously working a treat, even if the picture is upside down and a bit fuzzy. I tilt the phone; from what I can make out, it's a photo of a very cool retro-looking sunshine yellow camper van. And it's covered in white daisies. Oh my God. I quickly type a reply and press send.

Who does Daisy belong to Dad? xx

A reply pings back, almost immediately.

US OF COURSE ISNT SHE A BEAUTY XXX

But Dad never mentioned anything about buying a camper van. I'm not sure how to react. And aren't they for – like – young funky cool people? Not pensioners with a passion for *Cash in the Attic*. I type a reply.

Wow! Yes, she's lovely, can't wait to see her xx

I go to place the phone on the table, when another email arrives.

BE QUICK WE ARE DOING EUROPE IN HER AND GOING NEXT WEEK BOOKING EUROTUNNEL NOW XX

Whaaaat? Since when did Dad and Nancy 'do Europe'? He sounds like an over-entitled gap year student – not a pensioner who lives in the new retirement complex with a communal lounge. Surely he should be concentrating on the weekly bingo meet-up and looking after his lovely garden. And what about his black Labrador, Dusty? What will she do while they're off jollying around Europe? No no no. He can't just 'do Europe'! And what about his angina? I'm sure there must be rules around travelling with that . . . surely he needs to be close to the doctors' surgery at all times? How is that going to work, when he's cruising through the Alps or whatever? That's the beauty of where he lives – they have a GP on site! In literally one minute, he can be sitting in front of a doctor. No airlifting or mountain tracker dogs required . . .

'You OK?' Sam asks, bringing me back to the moment.

'Um, yes. It's from Dad. Reckons he's "doing Europe",' I make silly quote signs with my fingers and pull a face.

'Oh, good for him. How exciting,' she smiles, slicing off a chunk of chocolate cake as I type a last reply.

Tom and I will be over at lunchtime xx

A few minutes later, and he hasn't replied, so I can't resist sending another email.

PS – do not book Eurotunnel until we've had a chat!

'Say hello from me, will you honey?' Sam smiles, offering me the last of the chocolate cake.

PPS – Sam says hi xx

I go to slot the phone into my bag, and then realise – they won't be expecting us and I don't want Nancy panicking about having enough food in. She always makes a lovely effort to produce a banquet-like feast whenever Tom and I turn up. I quickly send another email.

PPPS – I'll bring something nice for lunch xx

7

'So are you going to tell me what this is all about?' Tom smiles, sliding an arm around my waist as he arrives. But before I can answer, he pulls me in for a kiss and I stand on tiptoe to reach his warm lips, my thighs tingling and my stomach flipping over and over. Even after all the kisses we've shared, it's incredible the effect he still has on me. After leaving the café earlier, I bombed up to his office, but he was busy on a Skype call so I left a note with his PA asking him to meet me here at the taxi rank. We eventually pull apart. 'Mmm, that was nice. I've missed you Georgie.'

'Aw, don't be silly, we only saw each other this very morning, just a mere few hours ago. Although admittedly it was very early when you left . . .' I tease.

'OK, smartarse.' He tweaks my nose affectionately. 'It may be just a few hours, but I can still miss you if I like. Then again, if you don't want me to . . .' He shrugs nonchalantly but his smile widens.

'No, no, it's fine, you can miss me, of course you can – but I'd hate for you to feel lonely, that's all,' I say, enjoying our banter.

'Then move in with me – that way you'd never have to worry about me being lonely.' He looks right into my eyes, his jovial expression turning serious and almost taking my breath away.

'Let's talk about it . . .' I'm just about to continue when the taxi arrives, and after stowing the carrier bags safely in the middle of the back seat, we jump in either side.

'Is that a yes?' Tom says, fastening his seatbelt and turning to face me.

'It's a *let's talk about it*,' I say, flicking my eyes towards the driver.

'Well, that's good enough for me.' He kisses my cheek. '*For now*. But only if you tell me something.'

'What's that then, Mr Carrington?'

'Why have you got four enormous carrier bags crammed full of boxes from the food hall? I thought you wanted to try out that new gastro-pub around the corner.' He gives me a quizzical look.

'I do. Really I do, but would you mind if we try it another time?'

'Sure. You're the boss,' he says easily.

'Well not really, you're the actual boss.'

'True. But only when we're inside the store.'

'Is that right?' I raise my eyebrows suggestively and whisper, 'I can think of several other places too where you can be *very* authoritative.'

'Only because you like it that way,' he teases, not missing a beat.

'Naughty!' We both laugh.

'Anyway, stop flirting and tell me what's going on.' He glances at the bags again.

'I need to find out what Dad is up to. I think he's having some kind of midlife crisis, so we're going over there for lunch.'

'I see,' Tom says, totally unfazed, and then a few seconds later, he adds, 'isn't he almost seventy though?'

'Well, yes. But that's not the point.'

'Well, it is a bit.' He shakes his head. 'Midlife is forty-something, isn't it?'

'Hmm.' I ponder for a moment. 'A three-quarter-life crisis then.' Frowning, I pat the bags as if to emphasise the point.

When Sam and I had finished chatting, I went with her to the crèche, and after enjoying big squeezy cuddles with the twins, I whizzed down to the Carrington's food hall in the basement and selected an assortment from the hot food and deli counters – lasagne (Dad's favourite), garlic bread, tapas selection, profiteroles and mini crème brûlées, a cheese board with those charcoal crackers that I know Nancy loves, grapes, and Tom's favourite, fruity coleslaw with hot chicken wings . . . I've got the lot.

'He's OK though, I hope?' Tom's forehead creases. He knows all about Dad's past.

'Oh no, it's nothing like that . . .' I shake my head.

A few minutes later and I've shown Tom the picture of Daisy, and he reckons we should keep an open mind, see what Dad and Nancy have to say first, before leaping in and getting them all worried with my anxiety. In fact, he made a very good point too – by 'doing Europe', Dad may have just meant they were popping over to Calais for some duty-free shopping; he does have a tendency to exaggerate, and they are partial to a nice bottle of red with a wheel of Brie. Oh well; I guess we'll find out for sure very soon . . .

'Have you stopped catastrophising now?' Tom turns to face me.

'A bit, I guess, but let's just hope you're right. Dover is only an hour or so along the coast from Mulberry, and the Eurotunnel takes no time at all. I'm sure it will be fine,' I reply, attempting to convince myself as I slot my phone back inside my bag.

'Exactly, and in the meantime, tell me about the regatta – have you finished your project plan yet?'

'I have. And it's looking very good indeed,' I say proudly, having spent every spare moment since the meeting on it. I went with a proper project-planning app in the end; it's on my laptop, but only after reading through one of those Dummies books for hours to get the hang of it. And of course my Pinterest page has evolved, too; in fact I have several now – one for each of the things I'm organising. 'Although I'm really struggling with the ice-cream vans. And—'

'Ice cream?' Tom jumps in, looking animated.

'Yes, I need to find loads of ice-cream vans. Mr Whippy. Lots of them.'

'Well that's easy,' he responds, casually.

'It is?' I crease my forehead. 'I've had a nightmare trying to find proper ice-cream vendors. I called the Catering Association, hoping they might have a list of vans in our area, but no such luck – told me they're in decline, sadly, which is a bit of a mystery as I thought everyone loved ice cream. And I even went to the promenade, to the place I used to go as a child with Mum and Dad, right next to the pier, and the man in the van there said he'd be happy to help out for a few hours if his lumbago behaves on the day. But we can't just have one ice-cream van, lumbago aside. No, we need lots, thirty at least. I've counted every street corner on Wayfarer Way, not to mention Market Square and the actual marina – we really need a fleet to line the route. And ideally someone to make a special regatta ice cream too.'

'No problem. I'll just call Uncle Marco.' Tom grins.

'Uncle Marco?' My pulse quickens.

'Yep, he's . . .' Tom pauses to ponder, 'Isabella's sister's husband's brother . . . I think.' He shakes his head, clearly losing track of his extensive family tree. 'Or something like that. Anyway, that's all irrelevant, what's important is that he owns an ice-cream factory, in Scarborough I think.' Oh my God. Wow! How exciting, an actual factory! I bet it's just like Willy Wonka's chocolate factory with enormous vats of sweets and sprinkles, only with ice cream instead, obvs. I want to give Tom a massive hug, and would if the food bags weren't in the way.

'I went to visit once as a child, and there were hundreds of those funny vans, the ones that play the tinkly music. It was amazing. I'd never seen anything like it.' Tom looks enthralled, and in an instant I'm reminded of the chasmic contrast in our backgrounds. Tom was home-schooled in Italy by a string of private tutors until he was fifteen, followed by a year at an exclusive polo school in Argentina and then on to Harvard when he was only seventeen. And that might explain why he calls his parents by their first names, almost as if they're strangers. No wonder he was fascinated by a mere ice-cream van. I can't imagine they featured much in his precision-built childhood. I'll call him this evening and get him on board.'

'Oh Tom, thank you so much.' He leans his head towards mine and I manage to reach carefully across the bags to give him a kiss on the cheek.

'No problem. I'll do whatever I can to help out. It's fun and makes a change to be talking about something other than sales projections and supplier contracts. Anything else you need?' he asks eagerly, obviously keen to embrace his lighter side – his face has even taken on a boyish charm. I love seeing him like this; it's such a stark contrast to the business-like demeanour he portrays instore.

'Don't suppose you have another uncle with a carousel, by any chance?' I still haven't managed to sort one out.

'Err, no! Sorry. Afraid not.' Tom laughs and shrugs apologetically.

8

We pull up outside the retirement complex over-looking Mulberry Common and Dad is walking down the path to meet us. He looks really well, all short sleeves and gardener's tan, and I'm sure his hair is a little longer than last time I saw him – darker too, come to think of it; he's obviously still using the Just For Men to hold on to a more youthful look to belie his near-septuagenarian status. Dusty, his very shiny black Labrador, is bouncing along beside him.

After paying the driver, Tom and I grab two bags each and head towards Dad. Dusty makes a beeline for me, licking the back of my hand before pushing her nose into one of the bags. Laughing, I stroke her silky ear and gently nudge her head away – I can't imagine she's starving. Dad dotes on her. Nancy too. And I know for a fact that Nancy cooks special dinners with rice and chicken all chopped up into little bite-size pieces, which I've then seen Dad hand-feed to Dusty while she's sprawled out in the middle of their sofa with a very regal look on her face.

'Georgie, it's lovely to see you. And Tom, how are you son?' Dad gives me a kiss before shaking Tom's hand and pressing his shoulder warmly.

'Very well, sir, and how are you?' Tom says politely, returning to his formal, business-like manner, and I swear his *Downton* accent (upstairs, naturally) just got a little more pronounced.

'As I said last time we met, I'd be far happier if you called me George. No need to stand on ceremony, Tom, not when you're practically family,' Dad pretends to chide, crinkling the corners of his eyes as he shakes his head.

'Sorry George.' Tom laughs.

'Come on then, let's get inside.' Dad rubs his hands together jovially. 'Nancy can't wait to see you both, she's just taken Daisy out for a run down to the corner shop to fetch some biscuits – she won't be long.'

'Oh Dad, she really didn't need to do that. I said we'd bring lunch – see here, there's plenty of food.' Tom and I simultaneously lift the carrier bags as confirmation.

'She likes to, sweetheart, you know how hospitable she is . . . and you can never have too many biscuits.'

Dad's smile widens as he places an arm around Tom's shoulders before leading him inside. I follow behind, pleased to see them getting on so well as always.

Dad is typing the number code into the security keypad on the communal door, when a spluttering noise followed by a loud bang behind us makes me jump – Dusty, too. She cowers sharply in shock before panting excessively. Dad grabs her collar and gives her a calming stroke to slow down her breathing. Dusty is a rescue dog, so who knows what has happened to her in a previous life? It's heartbreaking, if I let myself think too much about it.

'Ah, just in time. Here they are,' Dad says. We turn around. Oh my God. So this must be Daisy. My worst fears are confirmed – the camper van is ancient! Admittedly, it's very pretty and stylish, and it looks even better than it did in the picture, with yellow gingham curtains at the little windows and a couple of patchwork cushions propped jauntily on the back seat. But I can't help feeling panicky all over again. Especially on seeing that Nancy has abandoned it with one of the front wheels mounted on the actual pavement, having obviously misjudged the kerb's whereabouts. How on earth are they going to manage getting to the Eurotunnel, not to mention having to drive on the right-hand side of the road when they arrive on the Continent. What happens if they forget and end up going the wrong way along a motorway? Although, mind you, one saving grace – I reckon Daisy's top speed is only about 30 mph, so plenty of time for all the French drivers to spot them and swerve out of their way. But still, I can't help thinking it's a disaster waiting to happen.

Nancy climbs out and slams the heavy door behind her before bustling around to the passenger seat, patting her neat blonde hair back into place and pulling out a massive tin of shortbread biscuits, three packets of custard creams, two packets of bourbons and a cardboard cylinder of milk chocolate digestives which she piles up on top of the tin – she can barely see over her biscuit mountain. After quickly handing my two food bags to Tom, I dart forward to give Nancy a hand.

'Thank you, my dear, and I'm so sorry I wasn't here when you arrived. How are you?' Nancy asks, as I take the custard creams and bourbons from her.

'I'm very well, Nancy, but you really didn't need to go to any trouble on our account. I did spring the visit on you, after all.' I feel guilty now. I shouldn't have been so impulsive.

'And what a lovely surprise it is, plus I've got your favourites.' Nancy motions with her head to the chocolate digestives balanced on top of the tin. 'Come inside, I'll put the kettle on and we can have a nice catch-up,' she says warmly.

*

I can barely move, I'm that stuffed. Between us, we managed to polish off all the food and just about stagger to the lounge with its swirly patterned carpet and big squishy sofas, where we're now enjoying a cup of tea and a pile of biscuits. It would have been rude not to. Nancy laid them all out on a big silver platter and made a proper pot of tea with rose-patterned china cups on saucers, milk in a matching jug and sugar cubes in a bowl set out on a doily-covered tray.

'So, where are you planning on taking Daisy?' It's Tom who finally addresses the whopping big elephant in the room – somehow, the actual reason for our impromptu visit got avoided over lunch.

'Well, we want to cover as much ground as we can,' Dad starts. 'The glorious French countryside, I've always fancied wandering through a vineyard. Then, on to Spain. We might even hop over to Marrakesh to visit the souks.'

'Yes that would be marvellous.' Nancy joins in. 'I'd love a pair of those colourful canvas shoes they sell with the tassels on. Just like Aladdin wears. We could bring you back a pair, Georgie.' Nancy beams and I manage a smile, already concocting a plan inside my head as to how my new Aladdin shoes might mysteriously disappear. 'And what about Turkey?' Nancy continues.

'Oh yes. We could have a suck on one of those hookah pipes, love!' *Daaad. Nooooo. Just no!* My jaw drops – I stare at Dad and Nancy, goggle-eyed and speechless, as they both nod enthusiastically. What's going on? This isn't the Dad and Nancy I know – Dad, especially, is usually so traditional, set in his ways, with his old-school views and values, but now? Well, it's as if they've been possessed by a pair of much younger, and far funkier free-thinkers. Next they'll be doing t'ai chi on Mulberry Common and converting to Buddhism.

'The rose-fragranced hookah is supposed to be the best – that's what they were saying on that programme we watched last week. Have you seen it, Georgie?' Nancy says, earnestly. 'It's on the Discovery Channel and called *Travel the World Before It's Too Late*, or something like that.'

Ahh, I get it, now it's all starting to make sense – they've been watching too much television and have got carried away; turned into armchair explorers, only their armchair is sunshine yellow, camper-van-shaped and with a special pet name, Daisy!

'And Italy, we can't miss that out – Tom, you'll have to jot down the best places for us to visit.' Dad grins while Tom nods before glancing at me with a circumspect look on his face. 'We're not getting any younger, so who knows when we might get the chance again,' Dad finishes cheerily, before plopping three sugar cubes in his tea and giving it a good stir, seemingly oblivious to the enormity of the trip he's about to undertake.

'Wow, that's some itinerary you have there, George.' Tom looks impressed as he lets out a long puff of air. 'So, how long do you reckon you'll be away for?'

'Ooh, a good few months, I reckon. Certainly the whole summer. Back in September some time, I reckon . . .'

'*Months?* But Dad you can't go away for *months!*' I blurt out, instantly wishing I didn't sound like a moany teenager all of a sudden. Tom surreptitiously squeezes my hand.

'Why not?' Dad frowns.

'Well, um . . . what if something happens?' I ask, thinking: so much for a day trip to Calais . . . this is a proper road trip they have planned – they could be bombing around Lake Garda negotiating hairpin bends before the week is out!

'Like what?' Dad helps himself to a custard cream and then gives it a good dunk in his tea.

'I think Georgie's just a bit worried about your health,' Tom says diplomatically.

'Yes, what about your angina? I bet your GP won't be happy about you travelling so far and being away for such a long time. Don't you have to have regular check-ups?' I say, feeling panicky . . . and, if I'm being totally honest, perhaps a teeny-weeny bit jealous. I'd love to take off on a road trip to wander around vineyards and suck on hookah pipes. Maybe after the regatta!

'Dr Sanghera was very enthusiastic, wasn't he, Nancy?'

'Ooh, yes dear – said the sun, sea air and sense of adventure will do us both the world of good. Which reminds me, we must get some of that spray-on sun cream. I'll put it on our list. Have you seen it, Georgie? It's very good.' I nod politely, but the panic increases. What if something happens? 'It saves on all that rubbing in and messy hands palaver. Just one spray and away you go.' Nancy makes big eyes and waves a flamboyant hand in the air.

'But what if you need medical assistance?' I turn back to Dad, keen to check that he's at least considered the risks.

'Darling, we have it all covered – we got a superb insurance policy through the bank, and they do have doctors in other countries, you know. Besides, it's not as if we're going to the Gobi desert!' *Thank God.*

'And what about Dusty? Have you thought about her?' Ha! I bet they haven't. And on hearing her name, Dusty bombs over to me for a quick cuddle. I duly oblige by running my hand over her head. She thanks me by resting her chin on my knee and wagging her tail.

'Of course we have! And it really wouldn't be fair to keep her cooped up inside Daisy for such a length of time and then subject her to all that heat, so she's staying with Len and Beryl next door. Len likes a good stroll around the park of a morning, so Dusty will get her walks, and she often pops into theirs in the afternoon for a snooze on the sofa, so she'll be right at home with them,' Dad says in a very cheery voice. 'Nancy, can you add that to our list please, love? We mustn't forget to stock up on those treats Dusty loves.'

'Right you are, George, and we'd better get a dozen boxes and leave some money too so they can replenish when stocks run out.' Nancy reaches across to the coffee table for her notepad with the fridge magnet on the back. 'And I'll get some packs of cooked chicken for Beryl's freezer. We can't expect her to cook from scratch every day for Dusty, like I do.' Hmmm, so they have it all worked out then, it seems.

Dad turns to me. 'Georgie, we'll be fine sweetheart. Please try not to worry, we'll keep in touch.' He leans across the sofa to pat my arm.

'But this means you won't be here for my birthday,' I say, feeling a bit dejected, especially after all the birthdays he missed in the past; but then I quickly realise that I'm a grown woman, and not the child I was when he went to prison. Besides, I have Tom now, too, and my birthday surprise to look forward to – very exciting! I wonder what it is . . .

'Well, you could always come and join us for a weekend if you don't mind mucking in, and there's plenty of room inside Daisy, plus the weather on the Med is glorious this time of year,' Dad says jovially, and I shrivel a little inside. I can't imagine Tom has ever shacked up in a clapped-out old camper van covered in yellow daisies. 'It would be so much fun, especially now we have the awning. You know, it clips onto the side of the van just like a huge tent. And we can always take extra air beds and sleeping bags for the pair of you, save you having to lug them all the way over.' Oh God. I know he's trying to be kind, but . . . And I can just picture Isabella's face on hearing about our camping trip.

It's Tom who jumps in. 'Mr—' he manages, before Dad interrupts.

'Tom, how many times have I said . . . it's George to you, son, no need for such formality.' Dad smiles warmly and a pang of guilt hits me. He means well. I'm being mean – it could be fun, sleeping in a field or in a layby by the beach listening to the waves lap the shore . . . back to nature and all that. It could be an adventure.

'Sorry, George,' Tom smiles. 'We'd love to visit and camp with you in Daisy, but we already have plans for Georgie's birthday,' he starts, and I want to hug him, he's so kind. I know he'd hate sleeping in a tent; he told me he tried camping as a boy and swore he'd never ever do it again – he loves his home comforts far too much. Me too.

'Well, I'm sure there will be plenty of other times. You never know, we might really get the bug for it and venture further afield next time . . . The Australian bush!' Silence fills the little sitting room. I hold my breath. 'Only joking!' Dad laughs, but I'm sure I spot a faraway look in his eye.

Before I can grill him further, my phone buzzes with a text message. It's from Dan, replying to the text I sent him after the first regatta meeting.

Yes, count me in! If you fancy coming to my event on Saturday, we can chat at the aftershow party. I'll get details and invites sent over to you.

Ah, that's nice. I knew he'd be up for it. I quickly tap out a reply, and then realise the time.

'Dad, Nancy, sorry, but we're going to have to get going. I have a client this afternoon,' I say, hauling myself out of the armchair – I really shouldn't have had that fifth bourbon biscuit.

'Well, thanks for popping over, dear, it's always a treat to catch up.' Nancy gets up to see us out. I give her and Dad a hug; Tom does too.

'I'll call you, Georgie, before we head off,' Dad says, pulling open the front door and squeezing my hand as I step outside. 'And do stop worrying. We'll be fine!' he waves after us.

Oh God, I really hope so . . . I couldn't bear it if something happened to either of them.

9

The regatta plans are coming together really nicely now, and I needn't have panicked at all, as Betty, Annie, and someone from practically every department instore has volunteered to get involved and help out. #TeamCarringtons has had six weekly lunchtime meetings now in the staff canteen, and we've even managed to source a carousel – it turned out that Annie's Uncle Mikey used to work on the funfairs, so he put me in touch with a man just along the coast in Brighton who was more than happy to agree to turn up and spin the horses in exchange for a pound a ride. So, thankfully, I've managed to cross 'carousel' off my seemingly never-ending 'to do' list.

'OK, so everyone is agreed then?' It's Annie. We're in the staff canteen and just about to wrap up our seventh meeting. 'That I'm the deputy #TeamCarringtons boss?'

'Fine by me, dear,' Betty says, finishing the last of her tea. 'I've got enough on my plate at home with lazy Luke.' She smiles wryly before sitting back and folding her arms.

'And fine by me too,' Denise from Home Electrical says to Annie. 'But only if I can be in charge of the brochures – making sure all the ice-cream vans have a big bundle to sell. I want to liaise with that Matt from the council. He is hot,' she laughs. Matt popped instore last week to see how I was getting on, so I invited him to join in our lunchtime meeting, and now Denise is clearly smitten. 'Georgie, do you know if he's single?'

'Sorry, no idea,' Denise's forehead creases with disappointment, 'but I'll see what I can find out,' I quickly add, and she grins like a loon.

'Thanks, Georgie.'

'OK, so to recap, we're pretty much there then – we have a carousel, thanks Annie,' she nods as I click to update my project plan with Uncle Mikey's friend's mobile number. 'And you're going to be the go-between with the council to make sure he has permission to set up the day before – and that all the legal stuff, health and safety, etc., is sorted out. Would you like some help with any of that?'

'Nope. Thanks anyway, but I have it all under control,' she says, smoothing down her black uniform top and straightening her gold Carrington's name badge.

'Great. And thank you! I do appreciate all your help. So, that leaves the tunnel tours . . .' I tab through the project plan until I find the right place and type an update. 'Mrs Grace has agreed to conduct the tours; they'll be every hour and tickets are already available to buy on the Carrington's website, and the official regatta website, too, which went live last week. Plus, she's also liaising with her publicist to see about organising a series of short readings from her book, with the option to buy a copy and have it signed at the end of each tour, which is a very nice touch.'

'Oooh, I'd love to give her a hand with that, and every hour for two days will certainly take it out of her . . . those tunnels go on for ever.' Betty leans forward. 'And one of them is at least a mile long.'

'I'm sure she'd appreciate the help,' I say, typing in Betty's name under the 'tunnels resource' section. 'I'll let her know.' I go to make a note in my pad on the 'phone calls to make' page.

'No need love, I'll be seeing her at bingo on Friday, we'll chat it all through then, you've enough to be getting on with.' Betty smiles kindly.

'Thanks so much, I really appreciate your help, Betty. And all of you, really, I can't thank you enough.' I smile around the table. With their help, Carrington's first regatta sponsorship is going to be a massive success. When I first agreed to represent Carrington's, I had no idea just how much work would be involved, so having a team of helpers is an absolute godsend. I make a mental note to thank each of them with a gift – a bouquet of flowers or some champagne truffles, perhaps – when it's all over. If everything goes smoothly and to plan, Isabella is bound to be impressed, and Tom will be thrilled that Carrington's is represented so well in the community. I'm sure it will make a difference to his negotiations in trying to find a suitable location for the new store.

'You're very welcome, G.' It's Melissa, our sturdy plain-clothes store detective. She flings an arm around my shoulders and pulls me in for a big bear hug, practically winding me in the process. 'Right, what else is on that plan of yours?' she adds, eventually letting go of me.

'The stalls are all organised; we have a nice selection ranging from gourmet candy floss – I never knew it came in different flavours – to good old traditional mulberry pie with custard. Sam has got her cake menu finalised, and Max, the Carrington's food hall manager, is doing a Japanese-themed marquee.'

'Well, I heard he's already told that Meredith one from the committee what locations he's having,' Betty puffs.

'I bet he has.' Melissa rolls her eyes.

'Apparently, he went straight to the organ grinder, Dunwoody, and said he can't be expected to serve his finest food in a back alley without proper access for his special climate-controlled Carrington's food delivery van,' Betty continues.

'Yes, that's right,' I say, remembering the email I got from him this morning confirming this to be the case. And he's managed to book Mr Nakamura, the Japanese chef, to do a Teppanyaki demo *and* a sushi-making class. It's going to be brilliant – visitors to the regatta will be able to visit the special 'Japanese cuisine' marquee, which will be in a prime spot by the harbour, where for a small fee they can roll their own *temaki* and eat it right away. I'm going to make sure Isabella has a front-row workbench for that event. Tom has told me she loves sushi, and as a fluent Japanese speaker, she's going to be very impressed that we have Mr Nakamura here in Mulberry-On-Sea for her to chat to.

'And you know, Max is actually a proper trained chef, and he's friends with Gordon Ramsay, so I can't imagine he takes any crap, certainly not off the likes of that Meredith one. We all know what the sleb chefs are like.' Melissa shakes her head. *Hmm, good for you, Max!* 'And there's something not right about that bird.

123

Trust me!' Mel continues, and I stifle a giggle, thinking she's got a very good point. Meredith sure makes me feel uncomfortable – it's as if she has it in for me but I'm not entirely sure why. I know she has issues with Carrington's after her affair with the Heff, but still . . . 'Yep, I can always tell the shifty ones, comes from people-watching all day long as I follow them covertly around the store. I should have a master's degree in character profiling.'

I also got an email from Meredith, stating that she wants a woman from the WI to approve Sam's menu to ensure there isn't a 'conflict of interests' with the other cake sellers – Meredith really does seem hell-bent on making this regatta as difficult as possible for Carrington's. I haven't told Sam yet.

Talking of whom – she must be telepathic, as my mobile buzzes with a text message from Sam: spooky! I glance at the screen while the others chat about the last series of *Ramsay's Kitchen Nightmares*.

Just a reminder re. the nanny/manny interviews tomorrow. First one is at 10 so bring your clipboard and oversized geek glasses lol xxx

I quickly tap out a reply.

Can't wait, don't forget the running shorts! xxx

I slot my mobile into my pocket. We're not really supposed to have phones on us, but everyone does, and as long we keep them on silent it's OK.

'So, is that it for now? Only, I need to get back to the shop floor to sniff out the lifters. Had to body-slam a bloke with half of Home Electricals stock shoved up his hoodie this morning – must think I'm blind.' There's a resounding tut-tutting sound.

'Well, I'd like to see them try it on in my department.' Annie flicks her hair before leaning back in her chair. 'I'm like a hawk when it comes to my bags.' I smile, remembering how they used to be *my bags*. I sometimes wish I still worked in Women's Accessories, with all those luxury handbags. Nothing beats the smell and feel of buttery-soft leather on opening a new season delivery box from designers like Marc Jacobs and Mulberry.

'I think so. And thanks for coming – see you all on Monday for what could very well be our last meeting – not much left to do now, we're almost there,' I beam. We all push our chairs back and go to leave, and then I remember. 'Oh, hang on, I forget to say . . . who fancies a trip to an ice-cream factory?'

Tom put me in touch with his Uncle Marco and we've already exchanged emails and sorted out most of the arrangements, but he's invited me to the factory too – how could I resist seeing where ice cream is actually made? No way.

'Ooh, I'd love to do that . . . and then I can tell Jack all about it,' Lauren says, her eyes lighting up.

'Why don't you bring him with you?' I suggest, thinking he's bound to love it.

'Really?' She looks so excited.

'Sure, why not! We can make a day of it. I'll organise a date and let you know. It will have to be soon, is that OK?'

'Brilliant. I can't wait. And Jack will be so excited when I tell him. Thanks Georgie.'

10

When I arrive at Sam and Nathan's house, a white weather-boarded villa on a private beach estate just along the coast from Mulberry-On-Sea, I ring the bell. And wait. And wait some more. The lights are on and their cars are in the driveway. I'm pondering on whether to call Sam's mobile, when Nathan eventually pulls open the front door, looking frazzled.

'Georgie, am I pleased to see you. Come in.' He gives me a quick hug and a kiss on the cheek. 'Sorry about the wait. I was on the phone appeasing a client and Sam's going through Holly and Ivy's wardrobes trying on every single outfit they have – she wants them looking their very best when the candidates turn up. And a lorry-load of new gear arrived yesterday so it's taking forever . . .' He smiles, but there's a hint of frustration in his voice, which is so unlike him.

'Oh, no problem, I can see you have your hands full.' He has a half-empty bottle of milk in one hand

and a bunny-print towel slung over his right shoulder.

'Oh God.' He waves the bottle in the air. 'Trying to tidy up before the first candidate arrives. Come on, I'll make you a cup of tea.' He strides off towards the kitchen.

'Thanks, Nathan, but why don't I make the tea, and then you can give Sam a hand?'

'If you're sure! That would be fantastic. Thank you.' He throws the bottle in the sink and goes to leave, but then quickly turns back. 'You know where everything is, yes?' He rakes a hand through his messy blond hair before reaching down to retrieve a heart-shaped Hello Kitty cushion from the floor.

'Yes! Now go.' I grin, lift up the kettle and waggle it around as proof.

An hour or so later, and the girls are bouncing in their activity chairs, looking cute in matching red spotty pinafores over little white T-shirts, and Sam, Nathan and I are sitting around the breakfast island in the centre of their enormous kitchen. All marble counters and terracotta floor tiles. I know Sam is a professional cook and spends a lot of time in her kitchen, but it really is breathtaking, with whole-wall concertina glass doors that open out directly onto the grassy sand dunes leading down to the sea. And I'm a big fan of her rainbow-crystal-embellished food mixer too. Very blingtastic!

'Don't you think it's a bit casual to have the interviews

in here?' Sam grabs a packet of baby wipes off the counter and wings them into a drawer.

'We could use the dining room if you prefer, it's more formal – or how about my office? Then it would be like a proper interview. We could even sit in a row on one side of the desk as a panel and pretend we're in *The Apprentice*, hands up to be Lord Sugar. I want the pointy finger "you're hired" line,' Nathan jokes, but Sam doesn't laugh – she shoots him a fiery 'shut-up-this-is-serious' glare instead, which is so unlike her.

'Or how about the lounge? Nice and relaxed,' I suggest, wishing they'd both calm down – they look so anxious, anyone would think *they* were the candidates waiting to be interviewed. And the strained atmosphere between them is almost palpable. I've never seen them like this, and it's awkward. Horrible even. Sam seems so unhappy.

'Yes, good idea, not too formal, not too messy,' Sam says, eyeing up a pile of dirty plates stacked on the draining board. I breathe a small sigh of relief, but then she promptly adds, 'I'll just run the Dyson round,' and practically launches herself from the bar stool and towards the door in less time than it takes for me to swallow a mouthful of tea.

'I'll do it.' Nathan places a hand on Sam's arm.

'Oh for God's sake, I am capable of vacuuming my

own house, you know,' she snaps, wrenching her arm free. And I'm shocked. In all the years Sam and I have been friends, I can't remember ever having seen her like this. And definitely not with Nathan. I've never heard her utter a bad word about him, let alone to his actual face. And she's not usually so bothered by what other people think. I know she's exhausted, but there's something more to it – I'll talk to her when we're alone and see if I can get to the bottom of whatever it is that's going on here. Sam and Nathan are rock solid, or so I had thought.

'Does it even need vacuuming? I thought you had a cleaner!' I say, trying to quell the situation. I'm sure a prospective nanny or manny isn't going to be bothered about a bit of carpet fluff.

'We did. But she left. Went back to Poland to care for her elderly mother,' Nathan says in a monotone voice, looking as if he has the weight of the world on his broad shoulders as he shoves his hands in his pockets and avoids eye contact with Sam. But before either of them has a chance to argue some more about who's getting the Dyson out, the doorbell rings, signifying the arrival of the first candidate.

A few hours, and several pots of tea later, and the third wannabe nanny has just left, a twenty-something Russian girl with limited English – the agency had said she was fluent. It quickly became apparent that she really wanted to be a pop star, though, and even offered to sing for us, but Sam politely declined, saying it wouldn't be necessary. And the last candidate hasn't turned up yet, but she's already twenty minutes late, which isn't a good sign.

'Oh God, at this rate we're never going to find someone suitable!' Sam says, scooping her legs up into the armchair. 'They were all a nightmare. Did you see how Ivy cried when that . . . whatever her name was,' Sam waves a dismissive hand in the air, 'picked her up and squeezed her cheek? I have a good mind to call the agency and complain. She shouldn't be allowed to scare children like that.'

'But then she did have a very hairy wart on her chin!' I say, making light of it. I didn't think she was that bad, but Sam seems really upset – furious, even.

'Hmm, I could barely tear my eyes away from it; you would think she would have it removed, seeing as how she works with children. And she was way too rough – poor Ivy's little cheek. Did you see how red it was? It'd better not be bruised.' Sam folds her arms.

'Nooo,' I say, glancing towards the door as Nathan scoops both girls up, one under each arm, and heads into the kitchen. 'But I'm sure Ivy will be fine,' I add diplomatically. Ivy's cheek looked fine to me and I thought the woman was very gentle with both the girls, but then, what do I know about babies? Or how they're supposed to be handled? 'Sam, can I ask you something?'

'Sure. What is it?' she shrugs, staring at the carpet.

'Well, I just wondered if everything was OK?' I keep my voice low – the kitchen door is closed, I think, but I'm not absolutely sure. 'With you and Nathan?'

'Of course. Why wouldn't it be?' Sam frowns and I hesitate.

'It's just that you seem a bit . . . err,' I pause to feel my way, but Sam doesn't give me anything other than a blank face. 'Um, stressed,' I settle on.

'Do I?'

'Yes. I know you're tired—'

'Georgie, you have no idea, but take my advice and stay single and childless for as long as possible.'

'Um . . .' I start, feeling taken aback, but the doorbell rings, stealing my moment to probe further.

'Can you get it? I need a few seconds on my own without a baby screaming or tugging at me.' Sam rests her head back on the sofa and closes her eyes.

'Oh, err, sure.' I jump up, feeling confused and sad. We usually chat about anything and everything, but I guess I'll just have to find another time and try again.

I head along the hallway and pull open the front

door, but there's nobody there, only a sleek black limousine at the end of the driveway with a guy by the door in a chauffeur's uniform. Blimey, this candidate must be well heeled. And quite a bit older than the others we've seen today.

A woman wearing skintight black leather jeans and the highest stacked heels I've ever seen emerges from the car and sashays towards the house. *Hmm, hardly suitable footwear for a nanny!* She'll break her neck trying to run around after the twins in those. And I instinctively know that Sam will hate her on sight – way too much lip filler and volume spray in her super-big blonde hair. She looks more like an ageing rock star than Supernanny!

Not even bothering to acknowledge me, the woman strides past, pausing only briefly to hand me her cashmere pashmina. Flaming cheek – must think I'm a servant or something. I sling the pashmina in the boot box by the door and charge after her down the long *Dynasty*-style hallway, trying not to cough as a heady cloud of Oud perfume wafts my way.

'Oh hello,' Sam says, looking a bit taken aback as she walks out of the lounge and almost bumps right into the woman's chest. 'Err, you're a bit late.' Sam springs back, eyeing the wall clock before glancing at me over the woman's shoulder. I pull a face.

'Well, that's one way of putting it.' The woman plants a hand on her bony, leather-clad hip.

'I beg your pardon?' Sam stands square on to the woman, her eyes flashing.

'Look, why don't we sit down and start again?' I jump in, gesturing towards the lounge.

'I don't think that will be necessary. You're not really what we have in mind for a nanny. Sorry! I'll see you out.' Sam goes to walk away, but the woman grabs her arm. I move closer, wishing I hadn't left my bag in the kitchen now. I scan the hallway looking for a phone, just in case I need to dial 999. This woman is clearly a looper. Sam shakes her arm free.

'Don't be silly, darling. I'm not here to look after your babies,' the woman says.

'Oh! Then why are you here?' Sam says right back.

'To see you, of course!'

'But, I assumed . . . sorry, who are you?' Sam gives the woman an up-and-down look.

'Your mother! But you can call me Christy.'

Sam's face pales immediately.

She clutches the side cabinet.

Instinctively, I launch myself across the hall to stand by her side, but I'm too late. Sam's legs buckle and she crumples to the floor.

Oh my God.

11

Dan's gig was awesome; he's such an amazing singer and the crowd was mesmerised as he treated us to every one of his hit songs, ending with my all-time favourite – 'Sweet Sugar', a country/soul ballad that he co-wrote and originally recorded in Memphis. It's a very special song for me, as it was playing on the radio in the Carrington's staff canteen when I very first clapped eyes on Tom.

The aftershow party is in the VIP suite of a nearby Mayfair hotel, so Tom and I walked here. It's such a warm evening, it would have been a shame not to.

As the lift doors open directly into the suite, the atmosphere is already charged. Exciting. And very glamorous. All kinds of fashion and music types are milling around looking fabulous. Cara Delevingne is standing by the floor-to-ceiling window with the best billion-dollar brows I've ever seen. Tinie Tempah is chatting to a girl right next to me (I remember Dan

saying they have the same manager), and an exceptionally hot guy who looks incredibly like Benedict
Cumberbatch has just walked in. Swoon. I try not to
stare as I walk by on my way to the bar, which is
situated underneath a giant screen showing film
footage from Dan's performance.

'Shall we have Sex on the Beach?' Tom grins, waving
the cocktail menu at me.

'Oooh, why not?'

'As long as there isn't any sand . . . eh? We don't
want any chafing.' He nudges me and I laugh at his
schoolboy joke.

Tom orders while I scan the crowd looking for Dan.
And then I spot him, surrounded by people on the
other side of the room. He sees me, nods before smiling
and excusing himself, and heads towards us.

'Georgie. So pleased you made it. And this must be
Tom? Pleased to meet you.' Dan and Tom shake hands.

'Thanks for the invite, Dan; the gig was awesome.
Can I get you a drink?' Tom says easily.

'No, but thanks dude, I have a backlog already.' Dan
shakes his head and lifts a half-empty pint glass,
gesturing to the end of the bar where six full pints
are waiting plus two ice buckets with bottles of champagne chilling inside. 'In fact, you two could really
help me out . . . Fancy some bubbles?' Dan grabs a

bottle and plonks it on the bar. 'Let's crack this open and have that chat about the regatta.' He flips the cork out and fills three flutes, one for each of us.

'Cheers,' Tom lifts his glass.

'To Georgie, and the Mulberry Regatta,' Dan toasts.

'I'll drink to that,' I laugh, and take a big swig of champagne; thrilled that everything is pretty much organised now; #TeamCarringtons has done a fantastic job – my last committee meeting in the town hall went very well. Cher, Matt and Jared seemed impressed with my Pinterest pages, even if Meredith wasn't. And I spoke to Sam last night and she said Christy had booked into a nearby hotel and that they were 'chatting things through', but she didn't seem keen to elaborate and I wasn't sure how far to probe. In fact, she was surprisingly reticent, to be honest. I really need to go and see her at home so we can have a proper heart-to-heart . . . I've popped into the café loads of times, but she's not been there at all this week, which is understandable under the circumstances.

*

Dan and I have been through the logistics and I've explained that Jared, at Mulberry FM, is organising the mini-music festival, so his manager is going to liaise with Jared to get everything arranged for Dan's performance. He's not bothered about a full sound check and all that, as long as his band are looked after and he has somewhere to chill, away from the crowd, before going on stage. And he's agreed to do a set of six songs, including 'Sweet Sugar' (I told him it's my favourite). It's going to be amazing.

'I'll chat to Cher, she's the landlady at the Hook, Line and Sinker pub . . .'

'Oh, yes I know it,' Dan says. 'Great location for a music festival, on the beach overlooking the marina . . . very St Tropez!' Dan grins, and we all laugh. Mulberry-On-Sea is a trillion miles away from being as chic as the French Riviera, although at the last regatta committee meeting, someone did say the council had planted a row of palm trees along the promenade next to the penny slot amusement arcades, so I guess that's a start.

'I'm sure Cher will have somewhere you can use as a "green room", a VIP area, just like they have backstage at Glastonbury.'

'Awesome. We'll talk more before then, though . . . Have you said hello to Kelly yet?'

'*Kelly?*' Oh my God, is she actually here? And then I remember, Kelly and Dan go back years. It's how he came to be in the TV show, and subsequently how we met.

'Yeah, you know . . . Kelly Cooper TV. Green geek glasses, looks a bit like Ronald McDonald.' Dan laughs. 'But don't say I said so . . . you know what she's like.' He rolls his eyes.

'Oh, how could I forget?' My heart sinks. Instinctively, I can feel myself bracing, scanning in case a camera is nearby – which is ridiculous, I know, but I'm still paranoid after her filming me undercover and it being plastered on YouTube, which is exactly what happened when she rocked up instore last year and caught me twerking along to that 'Single Ladies' song. Hideous. I gulp down a big swig of champagne.

'I didn't realise Kelly would be here tonight; we must say hello,' Tom says and, right on cue, Kelly appears, wearing one of her trademark swirly patterned Westwood playsuits, teamed with diamanté-studded biker boots, which are actually pretty cool (I make a quick mental note to indulge in some online shopping to see if I can find a pair).

'Geooooorgie. Darling, how are you?' Kelly shrieks in her usual flamboyant way – wild orange Medusa curls bouncing all over the place. She pulls me in close and delivers two air kisses either side of my head before letting me go and grabbing hold of Tom. Kelly flings both arms around his neck and plants a big kiss on his lips. 'Oooh, the things I could do to you!' she jokes, stepping back and pressing a palm to his chest. 'But we mustn't tell your mother! Oh no. Isabella still hasn't forgiven me for hitting on that guy she was shagging in university . . . Not my fault if he just wasn't that in to her.' Tom coughs discreetly, and tactfully lifts Kelly's arm away. Oh God! I had forgotten just how inappropriate she could be. 'So, are you all getting on it? Hoovering lines of candy cane and necking the shots?' An awkward silence follows, but Kelly is immune. 'Wasn't Dan amazeballs?' she swiftly adds, making big eyes, while I stifle a snerk at her trying to sound all 'down-with-the-kids'.

'He certainly was, and he's agreed to perform at the Mulberry Regatta, so we have that to look forward to as well,' Tom says to steer the conversation into more conventional territory.

'Well, we have to support the local community. Don't forget I grew up in Mulberry, and everyone, from primary school to my first Saturday job in Tesco and everyone in between, has been incredibly supportive over the years.' Dan grins.

'Perfect!' Kelly jumps in and then hollers, '*Georgie!*', making me jump. Tom squeezes my hand as if secretly saying, *Just humour her and she'll go away very soon . . .*

'How's that column of yours going?'

'Very well, thank you.'

'Good. I just luuuuurved that piece you did on Scherzy's handbag. She's such a doll. Hilarious too! I met her recently at a TV awards do.' She pauses to do the crossed-arm *X Factor* thingy. Cringe. 'I'm hoping to do a special "Day in the Life" documentary with her next summer . . . Ooooh, have you met Gaspard?' she adds, suddenly changing topic. I stare blankly – it's a full-time job keeping up with her.

'Err, Gaspard?' I crease my forehead, wondering what the hell she's going on about.

'Oh, darling, you must. Come with me.' Taking my hand from Tom's, and before I have a chance to protest, Kelly whisks me away and practically propels me to the other side of the room, where an older guy, sixties maybe, with black-framed geek glasses and a flamboyant magenta-coloured velvet tuxedo, complete with frilly white shirt and bow tie, is chatting to a group of tall, incredibly beautiful women. I'm guessing he's very important as they're all hanging on his every word. Unperturbed, Kelly powers on through the throng and presents me, literally, to the guy.

'Gaspard. This is Georgie Hart. The girl I told you about. The one who loves handbags . . . From Mulberry-On-Sea!' A fleeting glimmer of disdain passes Gaspard's face as he gives me a quick up-and-down look, before frowning, reluctantly excusing himself from the group, who quietly drift away, and fixing his gaze directly on me.

'Ah, yes . . . I have a vague recollection,' Gaspard says slowly, with a French accent.

'The one from my last series . . . in the department store,' Kelly prompts, and I wish my cheeks would stop burning – it's obvious that he has absolutely no idea who I am. Awks! 'Talk to her, Gaspard, she's Isabella's son's girlfriend,' Kelly instructs. 'She's a huge fan of your work.' *I am?* Gulp. But before I can catch my breath, Kelly has disappeared, leaving me alone with a man who quite clearly would much rather be entertaining his fangirls than exchanging polite chitchat with me.

'So, tell me, Georgie Hart, what is it you do in Mulberry-On-Sea?' Gaspard slides a silver-embossed cigarette case from his breast pocket. He flips it open and offers me a cigarillo. Shaking my head, I politely decline. 'Then I shan't either,' he says smoothly, before slipping the cigarette case away.

'Oh, don't stop on my account. I love the smell – my dad used to smoke them when I was a child before he went to . . . err.' I stop talking, suddenly very conscious that I'm blabbering like a looper. A short silence follows.

'Went?' Gaspard's monobrow twitches. 'Where did he go?'

'Um, oh, it doesn't matter,' I say, trying to sound breezy, but wishing I could run away back to the bar to be with Tom and Dan. Gaspard is staring at me, waiting for a response, and I get the distinct impression that he's used to people answering him right away. He's very formidable.

'Of course it does. He's your father. Where did he go?' There's a short silence. 'Was it to heaven?' Gaspard's eyes go all Bambi and for some ridiculous reason I want to laugh, and mix it up with a tinge of hysteria.

'Oh no, nothing like that, he err . . .' I pause, suddenly shocked at how the feeling of people knowing, and judging, still catches me unawares sometimes. 'Went to prison.' I drop my gaze and study the sparkly flecked carpet.

'Is that all?' Gaspard booms. His face breaks into a broad smile. 'My dear, it's practically de rigueur these days,' and he actually nudges me conspiratorially. 'Dolce et Gabbana, John Galliano . . . they're all getting convictions.' And then he leans into me and lowers his voice. 'What did he do?' He looks intrigued and there's a hint of naughtiness in his voice.

'He, um, he . . . it was insider dealing, he sold information from the trade floor of the bank he worked at—'

'Pah!' Gaspard waves a frivolous hand in the air. 'And those who bought the information from him ran free, no doubt.' I smile wryly. 'Sooo, you still haven't told me what it is you do in the department store.' Gaspard's face softens as he tactfully changes the subject, thank God.

'Well, I used to run the Women's Accessories section, selling luxury handbags among other things, but now I'm a personal stylist and I write a—'

'Ahh, yes, it's all coming back to me now – Kelly said you stole the show, described you as an everywoman, the nation's sweetheart . . . She also said that you're very knowledgeable when it comes to women's accessories.' I smile graciously, but – *stole the show?* Hijacked it more like, by making an utter fool of myself, and as for being a nation's sweetheart, well – I'm hardly Cheryl Cole. But get me chatting about handbags, and, yes, I can do that all day long.

'So what's your favourite style of bag?' He looks amused as he tilts his head to one side.

'Oh, God, I'm not sure I could whittle it down to just one . . . I mean, there are so many – top handle, tote, crossbody; it really depends on the occasion. I love all the bag babies,' I gush, like a proper handbag fangirl.

'Interesting. But if you could have the perfect handbag, then what would it look like?' I ponder for a moment. And then I know.

'Well, that's easy.'

'It is?' He seems amused.

'Of course. It would look personal.'

'Personal?' His forehead creases.

'Yep, maybe with a unique sparkly keychain or a customised colour, you know – like the paint mixer in Homebase where you can mix up practically any shade of paint that you like.' I pause briefly but he looks completely baffled – they obviously don't have Homebase in France, or wherever it is he lives. 'Or, oh my God, what about this?' I say, getting really excited now. His eyes widen, scanning the room, most likely searching for Kelly to come and rescue him from this *crazeee* English shop girl talking about paint in places he's never heard of. Unperturbed, I keep on. 'A message of my choice, a poem perhaps, inscribed.' I clap my hands together in glee. I can't help myself, as I'm that into this whole design-my-perfect-bag conversation we're having now. 'Gold leaf lettering!' I practically gasp, clearly losing the plot. 'Or a cartoon caricature – I saw something similar, it was amazing . . . I'm not sure I'd have a cartoon of myself, though . . . no, someone far more gorgeous to look at, Ryan Gosling perhaps. Topless. Oh my God, can you imagine? Ryan embossed on the inside of your bag, naked torso winking every time you rummage for your purse?' I laugh, definitely venturing into crazeee looper-land now.

Silence follows. Oh God. And then Kelly appears.

'I knew you'd love her, Gaspard. Isn't she a doll?' Kelly says, adopting a weird American accent.

'She sure is! And exactly what I was looking for.' Gaspard eyes me up and down. *Whaaaat?* Oh no! He's old enough to be my dad, ugh. I turn to leave, but Kelly grabs my hand.

'Excellent!' She rubs Gaspard's arm affectionately, and then turns to me. 'Georgie, Gaspard is looking for a muse . . .'

Oh, right! No. Do I even look like Edie Sedgwick? I saw that film *Factory Girl* – so no! No, no, no, no, no.

But, 'Ummmm' is what comes out of my mouth.

'And now I have found her. You must come to my design studio at once.' Gaspard flings a hand in the air. 'I want to . . .' He pauses and looks baffled, 'How do you say it? Pickle your brain.' *Fuuuuuuck.*

'Oh darling, don't look so horrified.' Kelly pulls me in for one of her cheek-crushing cuddles before quickly whispering in my ear. 'Just smile and say yes.'

She swivels me back around towards Gaspard, and breathes, 'You're going to launch the new Georgie Bag range! How epic is that?'

Faints.

12

So it turns out that Gaspard is a famous international designer – up there with the likes of Dior
and de la Renta! That's right. So much for my fashion
awareness – I had no idea who he even was at the
party, or that he was at the helm of the famous House
of Mercier, for my shame – but then his pieces are for
a more mature woman and far too expensive for the
older Carrington's customers. I certainly know all
about him now, though! That's right, I Googled him
the very second I stepped outside that penthouse suite.
Of course I did. And then felt marginally more
on-trend when I discovered that he's very reclusive,
likes to stay away from the media spotlight, and his
surname is actually Pumphrey, far less exotic.
His mother was French. And he was at the party as
Kelly's plus one – they go back years, apparently.

Anyway, he's looking to branch out into women's
accessories aimed at a younger market and, rather

than consult with his usual panel of experts, he wants me, Georgie Hart, from Mulberry-On-Sea, to help him design a range of handbags to appeal to, and I quote his exact words, 'the ordinary girl-about-town', but – and he was very fastidious in pointing this out as well – to 'a girl who dreams of something more . . .' That's me, apparently. Gaspard reckons it emanates from my soul, and to quote him some more, 'quicker than a ray of light'. Hmm, interesting theory, or perhaps he's just been listening to that Madonna song for way too long, but whatever it is, I'm delighted to help out and can't wait to get involved.

And then Gaspard went off on one talking about monogrammed interior fabrics and metal work but, to cut a long story short, the party was last Saturday, seven days ago, and I'm now at Heathrow Airport waiting to board a flight to his funky design studio in the Tribeca district of *New York City* – it's where Robert De Niro has a restaurant. And Beyoncé and Jay-Z have a house there too. And I'm so damn excited I could actually burst. Of course, I also got straight on Google Earth the very minute I came off the phone from his PA, the day after the party, and the pictures I saw are just how I imagined, dreamed, they would be – a cast-iron building with huge windows and fire-escape ladders running down the front. Honestly, it was just like something out of *Sex and the City*, and I literally can-not wait to get there and see it all for myself.

Gaspard also told me that he caught a whiff of wanderlust wafting around me when we spoke at the party, and it's true, I have been hankering to travel, as you know, but it's funny how the universe sends a curveball when it's least expected. To be honest, it's not really the best timing, with the regatta and everything (the bank holiday weekend is only three weeks away), but there was no way I was turning down an opportunity this good. Even if I am a bit petrified of the potential consequences, both here – remember Isabella and her 'it would be such a shame' line re. the regatta – and abroad in NYC where, let's face it, it's entirely possible my design ideas could end up being a big pile of pony poo and I'll be on the first plane home and back in Carrington's personal shopping suite quicker than Gaspard can speed-dial a proper professional designer.

I turn to face Tom. 'Are you definitely definitely definitely sure?'

'Like I said the last time you asked, I'm definitely sure, a trillion times over, it will be fine.' He smiles and shakes his head before pulling me in close for a cuddle. 'It will be an adventure, Georgie. A once-in-a-lifetime opportunity. And if your Georgie Bag is any good then, who knows, we might even stock it in Carrington's . . .'

'Hey, what do mean, *might?*' I play-punch his arm.

'Only joking. Of course we will – just make sure it's a quality item.'

'Ha ha, like I'm going to help design a piece of old tat.' I pull a face. 'My bag will be epic.' I laugh and make big eyes before stretching a palm through the air for added impact. 'It will be the best handbag ever.'

'See, you're getting excited about it now, too, so why wouldn't you go? And please don't use the regatta as an excuse. Or Mr Cheeks – he'll be having the time of his life in that cat hotel you found for him, with his own room and a little chaise to lounge around on, while waiting for his daily pampering session in the grooming parlour.' Tom laughs. 'We've been over it so many times. Your team, the hashtag, or whatever it is they're called,' he rolls his eyes and smiles, 'will make sure everything stays on track; and besides, it's only for a fortnight. You'll be back before you know it, and certainly in plenty of time to make the final tweaks.'

'Well, four days, to be exact. I get home on Monday and the regatta starts on the Saturday . . .'

'Stop worrying!' He kisses the top of my head before pulling back to look me in the eye. 'Honestly, it will be brilliant. You've spent months organising everything, so it'll really just be a case of executing your best-laid plans on your return. And the team won't let you down.'

'True. I know I can count on them. And Annie was delighted to be made acting team manager while I'm away.' Although on hearing that Dan's a definite yes for the headline act, she was ecstatic and practically ripped the piece of paper with his manager's number on from my hand. I've also left her in charge of liaising with Cher to sort out the 'green room' for him.

'And I've rescheduled all my personal shopping clients – they can always Skype me, and Ruby in Womenswear has said she will help Lauren out with any emergencies. She's also happy to courier clothes on my behalf – sales are sales, at the end of the day, plus she's getting married next month, so is keen to get as much commission as possible.'

'So you have it all organised. I'm sure Carrington's can cope without you for a bit – see, nothing to worry about.' I glance away, knowing this isn't strictly true. Isabella was all for calling Sebastian in when Tom mentioned my trip on the phone to her the other day. I could hear her on the other end of the line. I'm sure she thinks I'm shirking my responsibilities just to run off on a jolly. And maybe I am a bit, but Tom's right, it is the offer of a lifetime, to work with a top designer on creating my perfect handbag. I'm sure chances like this don't come along twice. So I'd be a fool not to grab it with both hands. I just wish fate, the universe, or whatever, had sent this chance to me a few months in the future – when the regatta was over, and my best friend's estranged mother hadn't just reappeared after a twenty-five-year disappearing act.

I've tried calling Sam every day this week, but haven't managed to talk to her, so I've no idea how things are going for her with Christy. And in the end I had to leave a voice message to explain about the trip to New York, which certainly isn't ideal. And probably a bit insensitive. I should have gone to her house, but things have been so manic since Saturday, getting everything organised for the trip, I just ran out of time. I make a mental note to call her the very minute the flight touches down in JFK! Hmm, perhaps not, it'll be the middle of the night in the UK . . . but certainly soon. I'll definitely call as soon as I possibly can.

'Come on, let's get a coffee while we wait,' Tom says, picking up my carry-on bag and turning towards a nearby Costa Coffee.

'Sure, why not? Plenty of time.' I glance at my watch. Four hours left before check-in even opens.

'Indeed.' Tom smirks. 'I did say you might be giving

yourself just a bit too much extra time . . .' He laughs and holds up his left thumb and index finger in front of my face as a measure.

'OK, smartarse.' I bat his hand away. 'But you can never be too careful when it comes to getting to airports on time.'

I have an intense fear of arriving too late for check-in – or having to run at speed all the way to the gate with my name being Tannoyed around the airport so everyone knows I'm the one who will make them miss the flight departure slot when my luggage has to be chucked off due to me being a 'no show'! But I guess in this instance, I probably was a little overzealous in my timings. Oh well, more time together before we're apart for two weeks – the perfect opportunity to have that chat about us living together. We still haven't really talked about it, and Tom hasn't mentioned it for ages now. I'm going to miss him like crazy. We've agreed to call every day. It would have been great if Tom was able to come too, but he has back-to-back meetings lined up in his quest to find suitable premises for the new store. Apparently, the board has whittled it down to a shortlist of three now, but it's all top secret – Tom has promised to tell me the very minute he can.

We find a booth, just as my mobile rings. I quickly slip it from the cover, hoping it's Sam, but it's Eddie instead. Tom stows my carry-on bag under the table and heads to the counter, after asking if I want my usual. A milky tea. Smiling, I nod and give him a silly *Wayne's World* thumbs-up.

'Flower! Are you sitting down? Really bad news I'm afraid, I don't how to tell you . . .' Eddie says to open the conversation, and his voice has a weird seriousness to it that I haven't heard from him before.

'Oh no! Tell me.' A hand instinctively goes to my throat as I hold my breath, wondering what on earth has happened. 'Oh God, it's not Sam is it?' A horrible, hideous chill spikes the length of my spine. Why the hell didn't I make the effort to go to her house? 'Oh please, Eddie, not the twins, has something happened to one of them? Is that why I haven't been able to contact her?'

'Don't be ridic! Sam and the twins are fine. I assume, not that I've spoken to her since Christy, the rock chick, turned up. I've tried ringing, but she doesn't seem to want to take my calls . . .' *So not just me then . . . I must call her, and keep calling until she talks to me.* 'I'm joking! No bad stuff here.'

'Well, how the bloody hell was I supposed to know you were joking? You scared me with your super-serious voice.'

'Honestly, sugarpie, you really need to stop being

155

such a drama queen . . . Two and two makes four, remember? Not five trillion.'

'Well, you can talk; you're the biggest drama queen I know. In the whole world in fact, I bet, no, I *guarantee*. Actually!' Relief and irritation makes me shout, causing a breast-feeding woman on the opposite table to give me a really filthy look. 'Sorry,' I mouth to her, as the baby sticks its papery little hand out from under the scarf she has draped over her left boob and lets out a glass-shattering shriek. Oh God.

'O-M-A-G! What is that noise? I swear my eardrum just exploded inside my actual head.'

'I'm in Costa,' I tell him diplomatically, making sure I keep my voice low.

'Oh no. What for? You poor thing.'

'Oh Ed, purlease. Don't go all Kardashian on me . . .'

'Whatever do you mean?'

'You know very well what I mean.'

'Hmmm, anyway, I was just calling to say change of plan. I'm so sorry, but I can't make Mulberry this summer. NYC beckons instead!'

'You're bloody joking.'

'Darling, honestly, there's no need to sound quite so disappointed. I'll try and pop back for Christm—'

'No need. Ed, I'll see you there. I'm coming to New York for two weeks,' I whisper-yell right into the phone so as not to disturb the baby again. But rewind a second – Eddie is going to be in New York too! *See! The universe knows.* How bloody exciting.

'*Whaaaat?* When?' he yells.

'I'm at the actual airport right now. I'll be in New York in like . . . seven and a half hours.'

'*Scream.* Call me the minute you arrive. I'll be there on Monday.'

'Brilliant. And of course I will!' I'm practically hyperventilating – this is going to be so shamazing. My best friend is going to be biting the big apple too.

'OK sugarpie. Gotta go, Carly is glaring. Oh, really quickly . . . Have a good flight, flower, and pay for the upgrade if it's an option, sooo worth it! I practically floated through LAX on my return home.'

And he's gone, typical Eddie, he's not even bothered about knowing the reason for my trip. He's just straight to the fun bit . . . after scaring me half to death with his stupid jokes first though, of course.

Tom arrives back with the drinks and two raspberry ripple cupcakes.

'Can you believe this?' I say, waggling my phone in the air. 'That was Eddie! He just called and you'll never guess what . . . he is only going to be in New York too, at the same time as me . . .'

'Well, there you go! All the more reason why it's a

fantastic time for you to go and not worry about the regatta.' Tom grins, and a fleeting glimmer of guilt darts across his face.

'What's going on?' I ask, slowly.

'Nothing.' Tom sips his coffee to avoid eye contact.

'Tell me.' And he caves right away.

'I told him you were going to be in New York. Sorry. Did I steal your thunder?'

'Hmm, I'm not sure. Tell me more . . .' So Eddie already knew, hence the silly joke to wind me up. I'll kill him when I see him.

'He called me—'

'Why?' I jump in.

'Well, give me a chance,' Tom laughs, shaking his head.

'Sorry.' I take a mouthful of tea and shut up.

'He called for a chat and it kind of came out.'

'Hang on. Since when did Eddie just call you for a chat?' I ask, praying that Eddie wasn't tapping Tom for clues about his intentions re. us living together. Quizzing Tom about proposing, just to win a bet – I wouldn't put it past Eddie to try to engineer things.

'Since it's your birthday soon.'

'Wow. Really?' I say, my voice full of excitement now.

'Yes, he wanted to know what I was getting you, so we didn't duplicate . . . seeing as it's your thirtieth, he wondered if I was going big, whatever that means. But don't worry; I didn't tell him, definitely not, you know how useless he is at keeping a secret. I certainly wasn't going to take a chance on him inadvertently spoiling the surprise, all because he couldn't contain himself,' Tom grins, mysteriously.

'Aw, that's lovely. Eddie can be very thoughtful,' I reply. Maybe I won't kill him after all. Or, hold on . . . *going big*? Hmmm, on second thoughts, that definitely sounds like Eddie-talk for something extravagant, a statement piece, a special gift, or . . . God, he's incorrigible, jewellery! A ring! Perhaps I will kill him after all. He just can't help himself.

'Only if he likes you, of course,' Tom says, not missing a beat. He shrugs his shoulders. 'Well, it's true. And I wish I could be like him; it can be exhausting having to be nice to everyone all the time,' Tom adds, with a weary look on his face. I know he finds it hard sometimes, keeping up the nice, measured Mr Carrington image, especially when Mrs Godfrey from the WI is on the warpath about something or another that's not right in store. Just a few weeks ago, she beat a path direct to Tom's office on the executive floor to voice her concerns, loudly, over the giant Ann Summers display with its 'scantily dressed mannequins' in one of the side windows. Apparently, peekaboo bras have no place in

Mulberry-On-Sea and must be removed forthwith and certainly before the regatta.

'Indeed,' I say, on autopilot, still pondering on what Eddie is up to. He never normally calls Tom. I take another mouthful of tea followed by a big bite of my cupcake. Mm-mmm. It tastes good. Not as good as Sam's, but a very close second. Tom gestures to my chin before handing me a napkin to wipe the butter-cream frosting away – I find it impossible to eat cake without getting covered, but then that's half the fun, I suppose. I take another massive bite and relish the sugary soft sweetness.

'And he is your best friend – I'm sure the regatta will be fine . . . don't worry about it,' Tom says absent-mindedly, before tucking into his cupcake too. He's busy licking his fingers when he realises what he's just said. He stops licking and looks me straight in the eye.

'So you do have doubts?' I knew it.

'No, well, not really . . . it'll be fine. Like I said, the team will hold the fort, you'll be back before you know it . . . you have everything planned.' Tom grins and pushes a stray lock of hair out of his eyes, but he's not fooling me.

'But there is something, isn't there?' I probe. Maybe it isn't such a good idea for me to go after all.

'It's nothing, a minor detail. Look, let's not think about it now. Let's talk about us instead – have you decided when you're moving in with me?' Tom grins.

'Um, yes, err . . . or you could move in with me?' I start distractedly, and Tom nods his head slowly, but it's obvious he's not keen on my flat being his new home.

'Sorry, I can't really think about it right now. Please, just tell me what the "minor detail" is that I've overlooked.'

'OK. It's Uncle Marco. He also called, yesterday, asking about the stickers for the ice-cream vans – the ones with the Carrington's logo on . . . he's been trying to get hold of you. Weren't you supposed to be visiting him yesterday to deliver the stickers?'

'Oh my God!' A horrible sinking feeling rushes through me. I put the rest of the cake back on the plate. 'I'm so sorry – I totally forgot.' And what about Lauren, and Jack? They've missed out now. I'm not sure I even let Lauren know the visit was scheduled for yesterday – it must have slipped my mind in all the excitement over going to New York. 'I'd better call him, and Lauren too . . . to apologise.' I reach for my phone.

'It's fine.' Tom places his hand over mine. 'Don't worry about it. I've sorted it out. The stickers are being couriered up to Scarborough and he'll distribute them to the guys from there, so they can put them on the side of the vans before travelling to Mulberry for the regatta – he's called in about thirty vendors so far, which I gather is no mean feat, and it'll be fantastic publicity for Carrington's as they travel from all over the country.'

'Wow! Thank you so much. And I truly am sorry, I totally forgot.'

'Don't be daft, like I said, it's fine.' Tom smiles. 'And he said you had already talked about ice-cream flavours, so he's happy to just go ahead and choose a nice selection. He was telling me about a new bubble gum flavour, which sounds awesome. And he'll make sure the vans are stocked. So if there's anything else I can do to help, then you only have to let me know – I really enjoyed chatting about ice cream instead of shrinkage and stock figures for a change.'

'But I was supposed to be managing it all.' I feel rubbish now. And there's no way I'm adding to Tom's workload by getting him involved, and what would Isabella think? That I can't cope, that's what! Oh no. Maybe I shouldn't go to New York after all. But I want to. I *really* want to.

'And you have. Like I said, it's just one minor detail, everything else is going to plan.' I nod, to reassure him, as it's true – it is all on track. But I'm still cross with myself for lapsing on the stickers. 'You know, I asked him to bring some of those screwball things to the regatta, do you remember them? Raspberry ripple ice cream in a plastic cone with bubble gum at the bottom?' He's grinning like a big kid as I tap out a note on my phone reminding me to check that Annie follows my project plan to the letter. I've emailed it to her, and I've even left the notepads and the various highlighter pens in her locker in the staff room. I called in last night especially; to make sure they were there, waiting for her when she gets into work tomorrow morning.

'Yes, I was never allowed one – Mum used to worry about me choking on the frozen bubble gum.'

'Aw, well, we'll just have to make sure you get one at the regatta,' he says brightly, and I smile – he's so kind. I so want to make the regatta a success, not just for my sake, but for his too. He's trusted me with it, to represent Carrington's, his store, his business, and his reputation in the local community.

'I'll call Annie tomorrow for an update, and I can always ring Uncle Marco from New York to apologise,' I say, still feeling deflated. And I must apologise to Lauren; maybe I can make it up to her and Jack when I get back, organise another trip perhaps.

'Georgie, stop looking for things to worry about. It will all be OK.' Tom finishes his coffee before devouring the rest of the cupcake.

Silence follows. I check the clock on my phone, and then jump when it suddenly vibrates in synch with my ringtone – the 'Oh oh oh' bit of Lawson's 'Juliet', alerting me to a call.

'It's Dad.' I show Tom the screen.

'Quick, you'd better answer it!' he says, motioning to the phone with an urgent look in his eye, knowing what a nightmare it's been trying to get hold of Dad or Nancy since they went away. Dad still hasn't grasped the concept of keeping his mobile switched on at all times like the rest of the world's population – he says it's a waste of battery life, so he only puts it on to make an actual call, oblivious to the fact that some-body might be trying to get hold of him at times outside the designated 'mobile on' time! And Nancy doesn't even have a mobile – can't get on with them, she says.

'Dad! How are you? Where are you? Why haven't you called back?'

'Yes, yes, we're all fine. No need to panic. I just got your message; we were out of signal in a remote French village whenever you called, so I didn't bother putting the phone on. How are you, darling?'

164

'I'm fine, Dad. And really pleased to have the chance to speak to you before I go,' I say, trying to hide the concern from my voice. I left the message days ago. Common sense told me he had the phone off, or they were just in a bad signal area – Dad had tried calling me previously from Calais to say they had made it through the Eurotunnel, but all I heard was a load of static followed by some crackles, so he sent a text in the end which arrived the following day! Ridic, given that France is only a few hours away from Mulberry-On-Sea. And surely someone would call me if there had been an actual emergency, isn't that what the British embassy does – track down loved ones in times of crisis? I've seen them on the news, chaperoning suspected drug mules in Peru before the designated family member gets there . . . Nevertheless my irrational self was already imagining all kinds of dramas. I let out a big sigh of relief.

'Well, we were delighted when we heard your news. You're going to have a wonderful time, sweetheart.'

'Thanks Dad, and I hope you are too. How are you getting on?'

'Brilliantly, love. It's such a tonic. And Nancy is enjoying the break from all the cooking and cleaning at home, which is a surprise because whenever I've offered to do my bit in the past, she's been very reluctant to hand over the reins, but now she's happy to let me loose in Daisy's little kitchenette area. I made a superb Welsh rarebit for our breakfast today with lashings of Worcester sauce, just the way Nancy likes it.'

'That's nice, Dad.'

'And you know, she even went skinny-dipping in a lake yesterday . . . said she just forgot to put her bathing suit on, but she's not fooling me.' He chuckles. 'She's having the time of her life. So I whipped off my undies and ran in to join her.'

'Oh Dad, you didn't?' I say, shocked, amused and perplexed. I just can't imagine him, or Nancy come to think of it, skinny-dipping in a French lake. And it's an image I definitely don't want inside my head. Who would have thought it? Such a far cry from his more formal shirt, tie and trousers attire at all times, even when lounging at home watching those gardening programmes that he likes.

'I absolutely did. Mind you, I have got a bit of a raspy chest today.' He coughs in that way people always do when describing their symptoms. 'Don't think I'll be rushing into the water again in a hurry. Georgie, it was perishing.'

'Good, then take that as a warning,' I say, firmly. 'Honestly, Dad, you really must be careful. Have you been keeping up with your tablets?'

'Of course, sweetheart. I wish you would stop worrying. That's my job as a parent.' A short silence follows. 'I know I didn't do a very good job of it when you were growing up, so at least let me make up for it now.'

'Oh Dad! Please, you did what you could,' I say, remembering the birthday and Christmas cards every year that always arrived on time – albeit with the prison postmark on, but he never forgot. 'Anyway, it's all in the past,' I add to change the subject.

'Right you are. So, have you packed your camera? You must take lots of snaps for us to see,' he says, back in his usual jovial voice now.

'I don't have a camera, Dad, I'll just use my iPhone.'

'Ahh, yes, so much easier. Well, I'd better go, must keep an eye on the bill. I've heard these roaming charges can go stratospheric if you're not careful, so have a wonderful trip, love, and do look after yourself.'

'I will, thanks Dad. You too.'

'Thank you, sweetheart. I love you, Georgie.'

'And I love you too.' And I do. My heart lifts. And in an instant, I realise that I can't remember the last time we told each other . . . Certainly not since he came back into my life, and that must be at least two years now. I'm shocked. It must be back when I was a child, before he went to prison. I have to rectify this. I make a vow to tell him more often, as soon as he gets back.

I press to end the call, and slot my phone into my pocket.

'Is everything OK?' Tom asks, placing an arm around me. 'You look sad.'

'Yes, yes I'm fine. Sorry, I, it . . . I don't know, it just seems a bit weird, with Dad being so far away, and now I'm going to put even more distance between us.'

'Hey, come here.' Tom pulls me into him, and gently rubs my arm. 'It is OK for you to go away, you know.'

'Oh I know. And ignore me; I'm just being silly – getting overemotional, that's all. I feel like a fool now,' I say, quickly brushing a stray tear away. I can't believe I'm actually crying. What on earth is wrong with me? I wanted to travel – my wish has come true and I'm ruining it by getting all silly and sentimental.

'You're not a fool. It's a big thing being far away from your loved ones . . . I should know, I spent the best part of my life parted from my family.'

'I'm sorry.' I squeeze his hand, having never really thought about his past in this way, but he's right, and I guess our backgrounds aren't so dissimilar after all, except he got to feel lonely surrounded by luxury, whereas I didn't, but it's still the same feeling when it comes down to it.

'Oh don't be. I got used to it years ago – my parents were always off globetrotting, and then I was away at school or uni. Which reminds me, Isabella can't wait to join us for the regatta. She said to tell you that she's really looking forward to seeing what you've come up with.' He smiles, but I can't help wondering if there was an innuendo, a mixed message in her words. Oh God. Now I'm being paranoid, or am I? Blimey, I'm not even sure.

'Great.' I keep my smile in place. 'You did point out that it's not just me organising it all – that there's a big committee?' I ask, thinking of Meredith and the others, who were actually surprisingly OK with me taking two weeks out. 'I'm really only overseeing a smallish part of it.' Help. I don't want Isabella blaming me if the whole thing is a disaster.

'Oh she knows. But she's mostly interested in the Carrington's contribution, of course!' He beams obliviously as my worst fear is confirmed – he has no idea what she's really like. 'They're going to moor up in the marina so they can stay for the duration.'

'Lovely.' I gulp.

'Right. Close your eyes,' Tom says, rubbing his hands together and changing topic.

'Why?'

'You'll see.' I tentatively do as I'm told.

'OK, you can open them now.' And I do. On the table in front of me is a gold envelope. I pick it up and turn it over before going to open it. 'Ahem. Not until your birthday!'

'Ohhhh,' I say, sticking my bottom lip out like a petulant child. I'm dying to know what's inside.

'The day before, to be precise. Promise me you won't open it until then?'

'I'll try.'

'Nope, you must promise,' he insists, his velvety-brown eyes all sparkly and twinkling, his voice full of boyish excitement. And my heart flutters – I love seeing this side of him; he spends far too much time in business mode, being serious. It's wonderful seeing him relaxed and looking like he's actually having fun.

'Then I promise. Thank you.' I lean over to kiss him before slipping the card inside my handbag. I can't wait to open it. And then a little voice pops inside my head: *You could take a peek on the aeroplane. He'll never know.* Nooo, no no no, it's plain wrong. Besides, I'll know . . . and all that. Plus I promised! Eeek. I inhale sharply before breathing out. I'm not even going to think about it. I have willpower. I do. I sooo do. A bit. I bite my bottom lip.

'Stop it.'

'Whaaaat?'

'Thinking about the envelope.'

'I'm not.' And my damn cheeks let me down by flaming immediately.

'I shall know, you know, if you open it before the designated day,' Tom laughs. But before I can respond with a suitable comeback, he lifts my hair and whispers teasingly into my ear. 'But you can open this envelope now, if you really want to . . .' He slides another, much smaller, white envelope towards me. It has the Hilton hotel logo on it. 'Come on.' He pauses to check the time on his watch before reaching under the table for my carry-on case. 'We've got three hours to have ridiculously filthy sex!' He grabs my hand and kisses me hard on the lips. Oh my God. Show me the way. And my pulse is practically at fever pitch as we jump up and run, giggling like hormone-fuelled teenagers, towards the Hilton sign.

13

OMG. Oh my actual God! You want to see the apartment I'm staying in. In fact, scrap that, it's not really an apartment *at all*. Well, not like one I've ever been in – no, this is a proper bona fide Manhattan mansion. It has a concierge, with a man called Larry, who was waiting in a black uniform with gold trim and pristine white gloves on his hands, as my driver (the actual driver that Gaspard's PA has allocated to me for the duration of my stay, wahey!) pulled up right outside the green canopied entrance, where my luggage was swiftly dealt with as I was swept up to the top floor, the penthouse. And, the best bit of all – I have my own lift. Just like Edward's penthouse palace in that *Pretty Woman* film, the doors slide open directly into my hallway – the hallway that's bigger than my whole flat at home! In fact, right now, I actually feel like I'm starring in a film, where the pretty but very quaint little seaside town of Mulberry-On-Sea is a trillion miles away.

I drop my handbag on the hall table, kick off my wedges and run the length of the hall and into the bedroom. And gasp. The super-king-sized bed is set up on a platform, so high that I literally have to fling myself up onto it. It's ridiculous. The mattress must be at least three foot deep and I'm not even joking. It's a proper princess-and-the-pea bed. I fall backwards, my body cushioned by the extra-plump duvet and pillow mountain, before letting out a little gasp. Above me is a brocade canopy, with curtains making a four-poster bed. God, I wish Tom was here – the fun we could have. My legs are still aching from our marathon session at the Hilton, which started in the lift. Tom's magnificent body pressed up hard against mine, his hand up underneath my top, fingers teasing inside my bra as his other hand tugged my hair, tilting my head back while his lips caressed my neck. It was all I could do to keep it together until we made it into the actual hotel room. Where he kicked the door shut behind us, pushed up my skirt and delivered on his promise of gloriously filthy sex, right there on the floor, before fireman-lifting me into the bedroom to do it all over again. Multiple orgasms sure are the best thing ever. And Tom is an expert. Sweet Jesus. I'm tingling from head to toe just thinking about it. I close my eyes for a moment and savour the exquisite memory for a while longer.

There's a terrace leading from the bedroom, so I leap off the bed and fling open the glass doors. The warm evening air envelops me as I walk outside – it's stifling hot, suffocating almost, but I don't care, I'm in the most exciting city in the whole world, or so it seems. Glorious. Iconic yellow taxis, honking their horns, fill the street below, weaving in and out of the traffic. Illuminated shop windows span both sides of the street, a drugstore, a dog grooming parlour, dry cleaner's, a Chinese restaurant with Hello Kitty tablecloths and paper lanterns – it's all here, and they're open like it's the middle of the day. New York really is the city that never sleeps – I can't imagine ever dropping my dry cleaning off at 9 p.m. back home in Mulberry-On-Sea. It would never happen and, even if it got mooted as a possibility, the residents' association would certainly have something to say about it.

A loud banging sound breaks the moment, and I instantly dash back inside. It takes a few seconds to get my bearings and work out where the noise is coming from. I quickly smooth my hair and straighten my top as I leg it back down the hallway towards what I think must be the front door – I'm sure this is where I stepped out of the lift. I tentatively pull open the heavy, gold-handled door.

'Good evening, Miss Hart. These just arrived.' It's Larry with the biggest basket of flowers I have ever seen – he needs both gloved hands just to lift it.

'*Wow!*'

'Shall I bring it in?'

'Um, yes. Yes please.' I step aside and Larry heaves the basket up onto the hall table. I take the card and see that the flowers are from Tom.

Hope you arrived safely.
Chat soon
Love Mr Carrington xoxoxo

Ahh, so lovely. I miss him already.

'Are you settling in OK?' Larry asks.

'I so am. It's amazing – but can you tell me where I can find the nearest place to get food, please?' I'm starving, even though my body is saying it's two o'clock in the morning and I should be asleep, I can't, it's only nine in the evening here. And I'm sure I read somewhere that the fastest way to get over jetlag is to adapt to the local time right away. Anyway, there's no time to sleep – being here in the actual Big Apple is way too exciting for that.

'Sure. What would you like to eat?' he says, in a proper New Yorker accent.

'Oooh, what is there? Apart from the Chinese restaurant opposite?' I ask, figuring I can eat Chinese food anytime (for my shame, they know me by name in the Wing Hong takeaway at the end of my street back home). 'I'm thinking something more . . . American!' Larry throws his head back and lets out a big belly laugh.

'Lady, this is America: you can have whatever you like, whenever you like.'

'Really? In that case I'd love a proper American cheeseburger in an authentic American diner that I can walk to.' (I want to soak up the New York atmosphere from the ground floor, as it were.) 'Like the one in *Grease* where Rizzo chucks pink milkshake over Kenickie and says, "To you from me, Pinky Lee",' I say, optimistically, putting his bold statement to the test, but then instantly wondering if he's actually seen the film. Hmm, on second thoughts, he's bound to – hasn't everyone?

'No problem!' he confirms, not missing a beat. 'Go out of the building, take a right, go half a block and you'll see the red stripe canopy and the blue neon window sign. Ask for Don, he'll take care of you. He's my cousin!' And with that, Larry does a little salute before turning on his heel and heading back into the lift.

Twenty minutes later, I'm swinging my legs on a well-worn black leather bar stool, soaking up the buzzy, vibrant atmosphere and chatting to Don as he fries delicious-smelling onions, hot dogs and hunks of steak on a huge hotplate, in between taking slurps of the thickest, yummiest cherry milkshake I've ever tasted! Mm-mmm. I take a picture with my phone, thinking I must show this to Sam. I wonder if Don will let me have the recipe, her café customers would love it. And, like Larry said he would, Don has taken care of me; from the moment I stepped inside this epitome of American culture – with the chrome-legged square red tables to the banquette booths, to the black-and-white checked tiles to the waft of cinnamon, maple syrup and pancakes. There's even a giant jukebox in the corner belting out classic Fifties rock-and-roll tunes. Heavenly. It's so warm and cosy, and everyone seems very friendly. Even the two uniformed cops sitting at the bar next to me – who look like characters straight from *CSI:NY* central casting, as they tuck into giant hot dogs smothered in curly swirls of yellow mustard – gave me the once-over before saying, 'How you doing, ma'am?'

Instinctively, I go to text the picture to Sam, but stop just in time. I need to talk to her first – I can't be sending her pictures of milkshakes from American diners when we haven't even had a proper heart-to-heart about the whole Christy thing. It's weird, because whenever something major has happened in the past, we've always been in it together, rock solid, supporting each other. If I'm honest, I'm a bit surprised she hasn't returned my calls; she must have got my message about coming to New York. Maybe she just needs time to get her head around having Christy back in her life. I'll call her again, not now – with the time difference it's the middle of the night at home, and I daren't risk waking the girls – but as soon as I can.

'One *proper* American cheeseburger for a cute Brit chick,' Don winks, trying to imitate an English accent, and my jaw drops as he slides the plate towards me. The burger is gargantuan, easily an inch-thick beef patty with two rashers of bacon, lettuce, tomato, pickle, onion, melted cheese, mustard, mayo and ketchup, all piled up in between a big sliced sourdough bun with sesame seeds on top and held together with a stick the length of a skewer. Easily. It has a stars and stripes flag on the end. And, if that wasn't enough, next to the burger is a tin bucket crammed with skinny fries smothered in rock salt with a side dip of mustard mayo. Mm-mmm. I can't wait to get stuck in, but where to start? I opt for a fry and quickly pop one into my mouth. Delicious. Crispy, with a hint of salt and pepper.

'Thank you, and blimey, I didn't realise it would be quite so massive,' I say, reaching over to the chrome napkin dispenser and helping myself to a wedge – I'm going to need them for the burger. I'm not even sure my jaw will fit around it. Don is chuckling, his shoulders jigging up and down as he turns back to tend the griddle. I take another slurp of the milkshake and carve the burger in half – it's the only way.

Before I get stuck in, I take a quick look at my phone and see that I have an email from Annie, sent some time ago.

Hi Georgie Girl!
You're probably on the flight now, but this is just to say that everything for the regatta is ticking along very nicely. Nothing to worry about. I've got the project plan and I found the notebooks and pens in my locker. I popped into work just now to check on things and schedule a #TeamCarringtons meeting for Monday – I've put a big notice on the pin board in the staff room, so the others see it FIRST THING. I plan on being super-efficient while you're away; even though

everything is organised, you never can be too careful.

Lauren texted me earlier asking about the ice-cream factory visit, but don't worry AT ALL. I will sort it, I fancy a day trip so I will take her and Jack and go sample a few flavours. I know the flavours have already been chosen but I think I should taste every single one just to make sure they are up to scratch, we don't want to be dishing up anything dodgy. ☺

Now go and have an amazeballing time in the Big Appleland and know that your best girl Annie is on it all lol!!!!!!

Love and hugs from
Me XOXOXOXO ☺ ☺

I laugh. Ah, that's so kind of her. And she wasn't even working today, but she still went into Carrington's – she really has come into her own recently; no longer the young, inexperienced sales assistant who always hid in the alcove behind the counter if a tricky customer came instore, but a brilliantly organised supervisor. Hurrah! And it just goes to show that it is possible to delegate and trust others to follow through on things . . . I've been a bit of a control freak in the past when it comes to making sure stuff is done at work. I feel relieved knowing she's got everything in hand, and that Lauren's little boy, Jack, won't miss out after all. I smile contentedly to myself as I put my phone into my bag and flick open a napkin on my lap in preparation for getting stuck into this beast of a burger.

I'm licking the mustard, mayo and ketchup mixture off my fingertips when the door suddenly swings open. And I don't believe it.

'Eddie!' I scream, waving my arms around like an idiot. 'But I thought you weren't arriving until Monday. And how did you know I'd be here in Don's Diner?' I jump down from the bar stool and practically do a running body-slam towards him.

'Change of plans, flower.' Eddie hugs me back before disentangling himself and straightening his navy Jack Wills jacket. He follows me back to the bar and lounges against the stool next to mine. 'Kel told me. You know how close we are – she made me a star, after all.' He shakes his head and actually laughs out loud at his own giant diva-ness – ahh, so he's taking himself less seriously now; nice – before surreptitiously leaning around me to eye up one of the cops, who eyes him right back. So, nothing wrong with Eddie's gaydar then, I see. I roll my eyes, and whisper, 'Stop flirting.'

Eddie mouths, 'But he started it,' and smiles

naughtily before doing a fake cough to clear his throat. 'So, as I was saying,' he continues back in his normal voice. 'Kel gave me the number of Gaspard's PA, who told me where she'd organised for you to stay, and the concierge guy pointed me this way. So, boom! The party starts right now, a whole two days . . . well, a day and a bit, earlier.'

'Fab. I'm so pleased you're here too. I know we're both going to be working, but at least we can keep each other company for the rest of the time.'

'Honey, I'm not working – I'm here on *vacation*, as we say over here.'

'Oh, but I thought that's why you couldn't come back to Mulberry for the summer, because you had to work . . .' I frown.

'Hmm, to be honest, I just didn't fancy it in the end. It feels a bit suffocating sometimes, too small-town for me. Like being in a goldfish bowl. And then when Kel told me about the plan to help out her old friend Gaspard by making you his muse, and in turn give you the adventure of a lifetime – you know how fond she is of you – well, I thought why not? I need a break and I know where I'd rather be . . . Mulberry or New York City? Let me ponder on that difficult conundrum for a moment.' And he puts a little finger to the corner of his mouth before pulling a face. 'No contest.

Especially as I get to spend two weeks with my bestie.' He puts his arm around my shoulders and pulls me in for a hug.

'So, where's Ciaran? And Pussy?'

'Oh, they're here too. Well, Pussy is with the dog-sitter right now – we've taken a condo at the Plaza, overlooking Central Park. It's only a few blocks from here so we're practically neighbours for the duration.'

'Brilliant,' I say, all goggle-eyed and slightly over-whelmed, thinking, oh how times have changed. I remember when Eddie was Walter's, aka the Heff's BA, back in the day at Carrington's, and moaned about absolutely everything. With hindsight he was always destined for a more glamorous existence. 'Will Ciaran be coming out to play too?'

'Of course, he's in the car.' Eddie motions towards the window where a sleek black town car is waiting. 'Fancy coming to a pool party?'

'What, now?' I ask, glancing down at my top and comfy skinny-jeans-for-travelling combo.

'Yes, now. Get that burger down you,' he pushes the plate closer to me, 'and let's go. It's Saturday night in the best city in the world, so I for one am not wasting a precious second of it.' He rubs his hands together with glee.

'Oh Ed, I'd love to, but I'm hardly dressed for a party, and I'm actually exhausted. Plus, won't I need a bikini?' I say, shaking my head.

'Whaaaat? Are you kidding me? Come on, you can sleep when you're dead! The party is at Soho House, sweet pea. You know – pool on the rooftop, dancing, cocktails, and famous people. Cool, exclusive, *very* exclusive.' He sweeps a palm through the air to accentuate the exclusivity of the venue. 'And a VIP members' guest list with my name, plus two, on. You're sooo going to love it. And you can grab a bikini and sling on a party dress en route, we'll swing by your place on the way.'

14

I want to die. Or at least swim in a massive vat of water, I'm that dehydrated and hungover – and jetlagged! I roll over in my giant four-poster bed, and scream as something pincers my foot – I kick it away, hard, then immediately clutch my head and force myself into an upright position.

'Must you yelp quite so raucously?' Eddie says. It's all coming back to me now – the glorious hot summer evening breeze, the rooftop bar, the pool – oh, God, the jasmine-scented heated pool! I'm sure I jumped in fully clothed, or maybe not – I honestly can't remember for sure.

After a brilliant night, laughing and chatting with loads of media types who all seemed to know Eddie, and involving far too many Soho Mules followed by an even more obscene amount of tequila shots, I managed to crawl back to my Manhattan mansion with Eddie in tow. From what I can remember, Ciaran had had enough partying at about three this morning and took the car back to the Plaza, but for some insane reason, Eddie and I kept on going. I'm sure we watched a film too, inside a proper little cinema with gold velour armchairs and bottles of Grey Goose L'Orange and cocktails with names like Bramble and Canadian Rockies – a far cry from the Wetherspoon's back in Mulberry-On-Sea with its Monster Ripper pint specials.

But now I'm paying for it. Oh yes, I'm paying. I want the bed to open up and envelop me in its soothing softness and never let me go – I'm that fragile.

'Sshhhhhhuuuush,' I just about manage, reaching for a bottle of water. 'It's your own fault, plying me with all those drinks. And what's the bloody time?' I huff grumpily, while scrabbling around on the floor for something to wear. I'm sure I took off my dress before I collapsed into bed, about an hour or so ago, or so it seems. And then I realise that I'm still wearing it, with a slightly damp bikini underneath and my leopard-print Loubs too. Oh God. I think I might actually still be drunk. I can't even see properly, and what is that black spikey thing dancing on my left eyeball?

'Lash alert, darling,' Eddie says, as if reading my mind. He sits up and pulls a section of the duvet up under his chin. 'What a night!'

'Never again, Ed, you're insane.' And they're expecting me today – a welcome meeting at the design studio. Gaspard's PA said they want to get to work right away, and Gaspard is keen to show me what they've been working on so far and get my input. Oh God. I feel sick. And make a dash for it down the hall. But where's the bloody bathroom? I fling open a door only to find I'm in the kitchen – it will have to do – and I end up hurling into the sink. Jesus.

Two hours later, I have established that the bathroom is in fact through a door in the bedroom – an en-suite, of course it is! And I've managed to have a cold, rejuvenating shower and several cups of strong coffee, and now my driver has just pulled up outside Gaspard's studio on Franklin Street, in Tribeca.

I take a deep breath and haul myself out of the cool, air-conditioned car, gasping as the humid midday heat hits me like a steam train gathering speed.

'Thank you,' I say to the driver, steadying myself against the door before he has to almost prise my hand away to close it. Awkward.

'You're welcome, ma'am. Do you require any . . . further assistance?' he asks, delicately, giving me a brief up-and-down glance while fingering the silver crucifix that's on a chain around his neck.

'Oh no, I'm fine.' I wave an arm around. 'In fact,

take the day off,' I add grandly, as a cover for my embarrassment at still being half-trollied on a Sunday lunchtime.

'If you're sure. Have a good day!' And he wastes no time in jumping into the driver's seat, swinging the door closed behind him and speeding off . . . to the nearest church, no doubt, to pray for my redemption.

I stand for a few seconds, just to get my bearings, wondering where the damn entrance is. I can see the building spanning the whole block – five, or is it six floors? I can't lift my head up long enough to count them without feeling dizzy again. I'm seriously contemplating giving up and trying to find my way back uptown, when another car glides to a halt at the kerb behind me. I turn around. A window slides down.

'It is you! Georgie Hart. I wasn't sure, in those huge shades. Have you just arrived?' It's Gaspard.

'Yes, just now,' I say, attempting to sound breezy and desperately trying not to wobble on my wedges.

'Wonderful, I can't wait to get started.' I gulp, wishing my eyes would focus properly; thank God for the shades. When I last looked, they were a bloodshot mess. 'I shall escort you in.' Once on the pavement, he gives me his arm and leads me in like an old-fashioned gentleman.

Inside, and I'm taken through to an enormous

light-filled space with floor-to-ceiling windows, giving a spectacular bird's-eye view of the new One World Trade Center in the sky, it's amazing. And to my right are two breathtakingly beautiful guys wearing nothing but tight white Calvin's. I try not to gawp as a woman, who looks just like Betty Draper's twinsie (she's got the pearls-and-belted-puffball-dress look down to a T) motions for me to follow her.

'Don't mind them. They're here for the shoot – the fall/winter fragrance campaign,' she says, her kitten heels clipping across the solid wood floor. Ooh! I didn't know the House of Mercier had its own perfume range too. 'That's right. It's another new venture,' she adds, as if she can actually see inside my head. Eeek! And the way she says it tells me that she's not entirely on board with all the 'new' things – the Georgie Bag included – if the hostile vibe she's emanating towards me is anything to go by!

We reach a corner of the room that's been sectioned off with a thick white cotton sheet, which she sweeps aside.

'You can get undressed here.' *Whaaaat? What's she going on about?* 'And don't dilly-dally, the photographer is a real stickler for timekeeping.' *Hold on! Undress? What, me? A photographer?* Did she really just say all that? Oh God. I knew it was too good to be true – an all-expenses-paid trip to New York, with a driver, and a mansion to boot. Damn Kelly and her wacky plans, she's got me again, only this time I'm not showing myself up in front of a camera. Oh no. 'The gowns are on the rail, pick one and we'll take it from there.' She gestures to a long clothes rail against the wall, laden with a multicoloured selection of designer dresses, each one hanging in its own plastic protector bag. 'Understated, of course: the bags are the focus. Give me a shout when you have the first one on.'

'But, err . . . I thought I was here to talk about design ideas,' I squeak, wondering what she means by 'bags'? When they haven't even been designed yet.

'Oh no!' she pauses. 'Well, yes, of course you are doing that too,' she says blithely, planting a hand on her hip. 'But you're the "face" for the collection. The ordinary girl.' She gives me a disparaging glance. *Flaming cheek.* 'I thought you knew.'

'No!'

'Oh, well, you do now.' And with that she lets the sheet drop before clipping her way back across the floor. *Fuuuuuuck.* Instinctively, I pull out my phone and press to call Tom. I hate being in the spotlight, he'll know what to do – maybe he can call Kelly and explain that there's been a terrible misunderstanding, and she can square it all with Gaspard before things go any further. Maybe she can find him another muse, or even a proper model, a 'face' that actually knows what she's doing – because I sure as hell don't. The nauseous feeling from earlier makes a rapid return. I inhale sharply. Tom's number rings for ages, so eventually I give up and redial Eddie, instead.

'I can't move my face,' he mumbles on answering, and I'm imagining he's still in the same position he was when I left – semi-comatose on my bed, with the left side of his head wedged against the bucket I found in the cupboard under the kitchen sink.

'Ed, listen! Wake up and park that hangover for a minute. This is serious. I'm huddled behind a sheet in the corner of a warehouse and they want to take pictures.'

'OMG. Shit. OK, get off the phone, I'm calling 911 right now,' he says covertly.

'Eddie! Stop it. It's serious,' I hiss in a stage-whisper voice.

'Have they hurt you? *Oh God*. Do they want a ransom?' He sounds wide-awake now. 'Have they mentioned me? Do they know we're friends? Crack-addled crazeees will snatch anyone these days, just to get their next spoonful. Well, I won't pay! Sorry doll-face, but Carly warned me about this kind of thing . . . we must let the police deal with it.'

'*Eddie. Shut up.* I haven't been kidnapped, you fucking idiot. I'm at Gaspard's studio.'

'Oh darling, is that all? Why would you wake me up just to tell me that?'

'Because, well, because they want me to be the "face" of the collection. I had no idea. I was supposed to be helping out with some design ideas, or so I thought – you know, giving them the "everywoman" perspective. I'm not a flaming model. I'm going to make an utter fool of myself.'

'Well, it's too late to back out now!' And the line goes dead. Grrrreat. Thanks Eddie. Love you long long time too.

I toss my phone in my bag, pull off my shades, squeeze my fists and do a silent scream, instantly regretting it when the pressure inside my head intensifies to near explosive levels. I rest my forehead against the cold concrete wall instead. *Right. Get a grip! It's just a few photos, nothing to it; just say cheese, and all that, nobody will actually see them . . .* I hope. They'll be so awful that the Betty Draper wannabe will bury them at the bottom of a bin. I say the words over and over before caving in and pulling my clothes off, figuring the sooner I get on with it, the sooner I can make polite excuses and leave to go back to bed. Because bed is all I want. I wish I'd stayed at home now in Mulberry-On-Sea – I don't want to be a model. Or a 'face'. I thought it was all about the handbags.

*

Scrap that! I'm having the time of my life. Soon after Eddie hung up on me, Millie, the hair and makeup artist turned up. We had met before – she worked on *Kelly Cooper Come Instore* and is now based here, working freelance (Kelly owed her, so to get her started she sorted out this gig and a few others at glossy magazines with plush offices on Fifth Avenue). Anyway, she's transformed me, so now I'm glowing from head-to-toe, even my eyes are sparkling – she tilted my head back and squeezed in some magic drops. She has plucked, tweezed and teased me to perfection, well, almost. The headache is still there, and if you look closely you'll see the shadows under my eyes, but hey . . . Nothing a bit of airbrushing can't fix.

'Ready?' Millie says brightly, smiling over my head in the wall mirror.

'Think so. I can't believe that vision is me,' I laugh, fluttering my extra-thick navy lash extensions, which complement my turquoise eyes perfectly, and my hair has gone from being a frizzball – no time for serum earlier – to a sleek, glossy, swingy bob.

'Of course it is,' Millie laughs, selecting a midnight-blue floor-grazing gown from the rail. 'Try this; it will look sensational with those lashes.' I take the dress, letting my fingers brush over the tiny Swarovski jewels as I carefully step into it. Millie zips me up. And someone shouts out.

'Let's go, people. We're on a schedule.'

'Good luck.' Millie holds up crossed fingers and gently nudges me forward.

I step out from behind the sheet and wow! The floor has been transformed into a magical forest scene, the windows have been covered with wooden shutters, and a woodland backdrop canvas hangs the length of the wall at the far end of the room. There's even a floor-to-ceiling tree made from the pages of books and a chaise longue waiting for me to lie on. A production assistant shows me how to drape across the chaise and arranges the dress accordingly, so it puddles around my body, creating a flattering silhouette. She hands me a small Kelly bag with a garish gold buckle on the front – not my kind of thing at all – and positions it on my hip and places my hands around it like a frame. The cameraman starts snapping, over and over and over, until I'm convinced my middle-distance, 'draw-me-like-one-of-your-French-girls' faraway gaze has frozen onto my face.

'Stop! Stop at once!' Gaspard appears, powering down the room with an outraged look on his face. 'This is all wrong.' A hushed silence circuits the floor. 'Too contrived. I want normal, girl-about-town, not this glitzy, glamorous overproduced crap. This isn't the Louis Vuitton Christmas advert! And what is this monstrosity?' He gasps and clutches his chest as if he's been shot through the heart with a poison dart. A few seconds later, he recovers sufficiently to point at the bag still positioned in my hand-frame, before recoiling to flip open his cigarette case and select a restorative cigarillo.

'Get it out of my sight.' A minion darts forward and swipes the bag from my clutch before tossing it into a giant bin. 'Georgie, get changed.' And Gaspard extends his free hand towards me, which I gratefully accept, before unravelling myself from the chaise and standing up. 'We're going on location. And bring the cruise collection!' he instructs to nobody in particular. They all leap into action, dashing around gathering up equipment as Gaspard leads me back to the cotton-sheeted changing section.

Two hours later and I'm sauntering in Central Park, wearing an exquisite pair of cherry-red satin pedal pushers and a striped navy crop top with kimono sleeves – both from the House of Mercier cruise collection. I've got sparkly silver pumps on my feet and my hair has been shooshed up to create a breezy girl-about-town look, instead of the sleek, over-styled look I had going on earlier. Milly was a bit upset as the Betty Draper twinsie had specifically instructed her to 'Vogue me up', whatever that means, which as it turns out wasn't what Gaspard had in mind at all.

Anyway, Gaspard has explained that to start with he wants to see me in action, doing ordinary, everyday things but with wonderment and intrigue – apparently, it's how he must work to unleash his creative genius. And so I must saunter, while he mooches along in the distance behind me with just one cameraman snapping away. So far, I've admired the giant mosaic at the entrance, casually glanced at the lush green trees, run a finger over the arm of the bronze Alice in Wonderland statue, gasped at the glistening water, even smiled whimsically at the people – Lycra-clad women mainly, clutching hand weights as they exercise by running up and down concrete steps. How do they do it? And in this heat! It's so humid and clammy. I'm exhausted just watching them. And, to be honest, I feel like a bit of a plum, pretending to be enchanted. Don't get me wrong, Central Park is breathtaking, a beautiful green wide-open space in the centre of a bustling metropolis, but it's not the same wandering around on my own.

I find a bench overlooking the lake and sit down. The headache from earlier has eased now – the lunch-time pizza and giant pretzel washed down with an all-sugar Coke certainty helped, courtesy of Millie. The others all had carryout from a nearby Whole Foods, but I couldn't face any of the dubious-looking items from the raw food bar. And the chia seed salad with blackened chicken, dried cranberries, edamame, jalapeño, cayenne shrimp and avocado just seemed too healthy for my current state. It's all so different here – a far cry from Mulberry, where carbs and sugar are the standard cure for a monster hangover. I wish Sam was with me and could see the sights too; it would be so much better if she were here. I know she's never been to New York, surprisingly, as she travelled all over the world when Alfie was still alive, and we used to talk about doing an NYC shopping trip. This was before she had the twins, of course, when we'd spend winter weekends cosied up together on the sofa drinking hot chocolate while watching *Sex and the City* repeats – Sam was always Samantha, of course, and I was a hybrid of Carrie and Charlotte, according to Sam. As if on autopilot, I pull out my phone to call her, briefly checking the world clock app – it's 7 p.m. at home, that's OK. She answers on the second ring.

'Hello.'

'Hey you! How are you? Did you get my messages?'
A short silence follows.

'Pardon?'

'Um, it's me!' I say, feeling weird.

'Who?'

'Georgie.' Maybe it isn't Sam speaking. I don't think I've ever had to say my actual name to her on the phone before – we've always just known whenever one of us was calling the other . . .

'Oh, I didn't know it was you. The number came up as "unavailable" on my phone.'

'Ah, maybe it's an international thing,' I suggest, wanting to disperse the awkwardness between us as quickly as possible. 'So, how are you? God, I wish you were here, Sam. You'll never guess where I am? Central Park. And it's just like it is on the telly . . .'

'Lovely. Are you having a good time?' she asks, but her voice is stilted.

'I am, yes. Thanks. Be better if you were here though. How are things?' I ask tentatively. She sounds distant. A million miles away, which I suppose she is, but it's more than that. There's something else . . . and I can't put my finger on it.

'Georgie. I'm going to have to go, Christy is waiting for me – we're going out to dinner. Let's catch up soon. Yes?'

'Oh. Um, well sure. Of course. OK,' I babble, awkwardly. 'Love to the twins, and Nathan.' But she's gone. I clasp my hands together around the phone, grateful for the big shades because any minute now hot, confused tears are going to bounce onto my cheeks. I don't understand what's going on. She's been my best friend since school, we've known each other for years; we're like sisters, the kind of sister you imagine having when you don't actually have one, because I know plenty of sisters who can't stand each other, but Sam is the perfect sister, the sister who gets you and will laugh at the same things, love the same things, give you shoes and hold your hair if you vomit after too many margaritas – she's your very own personal cheerleader. But everything seems different somehow and I'm not sure how it happened. It's as if we're strangers now, there's a shift – like sand trickling through my fingers – and I don't know what to do about it. I can't stop it.

Out of the corner of my eye, I can see a filmy image of Gaspard tapping on an iPad mini, making notes about the weird English girl, no doubt. This was a mistake. Coming here. What on earth was I thinking? I need to be at home, in Mulberry, being there for my friend when she needs me most, not sitting on benches in parks in Manhattan. No wonder she was off with me, I've let her down. And she's never ever done that to me. She's always been there, right by my side, supporting me no matter what. I take a deep breath, and type out a text.

Wish I was there with you! It's just a park after all. Hope you're OK xxx

I press send, and then instantly regret it, when this reply comes back.

I'm fine. And you might as well enjoy it seeing as you're there now! x

15

My time in New York is nearly over now and it's amazing how much work we've managed to do – and how many sights, bars, restaurants and clubs Eddie, Ciaran and I have visited too. We've even done the *Sex and the City* tour! *Twice*. I sat on the steps of the New York public library – where Carrie nearly married Big – in the glorious summer sunshine. I seem to be getting used to it now and, given that the summer weather at home is so unreliable, I'm not complaining. I walked barefoot on the grass, wafting a Chinese paper fan that I bought on Canal Street in an attempt to create a modicum of breeze on my heat-baked face, through Jefferson Market Garden in Greenwich Village where Miranda really did marry Steve. I found some amazing dress bargains in Century 21 and had a hot dog with fresh papaya juice from the famous Gray's Papaya on Broadway, just like Carrie did after her book launch party. And Tom Hanks and

Meg Ryan went there too in *You've Got Mail*. I love that film.

Of course, we've been to all the ubiquitous designer boutiques – Tiffany & Co on Fifth Avenue with its timelessly elegant Art Deco building, where I got to stand on the same spot as Audrey Hepburn, and gaze at the glittery jewels, just as she did during breakfast. I almost cried happy tears in Marc Jacobs – from being surrounded by all of the beauty. It was then on to Kate Spade where I bought a gorgeous purse in lipstick-pink for Sam; next was Tom Ford where Eddie went mad and practically bought up the whole store – he had to use the boot of my town car as well as his own just to get his shopping haul back to the Plaza. And then in Manolo Blahnik I really did cry happy tears when Eddie and Ciaran treated me to my first pair of Blahnik heels in ruby red with a crystal strap – a birthday surprise! And last, but very much not least, we visited the traditional American stalwarts such as Saks, Bergdorf Goodman, Macy's, FAO Schwarz – all of them amazing and a trillion miles away from Mulberry-On-Sea. Bigger. Bolder. Carrington's does stock high-end pieces, but a limited range, I realise now, having seen the vast selection over here. And we really must expand our Womenswear and Footwear ranges. I'm going to talk to Tom about it when I get home. And see if we can section off parts of the floor space to create individual instore boutiques, too, like they have in the department stores here, with a red rope at the entrance, and Charles from Security waiting to unhook it so customers can feel special as they browse. We could have a Tiffany boutique. A Tom Ford boutique. A Louboutin boutique – I know my clients would love it. And the seasonal visitors from the boats in the marina too, I imagine. Don't all the swanky ports have fabulous shopping opportunities right there?

But the highlight of my time here was definitely travelling on the Staten Island ferry, with the cool refreshing breeze coming off the New York harbour water in my hair, and seeing the Statue of Liberty – it took my breath away. It really did. It's so iconic and exactly like it is on the telly. And I managed to get a perfect selfie with it in the background to text to Sam. I can seriously say that I've had the time of my life; a whirlwind of new experiences. That old adage of work hard to play hard is sooooo very true. I've been at Gaspard's studio every night – it's when he works best – and then back to the Manhattan mansion for a few hours' sleep, before sightseeing all afternoon.

And I'm exhausted, but Gaspard now has four designs. A satchel (in two sizes), a top handle, a clutch, and a coin purse with a detachable strap that can be worn over the shoulder or crossbody. All with the signature House of Mercier monogram on the interior fabric. I explained that just because an 'ordinary' girl might not have the money to pay designer prices, it doesn't mean she doesn't want a bit of glamour! But not in your face – he was then all for doing a Fendi and stamping his logo all over the leather, but I put a stop to it. Too Nineties. Understated is far better. Think Cambridge Satchel, not Gucci monogrammed bowling bag. So now we just need to work out where to have the personalised inscription – I've suggested the underside of the flap, or even on the strap would work. Or how about letting the customer choose? But this prompted a lengthy feasibility meeting with the design team, as Gaspard wants the inscriptions done at the point of sale and plans on installing a special instore embossing machine, which has 'limited capability'. In other words, it can't inscribe on uneven surfaces . . . So the proper designers are debating all the options and will no doubt decide what's best.

So, because today is Friday 15 August, my actual birthday, after presenting me with a gorgeous silver bracelet with a Big Apple charm on, Gaspard told me to take the day off. I'm celebrating with Eddie and Ciaran by doing one last big sightseeing marathon before I have to return to Mulberry-On-Sea on Monday – we got up really early and have already been to Bleecker Street and meandered around the quirky boutiques, we stood in awe in Times Square, breathing in all the flashing billboards, sidestepping the crowds moving in a multitude of different directions, just relishing in, and absorbing, the sheer enormity of it all.

We climbed up the Empire State Building; the Chrysler too. We saw kids open fire hydrants in the street just to cool down – of course Ciaran and I dived right in, splashing and jumping around like loopers while Eddie stood on the sideline angsting over his new $700 Tom Ford strappy sandals getting ruined with water damage. We popped into a Magnolia Bakery and had pumpkin cake with maple cream cheese frosting and toasted pecans for breakfast – oh God, it was to die for; they even popped a candle in after Eddie and Ciaran told the whole shop we were celebrating. Well, they are, I'm trying to forget that I'm thirty – I don't feel thirty. I was OK last year being twenty-nine, but thirty feels so much older. I feel as if I'm in limbo, not a twenty-something or really a thirty-something. And it's not like I've actually done very much with my life either, not like Sam – married with two beautiful babies – or Tom – building a business empire. And not forgetting Eddie, living his dream of celebrity stardom. Those are all solid, tangible things they've done. I'm still ordinary Georgie Hart from Mulberry-On-Sea and the best thing I've done is build a relationship with Tom, my one, which is breathtaking of course, but I can't help feeling that I want to do more, to see more, to achieve more – certainly before my next big milestone birthday of forty.

So I'm currently in denial, pretending it's just another day, which is surprisingly easy being so far away from everyone – Tom is in a meeting all day but promised to call the minute it was over so, with the time difference, I'm not expecting to hear from him for a while yet. I'm sure I'll hear from Dad at some point, just as soon as he finds somewhere with a decent signal – we last spoke when he and Nancy were whooping it up on a vineyard in the South of France; they had been crushing grapes in a giant wooden barrel with their bare feet. Dad was over the moon and a few sheets to the wind, too, I reckon, after all the wine they had tasted that day. He was very slurry during the call, and I could hear Nancy giggling and shushing him in the background, but it's nice that they're having the time of their lives too! Good luck to them.

And Sam is probably busy with the twins, although

we haven't actually spoken since that day in Central Park. She emailed me the following day and said it's really tricky to talk at the moment – Christy is there all the time, and they're busy trying to sort things out. So I sent a light reply back saying that I totally understand and we can catch up properly when I get back – I didn't want to get all heavy with her by asking why things seem to have changed between us, figuring she has enough emotional stuff going on right now. I attached a few pictures of New York for her to see: all the major sights, even a selfie with the bright city lights at night from the Soho House rooftop, which was very naughty of me, I know, as you're not allowed to use mobiles inside there at all, to protect the privacy of the slebs, apparently – but I sneaked one when nobody was looking as there was no way I was leaving without a picture of some kind. Who knows if I'll ever get another chance?

We've just arrived at the entrance to Grand Central Station, which isn't at all how I imagined it to be. Quite unassuming – I was expecting something far grander.

'Let's find the oyster bar,' Ciaran says, grabbing Eddie's hand and steaming in. I dash alongside, rapidly realising that I judged too soon – as we walk further into the station, it's utterly stunning! We arrive in the main ticket hall, an opulent vaulted atrium with three enormous arched windows at one end, streaming shafts of light, which catch and dance on the glittery chandeliers.

'Meet you at the clock,' I laugh, tearing towards a magnificent four-sided brass ball clock at the heart of the hall, set high above the information meeting point. Tilting my head back, I stare up at the ceiling, a velvety blue and gold astrological mural – this place is so magical. And oh my God, here's the staircase where Justin Timberlake stands and sings to Mila Kunis in that film, *Friends with Benefits*. It's just wonderful being here, in actual real life, to see it all. It makes me feel alive. It makes me feel like I'm actually doing stuff. It's brilliant.

'Isn't it breathtaking?' I gush to Eddie and Ciaran when they catch up.

'It sure is. See, I told you, it's the best place in the world, America!' Eddie beams, and he's so right. And it suits him to a T – in fact, seeing him here, where he can be whatever he wants to be, I totally get why he felt stifled at home. Mulberry-On-Sea is like a bubble, so insular, compared to the bustling, pulsing, vibrant metropolis that is New York. And I've never seen Eddie and Ciaran holding hands on the high street at home, oh no – Mrs Godfrey from the WI would be outraged, for sure, whereas here nobody cares at all, which is just as it should be. 'Let's celebrate. Champagne and oysters for lunch. Follow me.'

*

We've worked our way through a dozen Fire Island oysters, which tasted delicious, followed by a further dozen sweet Fanny Bay oysters, which also prompted a round of juvenile sniggers, started by Ciaran and exacerbated by two flutes each of champagne, and now I'm stuffed, and a little bit trollied as we wander back outside and into a nearby coffee shop. The guys are debating our next place to visit on this whistle-stop tour, when my phone rings. Ahh, I bet it's Tom. I quickly glance at my watch as I rifle through my bag in search of my phone. The meeting must have dragged on – it's one o'clock here, so six in the evening at home.

Moments later, I've accepted his FaceTime request and he's on the screen and my heart aches. It's ridiculous, we've spoken a few times while I've been away, though not for a day or so now as Tom has had loads of back-to-back meetings to discuss the new store, and with the time difference, and my work schedule here, it's been tricky to co-ordinate things, so we've only managed a surreptitious text or two – but even so, it's not the same as actually touching him, cuddling him, laughing with him, or simply being next to him. I've really missed him and can't wait for us to start living together, and I'm not even sure we need to talk about it first any more. Tom's right, we love each other and that's the most important thing. Being apart has just made me feel it more.

'Hello Mr Carrington!' I hiccup. 'Ooops, sorry about that,' I laugh, slapping my spare hand over my mouth. 'Too many bubbles at lunchtime always gets me giddy.'

'Where are you?' Oh dear. He looks really stern.

'Um, in a coffee shop,' I say, wondering what's going on.

'Hang on.' He's talking to someone off camera.

'Which one? Do you know the address?'

'I'm not sure, near Grand Central Station.' Ahhhh . . . Now I get it! It's a wind-up, of course it is. I crack up laughing, and the hiccups ricochet one after the other. I bet he's here, about to bounce out from under a table to surprise me. So exciting. I glance at Eddie and Ciaran, but they're huddled over an iPad mini lining up our next sightseeing attraction, and totally oblivious to me.

'I can't hear you with all that background noise – can you go outside?' he says, the narky face still in place.

'Ha ha, you're so funny. Sure I can,' I say playing along.

He's probably standing on the pavement. I motion to Eddie to watch my bag; he nods and loops it over his knee for safekeeping. 'Hang on a minute,' I say to Tom before leaping up and dashing to the door. Outside, and I scan the street. 'Surprise surprise,' I giggle in my best Holly Willoughby voice. 'I'm here!' I pull a funny face for good measure. I literally cannot wait to see him.

'Yep, I can see that. But what I'd like to know is, why?'

'Err, what do you mean?' I feel confused as I scan the street.

'Why aren't you here? I thought when you said you were in a coffee shop that you were nearby, but had got lost or something.'

'Sorry, I don't know what you mean,' I say, racking my brains, wondering what on earth is going on – and he hasn't even said happy birthday!

'The envelope! Did you open it?' A long pause. And then a horrible realisation dawns – he isn't here. Oh God! I feel sick. Shit. My heart plummets. The smile slides from my face.

'Um, err, I'm so sorry, I must have forgotten.' I tear back into the coffee shop and yank my bag from Eddie's knee before bombing back outside and down a side alley away from the traffic where it's marginally more private. 'I have it here!' I flip my passport from my bag

– I stored the envelope inside it for safekeeping – and wave it in front of the phone for him to see.

'Good. Call me back when you've opened it. And happy birthday!' And the screen goes blank. Tears sting as I rip open the envelope.

It's a ticket.

I scrub at my eyes with the back of my hand in an attempt to focus. Las Vegas. I scan again. Departure date – today! Departure time – six hours ago! Oh no. Oh God. It's too late. I missed the flight. I push the ticket back inside the envelope and see there's a card too, handwritten in Tom's writing.

Happy birthday Georgie,

 If you managed to hold out on opening the envelope, then I can't wait to see you tomorrow!

 Let's fly - we're spending the weekend in Vegas starting with a birthday picnic via helicopter over the Grand Canyon.

 All my love

 Tom, aka Mr Carrington xoxoxox

 PS. I've squared it with Gaspard for you to have the weekend off and he's sworn to secrecy so as not to spoil the surprise!

Noooooo! No, no, no, no, noooooo! I'm trembling. I feel like the lottery winner who lost their ticket. And oh my God, no wonder he was short with me – never mind Gaspard, I'm the one who has ruined the surprise. I don't believe it. Vegas! The Grand Canyon – so epic. Why the hell didn't I open the envelope? Because I was too blooming busy jumping into rooftop pools with all my clothes on, followed by gadding around town and generally having the time of my life with Eddie, that's why!

And now the man I love is going to hate me. I've ruined everything. I inhale sharply and let out a long breath before pressing to FaceTime Tom back. It rings for ages. And ages. *And ages.* I hang up and redial, just a normal voice call in case FaceTime isn't working now, given that we're at opposite sides of a foreign country. And it rings, again for ages, before tripping through to what must be the most infuriating voice-mail message in the whole world: 'The person you are calling is not available to take your call.' *No flaming shit, Sherlock.*

16

'Get the car. We're going to Vegas!' I'm back inside the coffee shop.

'Don't be silly, sweetie, we can't just drive to Vegas,' Eddie says, flashing Ciaran a look. 'Why don't you sit down, you look like you've seen a ghost, or . . . are, oh my God, are you actually OK?' He pulls a face. 'Only you're doing stary-serial-killer eyes . . . Eep, I'm petrified.' Eddie pushes a chair out for me and I slam it right back into the table.

'Is everything a joke to you?' I bellow, eyes flashing as I dig my nails into the palms of my hands to stem the tears that are going to splash onto my face any second now. I bite my bottom lip too, just to be sure, as my handbag slides off my shoulder and lands with a miserable thud on the floor next to my left foot.

'OK, why don't we all calm down?' Ciaran stands up and touches my arm. 'What's going on?' he asks in a way that makes holding back the tears impossible. I hand him the card from Tom.

Eddie is up on his feet too now, and Ciaran holds the card in front of them. After speed-reading it, they glance at each other and then stare at me. Silence follows, apart from the plinky-tinkly music coming from the speakers mingled with the muffled sniff of my nose after Ciaran hands me a napkin and tells me to 'blow hard'.

'Here. Sorry, I'm a ridiculous idiot sometimes, I know.' Eddie gently loops the strap of my handbag back over my shoulder. 'Ready?' he nods firmly, and I manage a weak grimace. 'If ever there was a moment that calls for action, then that time is now. Follow me.' And, after grabbing my hand, he runs us from the coffee shop with Ciaran close behind.

*

I've just stepped off an aeroplane at Las Vegas airport. Eddie's driver got me to JFK in record time and then I was lucky enough to get a flight here almost right away. Thank God I had a modicum of sense to keep my passport on me at all times. And with the time difference it's only early evening here – sixish, I think. I'm not even sure, but who cares, I'm here to celebrate my birthday weekend with Tom. I switch on my mobile, he's going to be super-surprised, hopefully, that I made it here after all. There was no time to call before – I literally had to run to the departure gate and was strapped into my seat with the 'trays in the upright position and mobile phones switched off' message ringing in my ears all ready for takeoff, before I could even call him to say I had managed to find a flight. He answers on the fourth ring, but before I can speak he says,

'Georgie, I'm too angry to talk to you right now.' And the line goes dead. I stare at the phone in disbelief, my hands shaking. For a few seconds, I have no idea what to do, so I just stand clutching my phone and holding my breath while my cheeks smart from his dismissal. I feel utterly crushed. Just like he did, I guess, when I ruined his surprise. But I can fix it now.

Some time later, I will myself to get a grip and put one foot in front of the other, slinging the strap of my handbag over my head, crossbody style. I proceed to make my way along the glass-walled walkway towards Arrivals, figuring I can call Tom again once I get outside. I'll just be sure to talk right away before he even has a chance to hang up, I'll say I'm here in Vegas, find out where he is and go to him. I have to put this right. Or, better still, I'll text him – yes, good idea, then he'll see that I'm here and . . .

Nooooo! No, no, no, no, noooooo. The white wheel is spinning on the screen. I press all of the buttons in a desperate attempt to make the phone come back to life, if only for a second, but nothing, it's no use, it dies.

And right now, that's exactly what I want to do.

I feel sick.

Now what?

'Fuck you, fuck, fuck, fuckity, fucking, fuck yoooooooou,' I mutter to myself, frantically stabbing the phone screen with my index finger over and over and over, then quickly apologise when an American family of four stare at me – the dad instinctively steering his two daughters away from the deranged English girl. Oh God.

Right. Think. I have to think. I rack my brains, searching for a solution to this hideous situation. I know, there's bound to be someone with an iPhone charger, or somewhere to charge phones – this is Vegas, after all, haven't they got everything here? There are fruit machines right in front of me, one-arm bandits at the actual airport, so a phone charger is probably considered a basic. My heart lifts, and with my mind made up, I run to the moving walkway, guessing it will be faster. I start jogging my way along it. I'm almost at the end. And that's when I spot him in the crowd. Tall, dark curls, broad shoulders and long strides.

Tom.

It's my Tom.

And my heart soars.

He's here, right in front of me. Well, on the other side of the glass, but still within touching distance and he's walking in the opposite direction. To Departures. With his head down and a leather holdall thrown over his shoulder. But why? He can't go. Not now. I have to get to him. Let him know that I'm here. It's OK now, we can start again, go on the helicopter, have the picnic, I'll make it up to him, I'll get us tickets to the Cirque du Soleil, or whatever show he likes, we could go in the Gondolas, we could go to the sand park and drive big diggers around, it'll be fun, I bet he'll love it. It'll be like nothing ever happened, that I didn't mess up at all; besides, it's not as if I meant to, and his wonderful surprise weekend can still go ahead.

I turn and start running the other way, keen to catch up with him. I run faster, banging on the glass as I go.

'Hey, lady, look out,' an all-American guy yells as I almost run right into his big beefcake chest.

'Sorry, it's just that, I, my—' I apologise, but he's off, keen to get away from me too. I keep running the wrong way along the moving walkway, apologising some more as people sidestep to dart out of my way. I'm almost there; Tom is practically adjacent to me now. *With his bastard big Bose headphones on.* For crying out loud, which is exactly what I do. 'Tooooooom. *Tom.* Tom it's me, Georgie, I'm here. Tooooooom!' I bang harder, my right hand bunched into a fist. I slam it against the glass, but it's no use. He can't hear me. So with both hands, palms flat against the glass, I slap it as hard as I can, over and over and until eventually he turns. He turns his head sideways towards me, obviously catching sight of something in his peripheral vision. Thank you God. Thank you so so sooooo much. I'm full of relief as I jump up and down and slap some more, but it's quickly followed by a wave of crashing devastation when he turns away, oblivious to me right here next to him in the crowd.

And then I skid and fall over. The side of my handbag caught around the wheel of someone's suitcase and they're pulling it away from me, tighter and tighter, unaware that any second now I'm going to be strangled to death. Jesus Christ. I fling my hands to my throat and manage to push my fingers under the strap to loosen it enough so I can breathe. Just about.

'OK. That's enough. On your feet, ma'am.' Two men dressed in blue uniforms covered in badges arrive, manage to stop the wheelie suitcase from garrotting me, fling me into an upright position, flank me and practically frogmarch me away.

'Hey, you can't take me, Tom's right there,' I gasp immediately on being untangled. 'My boyfriend. It's Tom. I need to see him . . . I have to explain—'

'Damn right you do. In the detention centre.'

Whaaaaaat?

'No, please, you can't.'

But it's no use.

17

The rest of my birthday was ruined, obviously. I felt so rubbish after being so near yet so far from seeing Tom in Vegas, and then having to explain it all to the two very unamused men from Homeland Security who, after listening to me babble on like a fruitloop for what must have seemed like forever to them – and yes there were moments when they both just stared, speechless, no doubt wondering whether they should call for someone to certify me, or just let me go; I know, utterly cringy and certainly a new record low for me – I think they eventually came to the conclusion that I was harmless and best removed from their airport as quickly as possible, so I was allowed to get a flight back here to New York, but only after Eddie's PA, Carly, had vouched for me and confirmed that I had a place to stay.

So I came straight back to the Manhattan mansion, via the liquor store and Don's Diner, and climbed up

221

into the big princess-and-the-pea bed with a bottle of Southern Comfort and an enormous cheeseburger with extra *everything*! And after watching back-to-back episodes of *Revenge* season 3 on Netflix, I must have fallen asleep, as I only woke up Sunday lunchtime when my car arrived and the driver with the crucifix came knocking on the lift door to take me to Gaspard's studio. We spent the evening going over everything one last time – chatting about fluoro colour schemes, neon brights and realistic prices that an 'ordinary woman' would be prepared to pay for a truly gorgeous bag baby. Gaspard kept apologising profusely for not telling me about my birthday surprise – he says if the Georgie Girl collection (the name he's chosen for the range) is a hit, then he'll personally fly me across the Grand Canyon. I think he feels partly responsible – for bringing me out here in the first place and for distracting me. It's ridiculous, and he was sworn to secrecy, so no, I've only myself to blame for missing out and making Tom hate me, which is exactly what I told him.

Anyway, it's Monday now, the morning of my last day in New York – my flight leaves JFK in a few hours. And Ciaran and Eddie, with Pussy under his arm, wearing a Wonder Woman outfit complete with tiny red cape, have just emerged through the lift doors and into my hallway.

'Oh sweetie, come here!' Eddie swiftly thrusts Pussy into Ciaran's arms, and pulls me in for a massive hug. 'Will you be OK?' He rubs my back and makes freaky cooing sounds – public displays of physical sympathy have always been a bit of an anathema to Eddie. He promptly drops his hands and steps away from me. 'Right. Are you all set for the airport?'

'No,' I say, despondently. 'I want to fly in a helicopter over the Grand Canyon with my boyfriend . . .' I let my shoulders droop as I stick out my bottom lip for added petulance.

'Well, you can't.' Eddie sighs. 'Besides . . .' he pauses to do an undercover sleuth left-then-right glance down the hallway, 'it's not all it's cracked up to be.' He purses his lips. 'Ciaran and I did the helicopter thing after our wedding in Vegas, didn't we lover?'

Ciaran nods, and then rolls his eyes.

'Ed, come on . . . Georgie doesn't want to hear all this, do you love?' Ciaran smiles kindly and gives my arm a reassuring rub.

'Yes she does,' Eddie quips. 'I just meant that once you've seen one lot of red rock with a river running through it, well, it gets a bit samey after the first ten minutes. By the end of our helicopter ride, I was struggling to keep my eyes open . . . *Thelma and Louise*, darling, the cliff scene at the end, that's all you need

223

to see!' he finishes with a flourish, while Ciaran and I exchange exasperated looks.

'I think it's the spoiling-the-surprise bit, the not-getting-to-see-Tom bit, that Georgie is most upset about,' Ciaran adds, tactfully.

'But you'll see him very soon. Come on, let's get you flight-ready. I'm picturing a romantic reunion at Heathrow Airport. I wonder if he'll bring flowers . . . will you run into his arms?'

'Stop it!' I snap. 'He's not coming to Heathrow.'

'Oh, I'm sorry – just trying to lighten the mood, honeypie. But why on earth not?'

'Because when my flight lands, he'll be in an all-day meeting which he can't get out of. Something to do with the new store,' I say dejectedly, remembering him telling me a few days ago, before my birthday, when everything was still good between us, which seems like a lifetime ago now. I've tried calling him since I got my phone charged back up in Vegas (the security men had to let me so I could call Eddie, who called Carly, a US citizen – Eddie figured it best that she speak to them), but Tom's phone has been off. I guess he was on the flight home or maybe he just wants to cool off before talking to me.

'Well, it'll just make it all the more thrilling when you do actually see him then. And all will be forgiven and forgotten, and he'll ask you to move in with him again and you'll have incredibly filthy reunion sex, you'll see.' Eddie smiles, seemingly pleased with himself for having it all worked out. 'And don't forget our bet. Only a matter of time before the cash is mine.' He winks before grabbing my hand and leading me like an obedient toddler into the bedroom. 'Ciaran will pack while I find something suitable for you to wear. You never know, Tom might try to surprise you – *second time lucky* – by turning up at the airport . . . You'll want to look your best,' he instructs, flinging open the lid of my suitcase, which is on the bed, while casting a disparaging eye over my floor-drobe. 'Honestly, Georgie, I know these are mostly Mango and Topshop, but really . . . you must look after your clothes. Hang them up!'

'Hey, nothing wrong with high street clothes. I love them . . . and I'll have you know that some of my Carrington's clients do too. Even the fabulously wealthy ones – it's not all Prada and Phillip Lim you know.'

'Hmmm. If you say so.' He pulls a face, unconvinced, as he plucks a pair of red pleather shorts off the floor and hands them to me. 'Put these on. Tom won't know what's hit him when you emerge through Arrivals.'

'No I can't. They go a bit camel-toe after a bit; they'll be hideous after a seven-hour flight.'

'Ew, oversharer!' He tosses them into the suitcase. 'What about these?' He hands me a pair of cotton buffalo print shorts instead.

'They'll do.'

'Good. And put the Manolo's on.' I do as I'm told.

'On seconds thoughts, no! Far too . . . *TOWIE* does Marbs.'

'OK, I'll decide,' I say, holding up a palm, figuring this could go on all day if I let him have free rein. I slip the coveted heels off and carefully place them in the suitcase and opt for my gold flatform trainers instead, figuring comfort for travelling is best.

'Fine. Now let's sort out your hair and face.'

A few hours later, having hugged and kissed Eddie and Ciaran goodbye, I've just checked in at JFK airport. I glance at the Departures board and see the flight to London Heathrow is scheduled to leave on time, and whilst I'm sad to be leaving New York, I can't wait to see Tom, apologise and try to make amends. Sam, too – I really need to talk to her – and then I must get stuck in to finalising the last-minute bits and bobs for the regatta. If I can make sure my elements of it go smoothly, then I might just be in with a chance of redeeming myself with Tom, Isabella too. I hope. She's bound to know that I let her son down on my own birthday!

I wander over to a kiosk and am flicking through a copy of American *Vogue* when my phone rings. My heart lifts. I bet it's Tom. I quickly retrieve it. Oh, it's Dad. Ah well, it'll be nice to talk to him. When he called on my birthday we only chatted for literally a few seconds. The signal was shocking, and when I offered to ring him back, he wouldn't hear of it. Didn't want me running up my phone bill.

'Dad! How's it going? What adventures are you having today?'

Silence follows.

'Georgie?'

'Oh hi Nancy, sorry, I assumed you were Dad, how are you?' Another silence follows.

'I, I, um, I . . .' She's crying. Oh God. A horrible sickly shiver engulfs me. I toss the magazine back on the shelf and head outside.

'Nancy, what's happened?' Tears fill my eyes.

'It's George, your father! He's had a heart attack. And, I, I'm sorry, it's . . . I don't know . . .' The airport sways. The harsh striplights flash all around me. I can't hear properly. And why is everyone moving in slow motion? Gawping at me. I reach a hand out to a nearby wall to steady myself. I swallow hard before drawing in an enormous gulp of air, just like the drowning person who manages to reach the surface.

'I'm coming.' And I'm running. Running back to the check-in desk. Ignoring the queue, I tear to the front and fling my bag on the counter. 'I need to change my flight. I need to go right now—'

'OK, ma'am. See right there behind you? It's a queue!' the uniformed woman states in a bored voice, pointing a graffiti-print acrylic nail in my face before beckoning the next person to step forward. It's a big beer-bellied guy wearing a cowboy hat and a bootlace tie with a metal sheriff badge clasped at his chubby neck.

'But you don't understand. I need to go *right now*.' I slap my hand on the counter.

'*Security!*' The pretend cowboy sniggers, elbowing me sharply out of the way before fanning his passport and travel documents out across the desk in front of him, as if claiming his stake as the rightful person next to be processed. *Not me*. A feral instinct takes over and I shove him right back before sweeping my hand across the desk, messing up his documents and then making them flip up in the air. They land in a jumbled pile on the floor right next to his lizard-skin boot-clad feet. 'Bitch, you better pick that lot up, y'hear me!' He clenches a fist, raises it, and then hesitates when I step forward; clearly not used to a woman standing up to him, he drops his hand. Twat.

'Don't call me a bitch, you fucking knobber. You're not even a real cowboy.' I shout in his face – spit actually skyrockets from my mouth and lands on his lapel. Fucking hell. 'Do you know that I'm a personal friend of Dan Kilby? That's right. *The* Dan Kilby. *World-famous* country singer. You've probably tried to line-dance to his music . . .' My heart is hammering so hard it feels as if it might burst right out of my chest. What the hell am I doing? I sound like some kind of lunatic. The words are coming out of my mouth but it's as if somebody else, another *crazeee* person's mouth next to mine, is actually saying them. A few seconds later, and a guy in one of the same blue uniforms as worn in Vegas has hold of my elbow. My heart sinks to a new low I never knew existed. Oh no, not again. Twice in one weekend. They'll deport me this time, for sure.

'OK, let's calm everything down here,' he starts, in one of those softly-softly negotiator-style voices. 'Ma'am, please step aside.'

'No, I need to go right now. My dad, he . . .' My voice trembles, 'Nancy just called. What if he . . . dies?' My voice quivers as I say the actual word out loud. 'And I'm not there . . .'

'And where is your father?'

'He, they . . . they're doing Europe,' I manage.

'You need to give us more than that to go on,' the negotiator man says.

'I . . . hold on.' The phone is still clutched in my hand. 'Nancy?' But she's not there. I instantly call Dad's mobile, praying she picks up. She does after the first ring. 'Where are you?' I ask immediately. There's no time for niceties.

'In the mountains,' she says in a small, shaky voice.

'Where, Nancy? Where are you? You must know where you are!' I say, fear engulfing me, and making my voice sound hideously shrill and accusatory.

'I don't know. We stopped to paddle in the stream . . . It's so beautiful and tranquil here. But where's the ambulance, they called an ambulance, the people here . . .' she babbles, incoherently. Oh God. I'm going to faint. I wobble and the security man grips my elbow to steady me.

'What country?'

'Andorra.'

'Andorra!' I breathe in relief. 'I'm on my way.' And I end the call.

'There isn't an airport in Andorra!' It's the moody check-in woman.

'What do you mean? Every country has an airport!' I say, desperately resisting the urge to launch myself across the counter and head-butt her smug face.

'Well, Andorra doesn't,' she snaps before doing a sarcastic smile. 'Too mountainous, can't land aeroplanes there.'

And this tips me over the edge – I sink to my knees and big, gulping, heaving sobs roar from me while I slap the floor with my left hand. I knew I should have stopped them going. I should have been more insistent. I should have pointed out all the dangers of visiting remote places that I've never even heard of. Places that don't even have an airport! Who even decided that was ever an acceptable thing? But I was so wrapped up in myself, worrying about how I felt about them 'doing flaming Europe' – I should have talked them into a cruise or something. At least they have facilities, doctors, and hospitals right there on board. Some ships even have helipads; they would have got him to hospital immediately, and he wouldn't be stranded on the roadside waiting for an ambulance to find him in some God-awful dump that doesn't *even have an airport*.

*

A trillion hours later, or so it seems, and I'm here, in the breathtakingly beautiful country that is Andorra – the negotiator man at JFK sorted it all out after I eventually calmed down, managing to get me on the next flight. I tried calling Tom before takeoff, but his phone was either switched off or he was on a call as it went straight to that annoying answer message again. And then I had to turn my phone off as the steward doing the seatbelt check gave me a daggers look. There was no way I was drawing attention to myself whilst still in US airspace – hell no, I was certain I'd be arrested or something. America probably has my details now on some kind of database, especially for crazeee fruitcake loopers who don't get a third time lucky chance, and instead have to shuffle straight off to jail in chains and one of those orange jumpsuits.

Seven hours later, I arrived at Toulouse Airport in France, the closest one to Andorra, and after hastily exchanging a fistful of dollars for far fewer euros, I took a taxi over the border and all the way here to the hospital – it turns out there is only one hospital in Andorra. Thank God. I'm shattered beyond belief, still wearing my buffalo shorts, and all I have with me is my handbag, albeit with a broken strap after the Vegas security guy yanked it free from the wheelie suitcase, so hard that it snapped clean in two. My suitcase, I'm guessing, is riding a left-luggage carousel somewhere at Heathrow, or maybe it's still at JFK, offloaded when I was declared a 'no-show'. Either way, I'm past caring, to be honest; my only concern now is Dad. I have no idea how he's doing as when I tried to switch on my phone to call Nancy – the minute we landed – the battery had died, and yep, you guessed it, the charger is inside the suitcase. But I had a good think, and a big cry or two on the flight, and have managed to get a grip, just about. I can deal with this, whatever happens; whatever the situation is when I get to the hospital. I have to, for Nancy's sake. She's my only family, after all.

I push through the swing doors of the hospital's main entrance and race up to the reception desk. An English-speaking nurse directs me to a family room, and the minute the door is opened, Nancy dashes towards me.

'Oh, Georgie, you're here,' she says, her voice tearful and her face ashen. And she looks exhausted, all dark circles hanging like parachutes under her eyes; she's wearing a floral halter-neck swimming costume underneath a matching floaty sarong. She looks as if she's just stepped off a beach and the contrast to the clinical surrounding of the hospital intensifies my fear. I give her a big hug before quickly pulling back.

'Where is he?'

'He's fine. Love, he's going to be fine.' She clasps my hands in hers and squeezes them tight. 'I'm so sorry.

I panicked. He was gasping for air, and then when he collapsed on the mountain road, I screamed for help and the rest was a blur . . . How did you know? How did you get here? Did I call you? I must have done.' She shakes her head vigorously, as if to rinse away the confusion in a desperate bid to gain clarity.

'You did, and thank God you did. I couldn't bear it if . . .' My voice trails off.

'I know dear, and I'm so pleased you're here. They've done all the tests, and it turns out he has gallstones – that's why he was bent double before he clutched his chest and keeled over,' she gabbles fast, fuelled by adrenalin, her eyes are like dinner plates. 'He's going down for keyhole surgery tomorrow morning to have his gall bladder removed.'

'So, it's not the angina then?'

'Oh no, they said that's all fine. Well, as fine as it can be . . . but it's stable, has been for years, as you know – no, it's just bad luck the gallstones flared up now.' Relief runs through me. Closely followed by more tears. Loads of tears – it's as if a dam has burst and now I can't stop. 'Oh dear, lovie, let it all out.' Nancy rubs my arm before pulling me back in for another big hug.

'Sorry. It's just that, he's all I have . . . and you, you're my only family,' I say, in between the tears.

'There there, no need to apologise,' Nancy soothes. 'He'll be as right as rain in a few days, you'll see. I'm the one who should apologise, silly old fool, scaring you like that when you were so far away . . . Georgie, I'm so sorry.'

'Don't be daft. I would have been devastated if you hadn't called me,' I laugh, relief giving way to near-euphoria now.

'Come on, they've dosed him up with painkillers so he's a bit dreamy, but he'll be thrilled to bits to see you.' After looping her arm through mine, she takes me to him.

18

Why does it take so long for an iPhone to come back to life? Mine's been plugged in now for at least twenty minutes, I'm convinced of it. Not that I can actually check, because, yep, that's where the clock is.

After a very restless night trying to get some sleep on the sofa in the family room (Nancy wanted to stay at the hospital 'just in case', so I stayed too), I made sure Dad was OK – he's in theatre and will be out of it for at least the next few hours – before going in search of Daisy. Nancy gave me the keys and a rough idea of where she was located. It didn't take long to find her in a layby next to a pretty stream, as Andorra is a small country; the first café I popped into, they knew all about the yellow bus with daisies all over it. A local guy, who spoke no English (and I can't speak Catalan, of course), kindly brought me to Daisy in his four-by-four after we managed to establish a few details in French – mainly with me nodding and saying, '*Oui, oui, voiture jaune*' over and over.

So now I'm sitting in the front seat of Daisy with the window down, the engine running, and my phone plugged into a charger connected to the cigarette lighter, which is a miracle in itself as, once I found Daisy, it then took me over an hour, firstly to work out how to actually drive her (changing gears is like stirring custard), then to negotiate the prospect of driving on the wrong side of the road, and finally to find an actual shop. In the end, I sputtered and stalled my way into a hypermarket car park where I abandoned her by finding a space I could drive straight into, and after buying some essentials to tide me over – knickers, a Hello Kitty T-shirt, pink velour joggers (I know, but they were the best option), toothbrush, deodorant, that kind of thing, I managed to find an electronics shop which, thankfully, sold in-car phone chargers. Hurray! I never realised, before recent events, just how much I depend on mobile technology. It's ridiculous, but I truly think I might be addicted to Twitter and Facebook, checking emails and nosing through total strangers' Instagram pictures. But being without my phone ... well, it has been like an actual part of me was missing. Ludicrous, I know.

I press the button again – still nothing! And then,

boom! The Apple icon appears, and I've never felt so relieved – I'm back on. Right, I scan the easyJet website and see to my relief that it's only an hour-long flight from Toulouse to Gatwick, the nearest airport to Mulberry-On-Sea. Perfect. I book the first available flight – Friday afternoon, not ideal; but at least I'll be home with time to catch my breath and hopefully see Tom and Sam before the regatta launches on Saturday. Phew!

And then my phone goes berserk as it kicks into life, pinging with tweets, Facebook messages, several voicemails – I scan my missed calls list, and my heart sinks when I don't see anything from Sam. But then lifts when I see a missed call from Tom. I call him back right away, but it goes straight to that annoying voicemail woman yet again, so I text Annie instead for an update, figuring she'll be behind the counter at work and therefore unable to actually talk. A few seconds later, she replies.

OH NO. Sorry about your dad, hope he's better soon. Everything OK here. **NOTHING TO WORRY ABOUT.** See you on Friday! **xoxoxo**

Ah, that's a relief. I knew I could count on Annie. I smile. Oh, there's another text message from her.

PS, that commando man on the committee, the one who owns the TV shop is super scary, barked like a sergeant major he did when I sat in his chair by mistake. And what is wrong with that weirdo Meredith? Why does she hate Carrington's? Honestly, I nearly thumped her at the last meeting. I didn't of course ☺ xoxo

Oh dear. The commando man is a bit scary, and I wonder what Meredith did to upset Annie? But she does have a very good point – Meredith is weird. And rude. She was asked to leave Carrington's years ago; you'd think she would be over it by now . . . Sighing, I call Sam, but it just rings for ages and doesn't even go to voicemail, which is very strange. Usually, her cheery, sunny voice kicks in. Maybe it's something to do with me being in Andorra, dodgy roaming service or whatever – I push away the worm of worry, the little voice that says: *Or maybe she just doesn't want to talk to you . . .*

A few seconds later, Tom calls, and my heart lifts. I swipe the screen to answer the call immediately.

'Georgie! What happened? Did you fall asleep? I didn't bother calling last night after the meeting, in case I woke you up. I figured you'd be tired with jetlag.'
Ah, my heart soars. It's as if my forgetting to open the

envelope never happened, he's still talking to me, and obviously just wants to forget it and move on – he's not even mentioned it. He still loves me, of course he does; everyone fucks up now and again, and I'll make damn sure it never happens again. 'How was the flight home?' he continues cheerfully.

'Well, I'm not actually home yet, Tom.'

There's a pause before he says, 'But it's Tuesday, you're cutting it very fine for the regatta . . .' And he's right, but there was no way I wasn't going to come straight here to see Dad – in that moment when Nancy called, it was all I could think of, I had to get to Dad, and nothing, absolutely nothing else mattered. Not the regatta. Not even Tom. My heart drops. Tom sounds disappointed and hasn't even asked me why I'm not home yet; his first thought seems to be all about the regatta – maybe he's not OK with me after all. 'So, when are you coming home?'

'Friday morning,' I state, still deep in thought. A long silence follows.

'What? Jesus, Georgie, what's going on?' There's another silence. 'Is everything OK?' he eventually asks.

'Yes, sorry, it is now!'

And I quickly bring him up to speed.

'Oh God, I'm so sorry, Georgie. Your poor dad. Wish him a speedy recovery from me, will you?'

'I will, thanks. And Tom, I really can't wait to see you, I'm so sorry about ruining everything, I didn't ...' I say, taking control and figuring it best to cut to the chase, I can't bear this awkwardness between us.

'Look, don't worry about it now; you need to take care of your dad. Let's get the regatta out of the way and then maybe we can talk. I've got a manic week ahead wrapping up plans for the new store, in any case. I'm going to be in meetings for much of it,' he says, ominously.

'Um, yes. OK.' Hardly the response I was hoping for. 'I'd better get back to the hospital,' I quickly add, because, right now, I really can't think of anything else to say.

'Yes, probably for the best.' And I swear his *Downton* accent just got stronger. Oh God, I hate it when he goes all formal and distant. It's as if he's a trillion miles away, and I don't mean geographically.

'I'll call when I land,' I say quietly.

'Sure. If I don't answer, then I'm in a meeting, but leave a message.'

'Will do.' I try to ignore the sand-trickling-though-my-fingers feeling that's building up inside me.

'Safe trip. And I hope it all goes well for your dad.' And he's gone.

I sit and stare at the scenery, drawing in the

241

whooshing sound from the stream, the steep cobbly streets on the other side of the road, leading up to the lush, grassy green mountains. It's so tranquil and calm, and in total contrast to how I feel inside. Just a few weeks ago, my life was perfect, but now it's in turmoil: my best friend isn't talking to me, my boyfriend has distanced himself after I managed to ruin my own birthday surprise, and my dad is having surgery in a foreign country. Talk about all change. Gaspard said he could see the wanderlust emanating from my soul, or whatever – and it's true, I was hankering to do something exciting, something out of the ordinary, before I become a thirty-something, or, shudder, a forty-something, still in Mulberry, and still doing what I've always done: picking out clothes for other people to wear in their globetrotting lives, while I'm writing about the contents of celebrities' handbags. I'll be like Mrs Grace before she got her break – seventy-odd and still doing the same thing.

But the adventure wasn't supposed to be like this . . . this isn't what I wanted. Because, the way I feel right now, I'd do anything to be back in Mulberry-On-Sea, with Dad there, too, of course, fit and happy and tending the roses in his little garden just like always, instead of lying in a hospital bed in a foreign country.

And with Sam on the fifth floor in the Cupcakes At Carrington's café sharing a cake or three – cracking up over something or another, just like before, before everything changed. And then Tom, I really need to make things right with him; move in with him immediately, if he'll still have me. It's true, I've missed him so much these last two weeks, I can't believe I hesitated even for a second. What is there to talk about? I love him, I want to live with him, I don't even mind where it is now, and it can be in a tent in the middle of a field for all I care. It'll be another adventure, of a different kind, only this time one worth having. Some relationships work out; some people have long-lasting, fulfilling, trusting, happy relationships. I pause for a moment to ponder and then rapidly realise that, actually, I don't know anyone who has that – I thought Sam and Nathan were rock solid, but now I'm not so sure. And what about Dad and Nancy? Yes, they may have known each other for decades, but they were both married to other people for much of that time, which sort of proves my point. But then when did I get so cynical? I take a deep breath. Maybe there never are any guarantees. And then again, maybe it can work for Tom and me. But I guess I'll just have to wait and see if it's still an option.

Then there's the regatta – will my elements of it go to plan? Or has my luck finally run out? If recent events are anything to go by, then who knows . . . . it could turn into an utter disaster and I'll be throwing another pity party for one, when it's *all my flaming fault*. Isabella is bound to think so.

*

Back to the hospital and Dad is wide-awake and sitting up in bed trying to get the portable TV to work.

'Hello love.' He dumps the remote control on the nightstand and squeezes my hand as I lean across the bed to kiss his cheek.

'How are you feeling?' I say brightly. He looks surprisingly well for someone who has just had surgery – if the hospital bed and the drip in the back of his hand were taken away and replaced with a sun lounger and a large cocktail, he wouldn't look out of place on the deck of a cruise ship. I didn't really notice yesterday, I was so worried; anxious about the angina and if it would scupper his chances of making it through the operation – the doctor had even said that a general anaesthetic is always risky, a little more so with Dad's condition. But looking at him now, he seems very perky indeed – his mahogany tan is glorious and his hair a little longer and lighter than it was before he went off to 'do

244

Europe'. And he looks fitter, his chest and shoulders more defined.

'Never better, but I'm gasping for a cup of tea,' Dad says to Nancy, who is sitting on the other side of the bed with her knitting needles tap-tapping away.

'I bet you are. I'll go in search of a nurse or a cafeteria and leave you two together for a bit to have a chat, but don't be overdoing it.' Nancy smiles broadly, before putting her knitting on the end of the bed and glancing at me. I nod by way of confirmation as she pushes the door open with her left hip.

'So what happened then, Dad?'

'Well, it's a bit of a blur to be honest, love. I remember we had climbed up a steep cobbled alley to get a closer look at a traditional stone-clad house – you should have seen the window boxes, sweetheart: bursting with colour, they were. Anyway, next thing I know, I'm bent over double thinking my time had come. And I can tell you, when something like this happens, it sure does put things into perspective. All the way here in the ambulance I saw my life in sharp focus: significant events, regrets – and it's like Frank Sinatra said, "I've had a few . . ."'

'Oh Dad, please. Don't say that.'

'It's OK, sweetheart. Seems the big man up there doesn't want me yet.' He rolls his eyes heavenward.

'Plenty of life left in this old dog. And even if there wasn't, at least I did it my way.' He winks and pats the blanket down over his waist, seemingly pleased with himself, while I try not to feel horrified.

'Dad, I couldn't bear it if—'

'I know.' He smiles kindly, crinkling his eyes at the corners. 'But it comes to us all in time – for some far too soon, sadly.' There's a brief silence while we share a thought for Mum.

'She would have been sixty this year, which reminds me; we must visit her grave soon . . . When you're better, of course,' I quickly add.

'Definitely. As soon as I'm home, we'll make a day of it.' He squeezes my hand again. 'Maybe Nancy will make one of her nice flower arrangements.'

'I do hope so . . . Dad, I'm so pleased you have Nancy. She's such a lovely, warm woman. She was devastated when she called me; she loves you very much,' I tell him, thinking back to my inner dialogue by the stream. I so hope they stay the course. 'And I do too, Dad – I love you very much.' There, I've said it. I've told him. And I feel so happy. Dad's eyes fill with tears.

'Oh Georgie, I love you too. You mean the world to me, sweetheart, always have, from the moment you were born. It just took me a long time to really appreciate all that I had. But I can't tell you what it means to hear you say this. When you allowed me back into your life, I was so grateful, after I had let you down so badly . . .'

'It's OK, Dad, I understand now how the chain of events unfolded. And I understand that addiction is a horrible curse. But you beat it every day. You do that, and I admire you so much for it.' I know he's been going to meetings since he left prison all those years ago – I went too, for a while, to understand, and I learnt that addiction never goes away, it's there, always, secreted away as a possibility that requires a strategy, strength, and purposeful tackling every single day. And he does that. And I thank my lucky stars that I don't have to . . . I'm not entirely sure I'd have the strength of character that he has.

'For a time, gambling took over my life, but no more. Don't get me wrong, the urge never fully goes away, but I've learnt over the years how to be its master, instead of letting it rule me, if that makes sense?'

'It does, Dad, and I know it can't be easy.'

'It's easier, now that I have so much going for me. Nancy. And having you back is a wonderful thing, and something I thought for a while might never happen. It must be a couple of years now . . . Time sure flashes by when you're having fun,' Dad grins.

'Oh Dad, I'm so sorry for cutting you out like that, and for such a long time. What was I thinking? Recent events have shown me I was a fool . . . time is so precious.' I think back to how I felt at the airport when Nancy called. I was devastated, scared, and instantly thought I was losing Dad. It puts everything into perspective. In the grand scheme of things, we're only here for a short time . . . And the minute I get home, I'm going to make things right with Sam and Tom. Whatever it takes.

'No you weren't. You were young, and naïve, finding your way, and – let's face it – you had plenty to be angry and sceptical about. I let you down. Your own father; it can't have been easy.'

'But it's in the past now,' I smile.

'It is. And we've come so far, it never ceases to amaze me how wonderful life can be – happy, exhilarating and exquisite one moment, and then devastating, lonely and heartbreaking the next.'

'I wish we could just have the happy bit all the time,' I say, thinking life would be so much easier then.

'We can!' I frown, wondering how he's worked that one out. 'Well . . . what I mean is, there are never any guarantees in life, of course there aren't, but that's the whole point. It's all about perspective at the end of the day, and the bits you pay attention to. If you accept the rough with the smooth, then you immediately eliminate the doubt, the worry, which is the worst bit.'

'Hmmm . . .' I say, deep in thought. Dad takes my hand.

'Sweetheart, don't you see? If we don't experience the heartbreak, how can we ever savour the sweetness? Appreciate the truly exquisite moments? Really cherish them and bask in the happiness they bring? This is the problem these days: youngsters like you are so busy trying to avoid getting hurt that you forget to enjoy the good bits.'

'But it would make everything so much easier.' I smile wryly.

'Of course it would, but then it sure wouldn't be half as much of an exhilarating rollercoaster ride either.' He grins and shakes his head. 'You'll see. You wait until you're my age. I bet you'll look back and feel pleased to have lived a life worth living, to have experienced every range of emotions, and had adventures. In my opinion, it beats a predictable, monotonous life, one of having never taken a chance,' he says wisely. I nod and smile, thinking perhaps he has a point. We sit in silence together, reflecting. And then, to lighten the mood, he says, 'Georgie, darling, I'm so pleased you're here, but if you need to get going, I'm fine, really I am. A couple of gallstones aren't going to hold me back. I'll be up and about before you know it.'

I laugh. 'Dad, are you trying to get rid of me now?'

'No, but what's the point of you sitting around here when you have so much else to be doing? Stuff that's far more exciting, I bet.' He grins and squeezes my hand. I smile, thinking how amazing he is, after everything he's been through – the gambling addiction, the shame of going to prison for fraud to fund his addiction, losing his family, then Mum dying and attending her funeral handcuffed to a prison guard. I remember it as if it were yesterday – his own brother, Uncle Geoffrey, refusing to look him in the eye. And then being alone for years in that horrible fetid bedsit; but Dad never gave up, he always called me, kept trying to make things better, even when I refused to have anything to do with him. And thank God he did, because otherwise I'd still be that insecure, sceptical girl, always trying to fit in, as I was back then. Well, OK, a part of her is still there and probably always will be, but hey, at least I'm muddling along, trying to do things right . . . The feeling lingers. I squeeze his hand back.

'The doctor did say that you'll probably be OK to come home in a few days, well, not *home* home as in

250

back to Mulberry just yet, but certainly out of here. I was thinking a nice hotel for a week, or however long you need. I'll sort everything out for you, Dad. There's bound to be lots of luxury five-star spa hotels close by, where you can rest and recuperate in style with full room service – Andorra is a very popular place for skiing in winter and tourism in summer, so we'll find somewhere really nice.'

'Love, don't worry about me. Like I said, I'll be fine, and there's nothing wrong with Nancy and me travelling on in Daisy.'

'Dad, no way! You can't. I'm not being funny, but that camper van has no proper heating.'

'Ah, we don't need heating, not in weather like this. It's gloriously warm, even at night.'

'But what about the bed? You can't recuperate on that tiny thin mattress; you can barely lie side by side on it – what if Nancy accidently bumps your scar in the night? Please let me sort out a hotel. I wish I could stay here to look after you, but . . .' My voice trails off as my mind races, wondering if there's any way at all I could stay with him for a bit longer, just to be sure he's OK; but it's impossible, I can't let Carrington's down, or Tom. Not again.

'I know, the regatta. And you don't want to miss out on that. It's exciting. A chance to really show what you can do. The old dears at home were all talking about it before we left. How is it all going?'

'Fine, I think. Everything was pretty much organised before I went to New York, and Annie, she's the girl who took charge while I was away, said it's all on track. It should be brilliant.'

'Well, that's really good news. It'll be a huge success, you'll see.' I smile, but it's too late. 'What is it, sweetheart?' Dad probes, not missing a beat and turning his head to look me directly in the eye.

'It's nothing, Dad. We've already chatted for far too long. Besides, you're supposed to be resting . . . Nancy won't be pleased when she comes back,' I chide, attempting to change the subject.

'Pah, plenty of time for all that. Tell me what's up? Is it Tom?'

I glance away. Silence follows.

'I've ruined everything, Dad. I just hope I can fix it.' I pick at the hem of my shorts. 'But talking to you has really helped,' I quickly add.

'Oh, I'm sure you haven't, love. Tell me about it . . .'

And I do. I tell him everything. Right from the start. How Tom has asked me to move in, and I've hesitated, and I'm not even entirely sure why – I thought I was being independent, sensible and mature about it, or perhaps I was just hankering for reassurance, something more from Tom to 'prove' his intentions other than it just not being practical any more for us to live apart. I've told Dad about Isabella and how I'm convinced she hates me. We even had a short interlude when Nancy popped back with two mugs of tea before asking if I minded if she went and freshened up in the family room – have a short nap, perhaps. So then it was on to Sam and how she was with Nathan that day in the kitchen, and then Christy turning up out of the blue. Followed by my biggest faux pas, the grand finale, the Grand Canyon surprise – or, to be more precise, my ruining of it with my inadvertent absence – because I forgot all about the envelope.

Dad mulls it all over before speaking.

'Georgie, the thing is, sweetheart, Tom is probably as devastated as you are underneath that stiff-upper-lip cool thing he has going on. It'll be his pride, you'll see . . . Leave him be for a few days, let him calm down. I imagine he's disappointed; angry perhaps, certainly upset . . . I bet he was chuffed to bits with himself for organising the birthday surprise – you know how us men can be when it comes to doing things like that. It's a very big deal.' I smile at Dad's old-fashioned views. 'And then, when it didn't work out . . .'

'But I can't help thinking I should have stayed at home and then none of this would have happened.

You too – at least at home you were safe, and everyone seemed happy, sort of. You know, Sam isn't talking to me now, Dad. I should never have left her when she needed me most.'

'But you can't change stuff that's already happened, love. The past is gone; what counts is the here and now and the going forward. And, in my experience, love, things that are going on for others are rarely all our fault, but we often assume they are. Talk to her, explain how you feel, apologise, do whatever it takes to sort it out. Ask her how she feels, ask her what's going on for her, take an interest, because at the end of the day, we have no idea what's really going on for somebody else. And she's been a wonderful friend to you, hasn't she?' I nod. 'Good, so now might be a chance for you to be a wonderful friend to her.'

'Do you really think so? That it's not too late?'

'It's never too late . . . you and I both know that. Look at us! Look at what we have now. And I bet you never would have thought it possible a few years ago.' Dad winks and squeezes my hand just as Nancy arrives back with a jug of water, three plastic beakers, a bag of grapes and an enormous bunch of wild flowers.

'I went for a walk after my nap to blow the cobwebs away, and found these.' She waves the flowers in the air. 'Thought they might brighten up your room,' she says, instantly getting busy by pulling open the night-stand door in the hunt for a vase. 'Oh dear, the nurse assured me there was one in here. Never mind, I'm sure I'll find one somewhere.' And she's off again. I smile. She really does love and care about Dad, so much. And about me too; she's so kind and caring and values the relationship Dad and I have, which is very special of her, she could so easily have resented me, and what I represent – Dad's previous life married to another woman. But Nancy has never been like that. She'd do anything for Dad, I reckon. Maybe they will stay the course after all. I truly hope so.

19

On arrival at Toulouse Airport, it seems there must be some kind of festival going on. The sound of drums and vuvuzelas fills the air as Nancy pulls into the drop-off parking bay.

I turn to give her a hug. 'Thanks for the lift, Nancy. I really appreciate it.' It's been lovely spending a bit of time together, just the two of us, on the journey here – three hours, and Nancy is going to do a bit of sightseeing and have a nice lunch somewhere before heading back to see Dad this afternoon. Dad is doing really well but was insistent that Nancy takes some time out, instead of being 'cooped up in the hospital all day long'. Secretly, I think he was looking forward to watching an old black-and-white film on the only English channel he'd managed to find after getting the portable TV to work, followed by finishing his book, lunch served at his bedside, and an afternoon snooze. I spotted the cheeky roll of his eyes every time Nancy flung back the sheets and encouraged him to do the exercises set out by the physiotherapist – ankle circles followed by leg raises to stop his joints seizing up.

So, on the way here, Nancy and I had a proper heart-to-heart. She even chatted about Natalie – her daughter who died in the motorbike accident. Not in a sad, maudlin way, though; she seemed to enjoy reminiscing, remembering the happy times. And I talked about Mum too, told Nancy about her teaching me to swim, to knit, to play the piano – only 'Chopsticks', mind you, but still, it's a cherished memory, and it felt nice to be able to chat about Mum in a lovely relaxed way with somebody other than Dad. Someone who didn't know her – it keeps her feeling real to me.

'My pleasure, dear. I've enjoyed it. And, Georgie, thanks for insisting on a hotel, love,' she says, patting my back. 'You know how stubborn your father can be when he has his mind set, but honestly, it'll be far better for him than being squashed up in here.' She motions to the back of Daisy. 'Don't get me wrong, I've really enjoyed our adventure, touring around and feeling the sun on our backs, but you know me, I'm a home bird at heart.' She chuckles. 'Better not tell your father, though; he'd be devastated to think I wasn't as enthused about us "doing Europe" as he was.'

'Ah, don't worry, your secret is safe with me.' I squeeze her hand. 'But I have to say that I'm a bit surprised. You seemed so excited, that day, when Tom and I called in for an impromptu lunch.'

'Yes, well, if truth be told, I think I got a bit carried away with the romance of it all. Don't get me wrong, I've loved the trip but I'm really looking forward to getting back to some normality now. I've actually missed our cosy little flat, the weekly bingo, putting the rubbish out on Tuesday mornings, listening to the *Archers* omnibus while preparing a nice Sunday roast lunch with all the trimmings – we had paella last Sunday, which was nice too, but it's just not the same. Not to mention Dusty – I miss her terribly. I know she's really George's dog, but I'm very fond of her, and when she's not here, well, it's like a part of me is missing . . . Silly, isn't it?' Nancy shakes her head.

'Oh Nancy, I had no idea. Have you said anything to Dad about how you feel?'

'Oh no dear. This might be his dream, but it really isn't a hardship for me to join him in it. I've had a wonderful time, but I do like my home comforts.' I nod, thinking of my bedroom at home. I know exactly what she means – the Manhattan mansion was awesome with the princess-and-the-pea bed, but it just wasn't the same as my bed with the fairy lights around the wrought-iron frame or my Art Deco dressing table with all the memories it holds. 'But I'd be lying if I said that I wasn't looking forward to getting home. Back to Mulberry, it might be a bit mundane, but it's *our* mundane, and I actually like the familiarity of it. I reckon a couple of weeks in the hotel will be fine, and then we'll be on our way home. Now that's something lovely to look forward to.'

'Indeed it is,' I say, giving Nancy another hug before reaching for the door handle. But a guy wearing a sandwich board with a cartoon picture of a guillotine on next to some French writing pokes his head through the window instead and proceeds to babble, animatedly, in French.

'Err, *pardon?*' I start, quickly racking my brains in a desperate bid to excavate some schoolgirl French. 'Um . . . *parlez-vous anglais, s'il vous plaît?*' I cave in.

'Ah, *oui, un peu*,' he shrugs, nonchalantly. 'No aeroplanes today!'

'Whaaaat?' A horrible sinking feeling comes over me.

'The airport is closed. The noise, it is a . . . how you say?' I crease my forehead in frustration thinking, *you tell me*. On second thoughts, I'm going in. I'm not taking the word of an overanimated French man wearing a sandwich board with a picture of a guillotine on it. Besides, I have to get home. I've got a regatta to launch in precisely one day, a boyfriend who is massively pissed off with me, and a best friend who I abandoned when she needed me the most.

'I won't be a minute, Nancy. I'll just whizz and see what the noise is about and then I'll pop back out to say goodbye properly,' I say, trying to keep calm.

'Right you are, love. See you in a minute.' And she pulls out her knitting, which for some reason makes the French man crack up laughing. He then starts jumping around and pointing to his sandwich board with one hand, while doing freaky chopping actions at his neck with the other. Oh, I get it: didn't old women sit knitting while people had their heads chopped off in the guillotine? Ha-ha, very funneee. Not.

Once inside, and the place is chaos. There are people milling around everywhere, but more ominous are the electronic departure boards – they are all blank, completely lifeless. And the whole airport is filled with the deafening sound of the drums. And I immediately see why. In the middle of the check-in hall is a group of men and women with the same sandwich boards as the guy outside; some are holding up placards too. Others are handing out leaflets. I take one, but it's no use, it's all in French, so I run over to what appears to be an information desk. A woman with two enormous wheelie suitcases and a sun visor on her head is pounding her left fist on the desk.

'What kiiiiiiind of goddam hell is this?' she bellows in a deep southern American accent when nobody arrives to deal with her.

'Perhaps it's some kind of protest? Sorry, I couldn't help overhearing,' I say, sounding very proper and English, and why am I apologising? I scan the airport desperately searching for someone in authority to explain exactly what is going on.

'You got that right! But for three days? It's an abomination.'

'What do you mean?' I swallow hard, praying this isn't what I think it is.

'French air traffic control are the culprits – something to do with your European Union,' the American woman states. Oh God. 'Brought the whole country to a standstill. I just wanna know where the train station is so I can get the hell outta here.'

'But I must get home, I have to, I have a regatta to sort out, this is a nightmare, I don't know what to do, I can't wait three days.' I blabber like an idiot.

'Me neither. Where are you heading?'

'England. Anywhere there will do,' I add, figuring if I can get to the same land mass, it'll at least be better than being stuck here.

'Then you'd better get the train to Paris with me. We can take the Eurostar from there to London,' she offers.

'Perfect. Let's do it. Come on, Nancy will take us to a station, I'm sure of it. This is an emergency after all.' And I grab one of her suitcases and start running back outside. The woman lunges for her other suitcase, does a spectacular U-turn with it and jogs alongside me, puffing.

'I have no idea who Nancy is but, right now, I wanna marry her, have her goddam kids and devote the rest of my life to her . . .'

20

It's Saturday morning when I eventually make it home. The journey consisted of a five-hour train journey from Toulouse to Paris, then the 07.13 Eurostar was the first one with available seats on – seems everyone stranded in France had the same idea; then I got a train from London to Mulberry-On-Sea. I'm shattered beyond belief and my iPhone packed up somewhere between Toulouse and Bordeaux as I didn't even think to fully charge it before I said goodbye to Nancy, figuring I'd be home in just over an hour or so on the flight, but how wrong was I? *Never again.* And if I never leave this island again, then it won't be too soon . . . so much for wanderlust and adventure, I've had enough to last me a lifetime. And there's only so much French countryside one can admire from a train window with a loud woman called Patti in one ear belting on about the 'European Union' and how 'this fiasco would never ever happen in America'.

Although Patti was very sweet when we got to Paris, and lent me a pair of her 'easy-fit pants', as she called them – I had dumped the velour joggers before I left Andorra as they were making my thighs itch, and the buffalo shorts were near on freezing my legs off it was that cold through the middle of the night while we waited to board the Eurostar. Or maybe it was the stress and lack of sleep that had made my body temperature drop; but whatever it was . . . never again. I repeat, never again! Just in case I hadn't made it clear.

As I drag my weary body along the landing, I'm welcomed by my suitcase, considerably more battered than when it left, all bound up with US Homeland Security tape and abandoned outside the door to my flat. I'm turning the key in the lock when my neighbour, Frank, pops his head out from behind his front door. It creeps me out; it's as if he's been standing there waiting for me. Eeeek!

'Oh, it is you, just making sure. I signed for the suitcase.'

'Yes it's me, and thank you. Really appreciate it,' I quickly say, trying not to be rude, but I've got like one minute to be at the regatta.

'Right you are. And just so you know, your phone hasn't stopped – been ringing and ringing all morning;

I can hear it through the wall. I'd say somebody is desperate to get hold of you . . . you know these walls are paper thin, I can hear everything, especially at night.' He pauses to pull a weird face. 'You might want to bear that in mind next time one of your gentlemen friends stays over.' Whaaaat? Err, excuse me. I open my mouth, I close it, I open it again, wishing I could think of a suitably witty comeback, but nothing comes. I close my mouth, figuring *whatever*, I really don't have time for this.

'Um, yes, thanks Frank. Anyway, I better get on. Thanks again,' I say, going to grab the case by the handle but, on seeing that it's broken, I have to crouch down and slide it with both hands into my flat instead. Frank is still staring at my backside when I swivel around to close the door behind me.

Inside, and I plug my phone straight onto the charger, then leg it down the hallway and into my bedroom, tearing off the now hideously rank easy-fit pants and buffalo shorts as I go. No time to waste, the regatta officially started an hour ago. I open my suitcase and on second thoughts, no, I can't wear any of this – the contents have been rifled through and everything smells weird, eugh! I drop a slightly damp T-shirt back into the case and find a clean sundress in my wardrobe instead. It's a bit crinkled, but it'll

265

have to do. There's clean underwear in the airing cupboard, and a pair of last summer's flip-flops, which I had put in a bag for the charity shop, so after brushing my hair in record time, I'm done.

I bomb back down the hallway, perform a spectacular flyby grab of my shades and phone (30 per cent battery, that will have to do too), fling it in my bag, slam the front door behind me and jump, two at a time, down the stairs before running full pelt into town.

I'm a wheezing heap on arrival, and am hiding behind a parked lorry at the end of Wayfarer Way wondering where all the ice-cream vans are, when Meredith clocks me and marches over, clipboard firmly in place.

'There you are. I've been searching for you for at least an hour. And why haven't you been answering your phone? I even tried your home number, several times, in case you had slept in or had somehow forgotten that today is the day!' She has a manic look in her eye. 'You know the committee agreed to keep in phone contact at all times. So where have you been?' she interrogates.

'Oh, all over the place,' I say in between gasps, and I'm not even lying – if only she knew. 'Can't believe how busy it is already, that'll be why you missed me.' She looks unconvinced, which is hardly surprising, as there aren't that many people around, certainly no more than usual. Maybe they will all turn up later, in time for the first boat race, which from memory I think doesn't actually start until two thirty. I just about manage to refrain from clutching at my collar. Sweet lord of exercise, I really need to do some . . . I feel as if I'm having a coronary; how did I get to be so unfit?

'What on earth is the matter with you? We've barely started and you look exhausted,' she sniffs. *OK, Meredith, rub it in, why not? I'm a lazy slob who loves food. But I do have gym membership – hmm, shame I never go . . .*

'Nothing. I'm fine,' I lie, desperately trying to ignore the pounding sound of my own blood as it pumps into overdrive.

'Good. Then you'd better get up to the common and sort out the fiasco that's going on up there. If the police turn up then it'll be all your fault for swanning off to America at the last minute.' And with that she stalks off. Flaming hell! *Rude.* And hold on a minute, the committee all agreed I could go. Nobody objected, from what I can remember, so it's a bit rich her berating me for it now. And what the fuck is she going on about? *Fiasco?* I'd better head to the common.

Ten minutes later, I'm now able to breathe – I cheated and hopped in a cab at the end of the high street, figuring it would also buy me a few minutes to call Sam and Tom, I can't wait to find them. I'm guessing Sam will be in the marquee setting up her cake stall – and Tom . . . ? Well, he could be anywhere. His parents' yacht, perhaps, might be a good place to start – but both numbers went straight to voicemail. Tom and I have barely spoken all week, with him being in meetings and me at the hospital, and it's impossible to have a proper text message conversation when he's only got snatched breaks here and there, and I'm sitting right underneath one of those signs that has a picture of a mobile phone with a big red cross through it.

And *fiasco* is a massive understatement. A riot, more like!

'Annie!' I yell, but she doesn't hear me, which is no surprise as that X-rated Rucka Rucka Ali rap song, 'Only 17', is fog-horning from giant speakers erected on scaffolding spanning the circumference of the common. A giant carousel takes pride of place in the middle, but it's not moving, and then I see why. And *oh my God*, a guy, who I'm guessing is Annie's Uncle Mikey's friend (he's wearing a blue cloth money belt around his waist), instead of smiling and pressing the button so the children can enjoy a gentle jaunt on the merry-go-round to nice, happy, fun-in-the-sun type

268

music, is busy snarling and punching another guy in the head. Kids are clinging to the horses and screaming. Parents are trying to scramble up onto the carousel to retrieve their children. A woman runs over to Annie and points a finger in her face while shrieking something about explicit and highly inappropriate lyrics. And we've just reached the 'all up in her muff' line, when a police car does a spectacular *Starsky and Hutch*-style swerve before skidding to a halt right up close to the throbbing electricity generator.

A female police officer, wearing body armour and with a baton at the ready, leaps out of the car and shuts off the power while two of her colleagues head towards the fracas. Uncle Mikey's mate clocks them and immediately does a runner. Oh shit.

'Right. Who is in charge here then?' the police officer demands to know, and Annie turns to look at me before bowing her head and mumbling, 'I am.' She walks towards the patrol car with tears in her eyes.

'Actually, I am. Um, Annie is the deputy team manager, so whatever has gone wrong here is down to me,' I say, clearing my throat as I step forward, wondering what the hell happened while I was away to turn this into such a disaster. A feeling of dread rattles right through me. I take a deep breath and try to get a grip. It's been a stressful few days, and everything always seems worse and disproportionate when I'm exhausted. It'll be fine, this is just a hiccup, the carousel is only one of the events, and I bet the others are already a huge hit. And we haven't got to the main event yet, the actual boat races. It'll be fine. Of course it will. I say the words over and over inside my head like a lucky charm mantra.

'In that case, I have bad news. This fairground attraction is closing down with immediate effect.'

'But why?' Annie cries, cupping her trembling hands together up under her chin. 'I organised the proper licences and everything. Ask Matt from the council, he dealt with everything.' She turns to me. 'Georgie, I definitely did it all, I know I did . . .' And she dumps her bag on the grass and proceeds to turf out all the contents. 'See, right here.' Annie finds a plastic A4 wallet, which she hands to the police officer.

'That may be the case, but these documents are specifically for,' the police officer pauses to flip over a page, 'yes, here it is, see . . . Jimmy Dyer.' She taps the piece of paper.

'Yes, that's him. Uncle Mikey's friend.' Annie nods, calming down a bit.

'And seeing as he's just been arrested . . .' The police officer points to the other side of the common, where two of her colleagues have caught up with Jimmy and are now bundling him back towards their patrol car. 'He's not going to be here for quite some time. Sorry, but you can't operate machinery like this unless the licence holder is in situ. I suggest you offer all the customers a refund and—'

'Hang on a minute. You can't do that. My kids have been waiting here for over an hour for their turn. This is ridiculous. It's a bloody liberty, that's what it is. And I want a refund,' the woman with the pointy finger yells.

'I'm sorry, madam. It's the law.' And the police officer is handed a roll of blue and white tape. She secures one end to the ticket booth and proceeds to walk it around the whole carousel like it's a giant crime scene. Oh God. People are grabbing their children and running, literally, away from the common now, terrified in case they're in some kind of danger.

'What about my refund?' the woman yells again.

'You'll have to take that up with the sponsors.' That'll be us, Carrington's then. I take a big breath before letting out an even bigger one. I swivel around when more people start complaining.

'Told you, Jade, it's not safe. That'll be why they've closed it down. Come on, let's get out of here,' a man shouts to his girlfriend as they charge past Annie and me.

'Load of old rubbish this regatta is turning out to be. Let's go to Brighton instead,' another guy says as he lifts his crying little boy onto his shoulders.

My heart sinks. I close my eyes and swallow hard. When I open them again – as if it couldn't get any worse – the bloody 'Big Fun on the Carrington's Carousel' billboard collapses, as a gang of yobs kick it over before legging it, sniggering and swearing. There's a sickening splintering sound before it crashes, tearing a massive gaping hole, which now has a painted horse's head poking right through the middle. Then more police turn up and instantly chase after the gang. It's shambolic; an utter disaster. And if that wasn't bad enough, a guy with a big camera and a *Mulberry Echo* press badge dangling on a length of nylon around his neck is snapping away, hell-bent on getting the money shot for the front page of the next edition, no doubt. Grrrreat. All I need now is for Isabella to rock up and give me another one of her lines, only this time she'll be spot on – I have 'somehow managed to ruin things'. And the regatta hasn't even really started yet . . . .

Annie is sobbing now. Crouched down on her haunches in the grass. I kneel down beside her.

'Hey, come on. There's no point in crying, these things happen,' I say, rapidly figuring optimism is the best course of action right now. What else is there?

I've already written the carousel off; there's nothing we can do until Jimmy gets back from the police station, if he ever does, and so what's the point in worrying? At least it's up here on the common, away from the main event, and with a bit of luck Isabella won't venture far away from the harbour, so at least she'll be none the wiser to my seemingly complete ineptitude, which I'm guessing is how she will perceive this fiasco. 'I'm here now, and I bet everything else is OK. What do you say we go and find out?' I place a hand on Annie's back and grin like a looper verging on hysteria.

'Oh God, Georgie!' she says, keeping her head bowed. 'I'm so sorry.'

'Don't be daft. Come on, let's go. There's practically nobody here now anyway.' I glance around the common, and the crowd has mostly disappeared, leaving just a few stragglers sloping off with slumped shoulders and the place strewn with rubbish. I make a mental note to call Matt and ask him to send the litter team up here.

'But I wanted it all to be perfect.'

'And I bet it is. Look, let's forget about the carousel – Jimmy will come back at some stage and then we can get it back up and running. We might have to dump the billboard though,' I laugh, trying to lighten the mood, 'but that's not the end of the world.'

'But there's something else,' Annie says, quietly.

'OK,' I say, slowly. 'What is it?' I add gently.

'It's the tunnel tours!'

*

Annie and I are outside the magnificent powder-blue Carrington's building on the opposite side of the road, staring at the length of the queue. People are standing two, three deep, in places, right back to the cinema on Pear Tree Avenue.

'See what I mean?' Annie says, gripping the strap of her handbag even tighter. 'It's a disaster!'

'No, it isn't. This is good, surely?' I say, delighted by the obvious popularity of this initiative. It's amazing that so many people want to see beneath the iconic Carrington's building and hear more about our history. But Annie doesn't look so sure. And on closer inspection, her eyes are brimming with tears. 'What is it?' I ask, gently, giving her arm a reassuring squeeze.

'I've messed up again!'

'But how come? What do you mean?'

'You'll see. Follow me.' And she darts across the road and up to the front of the queue.

'Hey, you can't push in – and if I have to wait much

longer I'm going to call it a day,' a man in the queue shouts out.

'It's OK, we work here,' I smile to cover the sinking feeling inside.

'Well, you'd better get it sorted then. I booked for the first slot and it's already gone eleven o'clock.'

'We will. I promise. Come on, Annie.' I grab her hand and we run through the staff entrance at the side of the building, and quickly make our way along the narrow, winding staff corridor, sidestepping a couple of stock trolleys piled high with flattened cardboard boxes, to reach the big Carrington's Tunnel Tour placard that has been erected next to the gilt caged staff lift.

And then it immediately becomes obvious what the hold-up is: Betty and Mrs Grace are sitting on the floor of the lift, next to six big boxes full of her auto-biography hardbacks, suspended just below the ground level.

'Oh, thank God you're here, lovey,' Mrs Grace says, poking a bony hand up through the bottom of the metal concertina lift door. I crouch down and push my arm through a gap to clasp her arm. 'This damn lift has broken down – an hour we've been sat here waiting for the emergency guy from the lift mainte-nance company to show his face. Emergency, my arse!

My Stan could move faster, and that's saying something; he hasn't managed to shift his backside away from the telly for decades now, unless it's to feed those filthy birds of his, of course, and then he's like a ferret up a drainpipe.' Oh dear. We all nod politely.

Betty manages to scramble up onto her feet first, and then helps Mrs Grace up before handing her granny bag to her. They both stare up at us – the lift must be stuck about two feet below ground level, so even if we could get the door open somehow, we'd still have to find a way for Betty and Mrs Grace to climb out of the lift.

'Oh God. This is a nightmare,' I say, gripping the metal door in frustration and giving it a shake, but it's no use, it's not budging. 'I'm so sorry.' Of all the days for it to break down – it's always been slow and rickety, I've even been stuck in it too on occasion, but Charles, Carrington's handyman, was always able to prise open the door for me.

'It's not your fault, dear,' Mrs Grace says graciously. 'I'm just pleased I had the sense to ask Lara to come along later. Can you imagine?' I stare blankly. 'Lara, she's my publicist; oh no, it certainly wouldn't do for her to be stuck in this lift for any length of time. You know she's related to William Shakespeare? Oh yes, they only take on the best at my publishers,' Mrs Grace says, proudly.

'That's nice.' I press my nails into the palm of my hand in a desperate bid to get some perspective on this precarious situation as I try to ignore the 'what if the lift plunges even further down the shaft' scenario that's currently playing out inside my head. The food hall in the basement is below us and then there are two floors with stock rooms on, and that's before we even get to the actual floor where the tunnels are, so potentially the lift could plunge a further four levels. 'We really need to get you out of here right away!' And then quickly add, 'There's a queue a mile long – seems your tunnel tours are in great demand,' to detract from the seriousness of the situation. The last thing we need is Mrs Grace and Betty to start panicking – they obviously haven't realised the danger they're in.

'Is there really? Well, I never, there was only a handful of people when our taxi pulled up this morning, wasn't there Betty?' Betty nods and sinks back down onto one of the boxes.

'Ooooh, I'm so desperate to spend a penny,' she says, crossing her legs and pulling a face.

'Oh dear,' I say, eyeing up the old-fashioned fire bucket full of sand that's chained to the corridor wall – if needs must, and all that. 'What did security say?' I ask, motioning with my head towards the emergency call button on the lift wall.

'I went to see Charles in the loading bay and he said that the lift maintenance company were sending someone,' Annie says, her voice all wobbly.

'That was first thing,' Mrs Grace interjects. 'Young Annie was very good – I called her mobile phone and she came here right away. But we're still waiting.' Annie perks up on hearing the praise.

'Annie, can you call the lift maintenance company and find out where the hell they are, please?' I ask. We need to get this sorted out right away.

'I'm on it,' Annie says, pulling her phone from her bag. We all listen while she talks. 'Right, I see.' She ends the call. 'The guy is on his way, but he's stuck in the regatta traffic. The main road into town is bumper to bumper, apparently, with everyone heading this way, eager to find a parking space before they all go.'

'Oh God. Right, I'm going to find Charles; he's got me out of the lift before . . . I don't see why he can't crowbar you out right now. And then we'll figure a way to pull you both up here to the ground floor. Failing that, we'll call the fire brigade. We have to do something; we can't just leave you in here or leave all those people standing outside. It's a disaster. Carrington's will be a laughing stock.' And I shudder to think what Tom will say when he hears about this, and I have to talk to him – I'll do it just as soon as

I've freed Betty and Mrs Grace. Besides, there's no point in alerting him to this utter fiasco if I can possibly avoid it. He'll only worry about the damage it could do to Carrington's reputation and be disappointed in me for seemingly taking my eye off the ball, again.

'Oh no dear. Charles can't help – we've already been through all of that. He was here with us until about twenty minutes ago, explaining it all. He was very apologetic, but he could lose his job,' Mrs Grace says, teasing her Julie-Andrews-style feather crop back into place. 'It's the new health and safety rules; he mustn't lift a crowbar without the proper training.'

'Whaaaat? But that's ridiculous; he's been doing it for years . . . because the flaming lift is so unreliable!'

'Sorry duck, it's the new Euro law. He's not allowed; anyway, he's gone now – had to bomb off to the Japanese marquee after Max rang him on the mobile demanding he get down there to fix a dodgy gas ring, and bring more supplies too, while he was at it. Seems they all went crazy for Mr Nakamura's battered lobster,' Betty says, folding her arms and clutching her body in obvious discomfort.

'Tempura!' Mrs Grace corrects. 'It's all the rage these days.'

'Well, whatever it is, it's a weird thing to have for

your breakfast. Even if it has been cooked by a famous chef,' Betty groans.

'Hmmm, and it'll be nearly lunchtime soon and we'll miss out because we're stuck in a lift shaft.' Mrs Grace purses her movie-star red-coated lips.

'OK. Then there's no other option . . .' And there's certainly no time for us to sit around chatting like we're on a tea break in the staff canteen. We need to get the queue inside and around those tunnels in record time, if we're to stand any chance of catching up and saving the day. 'I'll lift the crowbar myself, and be damned!' And, before any of them can protest, I sprint as fast as I can along the corridor and back out of the store, ignoring the now heckling queue, until I reach the loading bay. Right, now to locate the crowbar.

Half an hour later, and I've managed to prise the lift door open with just enough space to allow Mrs Grace and Betty to squeeze through. They're stacking the boxes on top of one another to form a step high enough to climb up and out of the lift when the engineer finally turns up. And, oh my God, Mr Dunwoody, the MP, is powering along behind him with a thunderous look on his face.

'What in God's name is going on?' Mr Dunwoody puffs, practically flinging the engineer out of the way. 'My office phone is going berserk! My constituents are in that queue, and I can tell you they are *fuming*. And I'm not surprised, having to stand around for hours while you girls get your act together!' He casts a disparaging glare at Betty as she takes a quick breather, having just hauled herself out of the lift with a helping hand from Annie and the engineer. She huffs, before bustling off down the corridor in search of a bathroom. 'And where's she off to now? No time to powder your nose, dear!' he shouts out after her in an extra-patronising tone.

'Hang on a minute,' I start, my hackles rising. 'These *women* – Mrs Grace and Betty – have been here for ages. They arrived especially early in order to be properly prepared for the first tunnel tour – it's not their fault if the lift packed up.'

'That's right. You tell him, Georgie.' Mrs Grace has also made it out of the lift shaft and is now standing opposite Mr Dunwoody with her bony hands on her hips and a disgusted look on her face.

'Well, it's not my fault either! But my reputation is at stake here. I'll be a laughing stock if this gets back to Westminster. So I suggest you crack on with the tours,' he nods in Mrs Grace's direction, 'and *you*,' he glowers down at me, 'stop gadding about all over the shop and make this regatta a success, because if it isn't then your boyfriend will have another think

281

coming if he wants my support for his planning application for the purposes of purchasing another store!' And with that he marches off back down the corridor. I gulp. So that told me.

21

Everything else is going smoothly. The food marquees are doing exceptionally well; Annie has headed off there to get some refreshments to take back to Betty and Mrs Grace – they quickly got the queue down by doubling up on the numbers for each tour and roping in lazy Luke and Stan to dish out signed copies of Mrs Grace's book to the people joining the back of the queue – thereby saving even more time as people didn't have to hang around afterwards. Thankfully, Mrs Grace had the foresight to sign all the books while she was trapped in the lift.

And I've managed to track Sam down – Annie had a regatta brochure with a colour-coded map inside. Her cake stall is inside one of the marquees near the Hook, Line and Sinker pub, so I'm going to head there next, just as soon as I've tried calling Tom again. His number rings, but there's no answer. I decide not to leave another message as I've already left three and he's obviously busy – it is regatta day, after all. He's probably with the directors making sure everything is going smoothly, eek! Let's hope they bypassed the common and the now-closed carousel. Besides, I don't want to appear all stalkerish-annoying-girlfriend-bothering-him-when-he's-working. And it wouldn't kill him to call me back – we're supposed to be adults, after all. I push my phone back into my bag, and try to ignore the swell of unease in the pit of my stomach. Bravado aside, it's obvious he is still angry with me, or disappointed, or whatever it was Dad reckoned he was; but still, he could at least talk to me, he was the one who said we would . . . *Just as soon as the regatta is over!* Hmm, it's coming back to me now. In that case, I'll do what he wants – I'll wait until tomorrow evening, when the regatta is over and deemed a monumental success. With a bit of luck, he won't know about the carousel or the extended wait for the tunnel tours, because hopefully he's having too much of a good time enjoying all the other regatta events with his parents. Yes, I'll go to his apartment, talk to him and get everything sorted out. I let out a long breath before taking a swig of water from my bottle. I feel so much better now that I have a plan, like a weight has been lifted. Maybe my luck hasn't run out after all . . . I can turn this around, I know I can.

Smiling, I smooth down my sundress and turn into Wayfarer Way. The afternoon sun feels glorious on my bare arms and legs, warm with a light breeze and the perfect weather for an ice cream, a proper swirly Mr Whippy cone with a chocolate 99 flake, just like I had as a child. But hang on a minute! Where are all the ice-cream vans? I can see one at the far end of the street – but there were supposed to be loads, one on every corner.

Speeding up, I make a beeline for the lone van. I think it's the man from the pier; his lumbago obviously isn't playing up today. His van is bright pink; it even has 'Mr Whippy' written in white lettering down the side, next to a picture of Snow White and the seven dwarfs, and two big plastic ice-cream cones are mounted on the roof at the corners of the windscreen – it's perfect, and just how I remember from my childhood with Mum and Dad sitting on the bench by the pier polishing off our banana sandwiches and ginger beer before getting stuck into a huge swirly-whirly peaked ice cream in a cone. And when it came to the toppings, I always went for the works – a chocolate flake, butterscotch sauce and rainbow sprinkles. Mm-mmm.

'Hey, where are all the other vans?' I ask the guy, in between customers buying Screwballs, strawberry

Mivvi and Fab ice lollies. I wait while he unwraps a vanilla ice-cream brick to sandwich between two wafers.

'Sorry love, I've no idea. This is my allocated pitch for the day – I was asked to move away from my usual place down by the pier. Yes mate, what can I get you?' he says, turning to serve the next customer – a man with a trillion children all bouncing up and down with excitement.

'You could try the marina; there were hundreds of them down there a few minutes ago,' a guy in a black-and-white London Grammar T-shirt suggests. 'They might be open now. None of them were earlier – too busy sounding their chimes and arguing. That's why I came here. I think there's some kind of turf war going on down there.'

Whaaaat?

'Thank you,' I quickly shout out as I hare off towards the seafront.

And oh my God! He's right. Leaning against a wall to catch my breath, I can see ice-cream vans every-where; there must be at least thirty – each one has a massive Carrington's sticker on the side, and they're all triple-parked up to form a blockade right outside the main entrance to the marina. The very heart of the regatta! And if that wasn't bad enough, the deafening din of their chimes – 'Greensleeves' and 'Pop

Goes the Weasel' – fills the air. It's a disaster. An utter, utter fucking disaster!

And the marina is packed with yachts – people are standing on their decks to get a better view. Jesus, one woman even has a pair of binoculars pressed up to her pillow cheeks. And I dread to think where Tom's parents' yacht is – I bet Isabella is horrified. Because right now, Carrington's is a laughing stock. And what is that whirring noise? I look up into the glorious, cloudless blue sky and see a light aircraft hovering on the horizon, above the glittery sea, hazy in the heat – and it's trailing a banner. Oh God. It's *Sky News*. Filming the whole thing, no doubt!

My heart sinks – could today get any worse? There's no way Tom isn't going to find out about this – that's if he isn't watching, aghast, on TV right now. Maybe that's why he hasn't called me back, he's too blooming busy appeasing Mr Dunwoody, because I wouldn't put it past him to have beaten a path straight to Tom's door to have a bitch about his reputation being ruined in Westminster.

I get closer and spot Matt trying to reason with a big bald guy who has a spider tatt on the side of his neck. But it's no use, as the guy just bats a dismissive hand in the air before bombing back into his van and sliding the plastic vending screen shut.

'At last! You better sort this out, now that you've deigned to put in an appearance. And not before time . . . Where have you been all day?' Meredith steps out from a doorway and taps her finger on my shoulder. And I snap! I've had enough. The last week or so has been a nightmare, not to mention today so far, and I've tried really bloody hard to make things right. I draw in a big breath before batting her hand away.

'Um, excuse me, but where do you get off being so rude? I've been fire-fighting all day, making sure the Carrington's tunnel tours happened, that people are having a good time – isn't that what this is all about?' I say, standing square on to her. 'What have *you* been doing all day?'

'I beg your pardon!' she huffs, indignantly. 'How dare you talk to me like this?' And she goes to march off towards the ice-cream van fracas that's unfolding before us.

'Don't play the victim here, Meredith. You've been arsey with me since the moment I turned up at the first committee meeting.'

'No I haven't.'

'Yes you have.'

'Well, it's not my fault if you swanned in late to the first meeting expecting special treatment just because you're dating *Mr Carrington*.'

'Hardly! And, for the record, I wasn't late – you started the meeting early.' Ha! Take that. 'So, what exactly is your problem?' I can feel my heart pounding with adrenalin. It's like she's jealous or something.

'I don't know what you're talking about.' I have to jog to keep up with her.

'Yes you do. Tell me!' I wince as my voice jumps an octave.

'OK. You really want to know?' Meredith stops and plants her hands on her hips, but before she can answer, a spectacular arc of raspberry sundae sauce catapults into the air before landing on her head. She turns to me with an outraged look on her face, pink gunge dripping down her cheeks. She opens her mouth, closes it, and then does a massive harrumph before stalking off.

I spin around and see, to my horror, there's a full-on war ensuing now. The ice-cream men are all leaning out of their vans and pelting each other with chocolate flakes, mini plastic spoons, wafer shells and Haribo sweets. One even has a giant tub of rainbow sprinkles, which, after flipping the lid off, he swings, strong-man-style to gather maximum momentum before spraying everyone within a mile radius, or so it seems. Jesus Christ.

'Georgie! Are you OK?' It's Matt, ducking down

with his hand over his head in a desperate attempt to avoid the raft of flying missiles. And then I spot Denise, standing right behind him, with a brochure held up in front of her face like a shield.

'Yes, I'm fine. I think,' I say, picking sprinkles off my face.

'You know Denise, yes?' Matt yells, before quickly grabbing her hand and pulling her close into his chest for protection.

'I sure do,' I grin, and squeeze her free hand. Despite the ice-cream paraphernalia raining down on us, she's beaming with happiness, having bagged a man 'so dreamy'. Aw, I'm really pleased for them. 'Do you know what's going on here?' I shout to be heard over the racket.

'I've no idea! I just got a call from Bob, the harbour master, asking me to get down here right away, I thought you might be able to shed some light on it . . . weren't the ice-cream vans one of your things to organise?'

'Um, yes they were. Hold on a sec.' I duck into a tiny alcove next to a nautical-themed gift shop and pull out my mobile. Annie answers right away and confirms that, as far as she is aware, the ice-cream vans are all in place at their designated spots, she checked first thing this morning, and each one has a plentiful supply of regatta brochures and is stocked up with the special regatta ice-cream flavours that she and Lauren chose when they went to the factory – bubble gum, mulberry and cinnamon crumble, Eton mess (strawberry with mini-meringue pieces in), lemon parfait, a traditional Neapolitan and the one that Jack chose – chocolate with Smarties sprinkles. She sounds so pleased with herself for having pulled it off, after I forgot to even visit Tom's Uncle Marco, that I don't have the heart to tell her what's going on here. I hang up after thanking her.

'Right. I'm going in!'

'Are you mad?' Matt bellows.

'Probably. But someone has to stop them!' I head straight towards the van that has the guy with the spider tatt inside, and tap firmly on the plastic screen. A few seconds later, he appears and slides the screen open.

'Please can you tell me what the hell is going on?' I say, ducking quickly, but I'm too late – a lump of vanilla ice cream hits my shoulder and slides down my bare arm.

'You'd better hop in, love. Come on,' he says in a lovely Northern accent as he flings open the door for me to climb in. He hands me a paper napkin.

'Thank you.'

'Hang on.' He slides the screen closed. 'That's better. Bloody fools. They've ruined it for us all now . . .'

'What do you mean? Why are you all here? You were supposed to be dotted around the town,' I say, wiping my arm.

'And they were. I was the one supposed to be here at the entrance to the marina – it's the prime spot, you see, and seeing as how I organised everything, then fair dues. But they didn't like it – ice-cream vendors can get very territorial, you see, if their pitch isn't doing well. Hence they took it upon themselves to move here looking to up their takings. They're all self-employed, love, and times are hard I guess . . . But none of that excuses this behaviour, fighting like kids in a playground, it's blooming embarrassing.' He shakes his head.

'Ah, so you must be Tom's Un—'

'Marco,' he says, holding out a hand for me to shake. 'I'm Georgie.'

'You're our Tom's lass! Well, lovely to meet you at last. And don't look so surprised . . . I'm not what you were expecting, eh?'

'Um, err . . .' I start, not wanting to be rude but he's right – he isn't at all how I imagined a relative of Tom's to be.

'Don't worry, love, I get it all the time. I'm from the

normal side of the family. My brother is the one who married into the money, the Rossi dynasty – not that they always had it, mind you. Wouldn't think so, though, where Isabella is concerned, not with all her airs and graces.' And he laughs, while I wonder what he means. 'Anyway, I guess we had better get this riot stopped.'

'Yes, it's madness. It needs to stop right now or I'll have to call the police,' I say, really hoping it doesn't come to that – knowing my luck it'll be the same police officer who shut down the carousel, and I'll be deemed doubly incompetent.

'Trading standards, more like! Here, tell them.' And with a mischievous glint in his eye, he hands me a megaphone. I take it and, after flicking a switch, I pull back the plastic screen, lean my head out and bellow as loud as I can.

'Trading standards are on the way! I repeat, trading standards *are on the way*!' And a few minutes later, the vendors miraculously leap into their vans and drive off, convoy-style, towards Wayfarer Way.

'Thank you.' I turn to Marco.

'Ah, don't thank me, love; I'm just damn sorry they caused such a scene. And if you don't mind me saying so, you sure gave it some – petrified, they were. Petrified!'

293

22

I've managed to find Sam's stall, it's next to the new bakery one, but she's busy packing up cakes into huge white cardboard boxes when I arrive.

'Georgie!' she says, looking taken aback. I step forward to give her a hug but she carries on packing.

'How are you?' I start awkwardly.

'I'm fine,' she replies. But it's obvious she isn't.

'I can see you're busy, I, um, maybe I should go,' I start, desperately trying to keep my voice even, but I can't bear the way things are between us. It's as if we're strangers. I know I've let her down, but she shut me out too.

'OK.' Silence follows while I scan the marquee nervously, feeling unsettled and unsure of what to do next. And then I remember Dad's advice in the hospital that day. *Whatever it takes . . .*

'Sam, look, I'm really sorry; I know I've let you down . . . But please, let me apologise. At least hear me out . . .' She stops packing and I hold my breath, willing her to give me a chance to somehow fix things between us. Another silence follows.

'I'll be finished in a bit. Why don't you come back in half an hour?' Sam keeps her head down as she places the last cupcake into a box.

'Um, sure, I'll do that.'

I wander off into the crowd, hoping the bubbly party atmosphere will lift my mood while I wait for Sam to finish up. I find a gap at the railings overlooking the finishing line and watch in awe as four speedboats race through the waves making the water jet up and spray all over us. The hooters sound out as the sleek silver boat wins – the two women crew cheering and hugging each other as Bob, the harbour master, hands them their prize bottle of champagne. I glance around, relishing in the smiles, the laughter, the perfect blue sky, the warm sun glistening on the sea and feel pleased, relieved, this is exactly how I imagined Mulberry-On-Sea would be on regatta weekend. Everyone seems to be having a brilliant time, the boat races are exciting and exhilarating, and that is the whole point of a regatta after all.

*

Sam and I are at the Hook, Line and Sinker pub, sitting either side of a wooden bench table outside on the beach, when Cher appears with two glasses and an enormous jug full of Pimm's with sliced cucumber and mint leaves sloshing around inside.

'There you go, girls. You look as if you could both do with this.' She puts the jug in the centre of the table. 'Who died?' Chuckling, she wipes her hands on a cloth that's slung over her left shoulder. 'Right, I'll, err . . . sod off and leave you to it then,' she adds after clearing her throat when neither of us replies, and heads back over the beach towards the pub.

Sam lifts the jug and pours us both a drink while I watch the iridescent green waves swooshing and swaying back and forth, nudging the brown pebbles like a giant penny slot machine.

'Thank you.' Sam hands me a glass and I take a sip of the fruity mint concoction before placing the glass back on the table and pushing my hands under the sides of my legs, unsure of where to start. We're both studying our drinks when we say,

'I'm sorry,' in unison. I glance at Sam, feeling relieved that we are at least talking now, it's a start; but she keeps her head bowed. I reach a hand across the table and gently touch her arm.

'Sam, I'm so very sorry for abandoning you when

you needed me most. You've always been here for me, and the one time you needed me . . . I disappeared to New York. I don't blame you for hating me . . .' My voice trails off, and then I'm horrified to see silent tears snaking a path down her face before collecting in a little pool at the groove above her collarbones. I saw Sam cry when Alfie died, and then when she had the miscarriage, but those were both major, massive things. Sam doesn't cry easily. I jump off the bench and dart around the table to sit next to her. I put my arm around her and, after a while, her shoulders soften as she leans into me.

'Oh Sam, please, I can't bear to see you like this . . . tell me what to do to make it better. Please . . . I'll do it, I'll do anything.' She rests her head on my shoulder and we sit together in silence, in the still-warm evening air, for what seems like an eternity, with just the sound of the seagulls caw-cawing above us and the laughter in the distance from the last few revellers enjoying a drink before closing time.

Sam starts laughing. It throws me. I don't know what to do. But for some unfathomable reason I start laughing too.

'Why are we laughing?' It's Sam who recovers first.

'I have no idea . . . Um, that's actually a lie, I know why I'm laughing . . .' I hesitate.

'Go on.' Sam nods, swilling her drink around inside the glass.

'Relief, I guess. A bit. That we're here, talking, sort of . . . I thought I had lost you . . . you know, when I was away and, well, it's never been like that between us, has it? And I know I messed up, but we've always been so close. I'm really, really sorry.' I look away.

'Me too,' Sam says, quietly.

'You have nothing to be sorry about – I was the one who buggered off when you needed me most; I should never have done that.'

'And I shut you out. I should never have done that either.' We sit in silence; it's me who breaks it.

'What's going on, Sam? Well, I know a lot has gone on, with Christy turning up and stuff, but what I mean is . . . something has changed, and it changed a while ago. You're . . .' I pause to choose my words carefully; I don't want to upset her even more. 'Not like your old self.'

'Oh Georgie, how long have you got?' she sighs, wearily.

'All night! And longer, if that's what it takes.' I give her hand a squeeze.

*

Sam lets out a long breath. She's told me all about it. How she always thought she knew what she wanted, how being a mother with lots of children was her destiny, to have a big family, something she never had as a child and always dreamed of, to be a part of something, to be the perfect mum, the mum she never had . . . or so she had imagined. Only it didn't turn out that way. And it changed everything – what she had always believed turned out to be something entirely different.

'Oh Sam! I thought you were blissfully happy. OK, I knew you were tired, but aren't all new parents? I had no idea, I'm so sorry . . . Why didn't you tell me?'

'For a while I was in denial, I guess. I tried to ignore it, hoping the feeling would go away. And then, we seemed to be going in different directions – our worlds seemed so far apart. How could I? You were loved up with Tom while I was crying from sleep deprivation at four in the morning. And then when you cleared off and didn't look back . . .' I feel my cheeks flush, but quickly decide to keep quiet, knowing that what she's saying is true. I did leave her when she needed me, but not on purpose . . . It just sort of panned out that way; but still, I didn't hesitate in going, and for that I'll always feel bad. Not for actually going, but for going when I did. The timing couldn't have been any worse. 'It made me feel that you were taking everything for granted, everything you have here in Mulberry-On-Sea, including me – like it wasn't enough. And somehow that made me feel insignificant. Like I wasn't important to you . . .'

'But Sam, you're the most important person in the world to me – you, Dad and Nancy, and Tom. You're everything. You're my family.'

'But you were having the time of your life in New York, sending me selfies from rooftops with breathtaking views, while I was stuck here with two babies, feeling inadequate and frustrated because I've always been in control, been good at stuff, felt important I guess . . . and that had all gone. I was muddling through, making it all up as I went along – babies don't come with a manual, and for the first time in my life, I had no blooming idea what I was supposed to be doing. And part of me was jealous, too. I wanted to be having the time of my life in New York, not be scraping poo off my beautiful kitchen counters because one of the twins had ripped her nappy off and decided to lasso it around the joint. And that in turn made me feel as if I was failing all the time.'

'Oh God, Sam, I didn't realise. I had no idea. And there was me wishing you were there with me. I didn't stop to think how you were feeling . . . Or just how impractical the notion was, I understand now – you can't just pack a suitcase and jet off . . . your life is different now.'

'Please, it's not your fault. Like I said, it's my fault. That part of it started way before you went away – the feeling of not being a good enough mother, and then when I saw the mums in the café, seemingly perfect, doting over and all-consumed by their babies, discussing the virtues of blending up purple broccoli over sprouting broccoli – broccoli is broccoli, for crying out loud!' She lets out a long breath. 'But deep down, I felt guilty, because it doesn't interest me – and it just got worse when you went away. My only outlet, besides baby talk, had gone, and that's why I couldn't talk to you on the phone. I was cross and confused – I just wanted my old life back; the one where we laughed together and gossiped, and basically had a good time . . . Does that make me a bad mother?'

'I don't think so. Do you feel the same way now? Because, if you do, then I'm here now, I'll help you in whichever way I can . . . We'll go out, we'll do spa days again and go shopping, clubbing, have lunch at the swanky bistro, just like we used to. We could even do stuff together, you, me and the twins – the cinema or one of those soft play centres.' Sam grimaces. 'OK, maybe not that . . . but I'll babysit them, so you and

Nathan can have time together. How about that? I'll set aside a weekend once a month, it'll be my way of making it up to you.' And the minute the words are out of my mouth, I feel even more terrible – like the worst person on earth – because I made that promise once before and didn't follow it through. But I will now, I definitely will. Things have changed for me too – going away, ruining Tom's surprise, and then Dad being ill; it's all just made me realise what I really want, what's most important, and it's the people closest to me. That's what matters.

'It's all right,' Sam says, graciously. 'Not sure I'd want to babysit a pair of teething toddlers unless I really, really had to. It's hard work, and I realise now that I'm just not the earth mother I always thought I would be. Baking is my passion, not eco nappies and broccoli blending! Don't get me wrong, I love the twins, I adore them with every fibre of my being, I really do. But I'm just not cut out for childcare – I get bored. No, that's a lie; I don't just get bored. I get scared. Scared of what I might do.' Sam pauses and finishes the last of her Pimm's.

'Go on,' I say gently.

'Oh, please don't look so worried, it's not so bad now.' She manages a wry smile before lifting the jug to pour us both another drink.

'So what's changed then?'

'Talking to Christy. My own mother, the one who ran away when I was a child! Because, Georgie, since having the girls,' she pauses to take a deep breath, 'I've felt exactly the same way on occasion. I've wanted to run away. Hell, one night I even packed a suitcase and drove off for a few hours or so along the coast, leaving Nathan on his own wondering what was going on – it was the night before the nanny interviews and I had convinced myself employing a nanny meant that I was a rubbish mother. A failure.' Oh God, it all makes sense now. No wonder there was tension between Sam and Nathan on that day. No wonder Sam was hypercritical of the candidates, convinced one of them had bruised Ivy's little cheek – she was feeling vulnerable and inadequate. 'And that really scared me . . . because I could so easily have jumped on a plane and gone far, far away.'

'But you didn't. You came back, and that's the difference.' My mobile rings. I ignore it. This is important. Very important. And if it's Tom calling, I'm sure he'll understand when I explain later. But right now, I have to be here for Sam. 'I'm so sorry for disappearing when Christy turned up out of the blue like that,' I continue, unsure of what else to say.

'Don't be. I should have told you,' Sam says.

'What do you mean?' I crease my forehead.

'I asked her to come!'

Whaaaat? I had no idea.

'But how? When?' *And why didn't you tell me?* Is what pops into my head. But I quickly figure this isn't about me – it's like Dad said, we never really know what is going on in someone else's life.

'Well, I had been pondering on it for some time. Being pregnant made me think a lot about my own childhood, which naturally led on to Christy and how she could have left me. Anyway, I got a private investigator to track her down,' Sam says calmly, and I feel terrible that she went through all this without telling me. She senses how I feel and adds, 'Nathan didn't know either . . . it was something I just had to do on my own. I was worried that if you or he were involved, got to know her, then she'd have a connection, a hold if you like, a way to reach me later, if I didn't like her or want her in my life after all.'

'It's OK,' I say softly. 'The most important thing is – how do you feel now?'

'It's strange, but Christy and I get on really well. I don't hate her, or feel any resentment. We've talked so much and she's been really honest with me. She says she tried really hard too, to be a good mother, but felt inadequate. She says at the time, all those years ago, she thought I'd be better off without her, which is why she went.' Sam stops talking and we sit together in silence for a while, just sharing unspoken thoughts.

'Oh Sam . . .' It's me who eventually speaks.

'It's OK. I was in a bad place but I did something about it. I made changes; I got some help, at home and at work. It's all good now. Promise.' She grins.

'You got a nanny?'

'A manny! He's called Benedict, or Ben, as he prefers . . .'

'Mmm, well, that's a bonus,' I say, as an image of Benedict Cumberbatch instantly springs to mind.

'Ha! I know what you're thinking, and I'm not ashamed to say that my interest was definitely piqued when the agency called to "talk about Benedict". They had another manny too, but he was called Malcolm . . .' She pauses, and we both pull a face before going, 'Naaaaaahhhhh,' like a pair of silly schoolgirls. And it feels brilliant to be sharing a joke with Sam again. I've missed her so much. And the relief that we've managed to find a way forward is overwhelming, but then we have been friends since childhood, and friendships like ours don't crumble and disintegrate that easily, I know that now. It's like a marriage in a way, through good times and bad, we have to work at it . . .

'Sounds as if things are sorting themselves out then?' I say.

'Yep. I feel so much better now. It's as if I can breathe again, especially now we've had this conversation – a part of me hated not sharing it with you. You're my best friend – no, scrap that, you're like a sister, the family I never had.'

'Ah, well, I think you're amazing. And that's why I love you.' I put my arm around her and she rests her head on my shoulder.

'I love you too, Georgie.' I squeeze her tight with my free arm. 'You know, I also feel as if a huge burden has been lifted off me now, that it wasn't my fault Christy left – you know how I worried as a child.'

'I remember.' The Haribo Strawbs. The stories of princesses in castles. I remember it all.

'Christy said that at first she chased after the glitz, the glamour of LA as a way to block everything out, but soon regretted leaving. The problem was, it then became too late – she didn't know how to come back.'

'But she's here now.'

'Yes. And plans on staying. She's making a real effort. It's made me realise that not everyone is perfect but, as long as we try, then that's all right!'

I nod. I couldn't agree more . . .

23

The following morning, I wake up to the sound of my mobile vibrating across the nightstand, but before I can answer, it rings off. And it wasn't Tom calling me last night – it was a number I didn't recognise and there was no message. Then, when Sam and I had finished talking, we went for a walk along the beach, so it was after midnight when I fell into bed – too late to try calling Tom again.

My mobile rings again. Ah, maybe it's him. My heart lifts. Oh. My heart sinks. It's another number I don't recognise. I quickly answer, guessing it must be something to do with the regatta that starts in . . . I glance at the clock, about two hours. OK, at least I won't have to run into town today. Phew.

'Georgie! My dear, how are you?' Gulp. It's Isabella. I fling myself into a sitting position. I'd recognise her breathy Italian voice anywhere. But why is she calling me? On my mobile! I didn't even know she had my number. Oh God, here we go, I bet she's calling to have a word about the disaster that is the Carrington's sponsored regatta. Eeeep!

'Um, err, yes, I'm fine thank you.' Silence follows. 'And I'm so sorry, I didn't mean for any of it to happ—' I start blabbering like an idiot, quickly figuring it best to get in there first before she berates me for 'somehow managing to ruin it all'.

'Let's do lunch. Today!' she cuts in, leaving me to wonder if she even heard what I said.

'Oh, um, sure . . . That would be lovely,' I fib, crossing my fingers and praying that by lunch she actually means at lunchtime – the music festival kicks off at 3 p.m. and I *must* be there to make sure everything runs smoothly for Dan. I can't afford another disaster, certainly not with someone as high profile as him; that would be insane and bound to push Mr Dunwoody over the edge. But then I really don't think Isabella is going to take no for an answer.

'Good. We'll dine on board. Do you remember where our berth is from the soirée?'

'Yes, I think so.'

'Wonderful, see you at one.' And she hangs up. Eeek, two hours, blimey – should be OK. I hope. At least the festival is right next to the marina, so not too far to run, again, if I have to. And then I realise . . . I forgot to ask if Tom was coming for lunch too. He's bound to be, surely, isn't he? And he must have calmed down by now as I can't imagine he'd be OK with Isabella inviting me to lunch otherwise. Brilliant. Today is going to be so much better than yesterday. And I can't wait to see him – to get everything sorted out. Sam and I are back on track now. I just need to talk to Tom and then things between us will be like they were before I went away too. Happy and totally loved up. I send him a text.

Looking forward to lunch later, can't wait to see you xxx

*

The second day of the regatta gets off to a great start. I've just popped into Max's gourmet food marquee and been shown how to roll a *temaki* by Mr Nakamura.

'Mm-mmm. This is delicious,' I say to Sam. She's taking a break from selling cakes, while Stacey and the rest of the waitresses from the Cupcakes At Carrington's café hold the fort. Nathan and Ben have taken the twins over to the face-painting tent and Christy has gone to view an apartment just along the coast in Brighton – seems she really is planning on sticking around this time.

'Try this. It's incredible.' Sam pushes a California roll into my mouth. 'Good, eh?' I nod in between chewing and swallowing, feeling pleased that she seems to be back to her usual cheery self.

'Oh God, that's so good. What shall we go for next?' I say, eyeing up the giant wok where Mr Nakamura's assistant is tossing succulent garlic-coated king prawns into coriander-infused noodles. 'On second thoughts, I probably shouldn't eat any more; I don't want to spoil lunch.'

'No, you don't!' Sam pulls a face. 'Georgie, do you really have to go?'

'Well, I can't really back out now. As much as I'd love to spend the day with you . . .' I grin. 'Plus, it'll be really nice to actually see Tom and start sorting things out.' Last night on the beach, I told Sam all about Vegas and Andorra and . . . well, the whole blooming lot.

'Hmmm, well, rather you than me. Not that it really matters what she thinks . . . What I don't understand is why you are so bothered?'

'Well, she is Tom's mother, and they're really close,' I say, feeling a bit feeble because, actually, Sam has a very good point.

'But he's a grown man – you don't need her approval. Tom loves you, that's all that matters. And it's not as if he's a mummy's boy; he doesn't live with her, or let her rule his life. OK, they may be close as in they chat on the phone, but that's probably because she's travelling all the time. That'll be why she calls him every day – guilt! And trust me, I know all about that.'

'True, but if we're to have a future together, then it'll be so much easier if we get on. I just want her to like me, I guess.'

'Fair enough. And she did seem a bit frosty towards you that time at the soirée . . . Luckily, Nathan's mum Gloria and I get on really well. I can't imagine how strained it might be if we didn't, even if she did tell me I should give up work and make it easy for myself by being a stay-at-home mum.'

'She said that?' I pull a face. 'Oh dear. But you love your café.'

'I do, and it's a part of me. You know how special it is. It's like a legacy from Dad; he helped me get it in the first place, remember, and I'd quite like to pass it onto the twins one day, that's if they're interested in baking and keeping the good people of Mulberry in cakes. They may want to join a circus, for all I know, and that's fine as long as they're happy.' Sam shrugs. 'But, still, Gloria meant well. I just don't think she realised that going to work is my way of having a break. Toddlers are a lot of work, it's a marathon sometimes. I take my hat off to stay-at-home mums;

it's a full-time job in itself. Exhausting, and the last thing you want is a difficult mother-in-law – not that she is that yet, but maybe, perhaps one day. Oh, you know what I mean. So I guess I can see your point. But can I give you a tip?'

'Sure. I've really missed your advice, Sam,' I grin, and she grins back.

'Just don't try too hard. You're brilliant as you are, good enough, and Tom is lucky to have you. His mother, too. She may be Queen Isabella, but that doesn't make her the boss of you, superior somehow . . . Remember that!' Sam says firmly, shaking her head and making her blonde corkscrew curls bounce around furiously.

'I'll try. It's just that it's hard sometimes. You know, Tom and I come from such different worlds. He grew up in a castle set high up on an Italian hillside over-looking the Mediterranean Sea. Bit of a contrast to the cramped maisonette that was my foster carer's home.'

'So! It's not where you come from. It's who you are inside.' Sam folds her arms as if to underline the point.

'But what about the carousel and the ice-cream van turf war? Isabella might blame me.'

'Ah, don't be daft – it's not your fault the carousel guy got into a fight, or any of the other stuff you told me about. You did your best. Honestly, Georgie, stop blaming yourself for everything.'

I raise my eyebrows. 'Err, you're a fine one to talk.' I grin and nudge her gently with my elbow.

'Hmm.' She pauses, seemingly deep in thought. 'God, I've been a nightmare, haven't I?' Sam rolls her eyes.

'No you haven't. Besides, didn't you know? It's all my fault. Everything that goes wrong in the world is always *all my fault*.' And we both laugh.

'Come on you, let's get you to Her Majesty's luncheon,' Sam says, calming down. 'You mustn't be late or we'll never hear the end of it – how you "somehow managed to ruin" that too! Honestly, if she starts going on, then just tell her to shove it, and then come and find me. I'll feed you cake, lots of it, just like I always have . . .' Sam loops her arm through mine and we practically skip off towards the entrance to the marina. And I can't stop grinning; I'm so glad to have her back. My best friend, Sam, she really is incredible. And after everything she's been through, it sure does put things into perspective.

*

It's exactly 1 p.m. when I arrive at the yacht, and a guy wearing a navy blue polo shirt with matching shorts is waiting to greet me.

'If you'd like to come this way,' he smiles, and leads

me onto the main deck where Isabella is ensconced in amongst a mountain of cushions, next to a table laden with every kind of delectable food imaginable – there's even a centrepiece silver platter piled high with oysters packed in ice. I inwardly breathe a sigh of relief at having managed to resist Mr Nakamura's prawn noodles. And I'm guessing there must be other guests coming, as there's enough food here to feed a trillion people several times over. With a bit of luck, Tom will be here very soon.

The guy disappears. Isabella has her head bowed in a book. She doesn't seem to be hurrying herself to acknowledge me, so I seize the moment to glance at my mobile (Tom hasn't replied to my text) before stowing it in my tote. I wonder if I should sit down. Seems a bit rude to assume, so I hover. And hover some more, before Isabella eventually snaps the book shut and beckons for me to sit opposite her.

We sit in silence before she finally lifts her shades and says, 'You know how it is when you're nearing the end of a book? I find I can't possibly put it down until the last word has been read.' I nod by way of agreement, although I'm not sure I would ignore the arrival of a guest in favour of finishing a book – no, I'd much rather savour the last chapters to enjoy alone. But, each to their own, and all that. 'So, how are things, my dear?'

'Um, yes, good thank you. The regatta seems to be going very well today, so far . . .' I start, feeling uneasy. I wish Tom would hurry up and get here, this is really awkward – I feel as if I'm in an interview or something for an important job, which I guess I am in a way – girlfriend to her son! But surely it's up to Tom and me to decide on our own personal business, not her. I always feel as if she's scrutinising me, seeing if I measure up. And then, as if she can see inside my head, she says,

'Splendid. And do try to relax, please! You look nervous, and there really is no need to be – I'm so happy that we're having this time together, just the two of us.'

'Oh, are Tom and Vaughan not joining us then?' I reply, trying to keep my voice breezy and even.

'Vaughan has gone to watch the yacht races on the other side of the marina. And I didn't invite Tom. I thought it would be nice for us to have some girl time together.' And she actually grins. Oh God. I swallow hard and try to relax as she suggests. But it's not easy; she's not like anyone else I've ever had lunch with. She's so – I ponder momentarily – *regal*, is the best way to describe her, and it makes me feel inadequate, despite what Sam says. I know it's all about who we are as people and not the material stuff but, truth be told, she scares the life out of me.

'So, I understand that you met Marco yesterday.' Uh-oh, too soon . . . She knows about the turf war! She must do.

'Um, yes, that's right,' I say, helping myself to some water and wishing my hand would stop flaming shaking as I lift the bottle. And then, as if by magic, the servant, or whatever he is, appears to relieve me of the tedious task of having to open the bottle all by myself.

'Thank you,' I say, after he fills a glass and slides it towards me. Isabella shoos him away when he offers the bottle to her.

'Oh, Marco is such a character! But you mustn't be put off by that ghastly tattoo.' She shakes her head. 'He was very impressed with your organising of the regatta.' *He was?* Blimey! And after I forgot to visit him in his factory and all. But how nice of him not to land me in it with Isabella. I make a mental note to swing by his van later to thank him. 'Yes, he said that you and your team were very "on the ball", I think was the phrase he coined. That you "stepped up and could definitely be counted on in a crisis". So that's nice.' She flicks her hair back before popping a big black grape into her mouth.

'Wonderful, he's very kind,' I say, thinking: *if only she knew*.

316

'Yes.' She pauses and pulls a curious face, as if the notion had never occurred to her before. 'I suppose he is.' She nods by way of clarification. 'So, dear, tell me, did you enjoy your trip to New York?'

'I did, thank you. Although, with hindsight, the timing could have been better.' I take a sip of water.

'Yes, sorry about that! It was a little naughty of me.'

'Pardon?' I splutter and inadvertently knock over the glass. Water cascades onto the table and over the side. 'What do you mean?' I grab a napkin and dab at the crisp white linen tablecloth. The servant re-appears, but Isabella shoos him away and carries on talking as if nothing has happened. Cringe.

'Oh, Kelly and I go way back, that's how I organised the trip for you,' she says, nonchalantly, before helping herself to an oyster, tossing her head back and devouring it in one.

'Organised it? But I don't understand, I thought Kelly had spoken to Gaspard as he wanted some help, to, um, design a collection for . . . the ordinary woman,' I say, suddenly feeling very conscious of how small-town I sound. Oh God. I ponder on an oyster, not having tried one before, but quickly change my mind – what if I don't like it? I can hardly spit it out now.

'Well, yes, he did. And it was such fun organising it all. But don't you see?'

'See what?' *See that you deliberately engineered things so I'd be three thousand miles away, and right before the regatta, such an important event for Tom, not to mention Carrington's. Why would you do that? Why would you go out of your way to make things difficult for me? And potentially ruin things for Tom and Carrington's after you specifically warned me not to?*

'That I had to be sure,' Isabella says, wiping her fingers on a linen napkin.

'Sure of what?'

'That you weren't like the other one . . .'

'Other one?'

'My dear, you're not the first woman my son has been in love with.' She has the grace to avert her eyes while I inhale sharply through my nostrils before surreptitiously letting out a long breath. I don't want her thinking I'm getting huffy. I can handle this. I hope. I'm a grown woman, even if I do feel like a ridiculous jellyfish right now. I'm literally trembling all over. This is hideous. I wonder if she's barking, you know, as in proper bonkers, because I have no idea what's going on here.

'Um, sure . . . of course, I know that,' I fib, but what else can I say? When the truth is that Tom has never really talked about his previous relationships. I know he's had girlfriends, but I've always got the impression

318

that it was casual, that he was more focused on his career; he's certainly never mentioned actually being in love with anyone before. Not to mention that this is as awkward as hell. I really don't want to be chatting about my boyfriend's relationship history with his mother.

'Then you'll know how she broke his heart. How devastated he was, how it ruined everything. He lost his focus – his mojo, if you like – and he very nearly lost everything he had worked for. It wasn't long before he got involved in Carrington's – Camille, his aunt, had sold him her shares, hoping it would help to refocus him, and it did, although somewhere a little more,' she pauses to pick her words carefully, 'exclusive, would have been preferable . . .' Ah, I see, so that's why she went with the Mulberry Grand Hotel for her catering at the soirée – Carrington's is too provincial for her. 'Anyway, I was wrong,' she carries on. Oh! Maybe I judged too soon. 'I allowed myself to be swayed by my husband's lack of interest in Carrington's but, after seeing it for myself, I popped instore while you were in New York, and it's actually really rather splendid. I was very impressed with your personal shopping suite, and the girl that you had left in charge is so sweet. Nothing was too much trouble; you've trained her very well, my dear. In fact, everyone was full of praise for you.' I do a half-smile, thinking, that's nice, but I do wish she would get to the point. 'But you see, I didn't know very much about you before then, and I wasn't going to stand by and let the same thing happen to Tom again.' I drop my eyes to my lap and study the pattern on my dress, wishing I were anywhere but here. Surely this is Tom's business, not hers. Isn't it up to him who he goes out with?

'What I do know is, that if Tom had wanted me to know about his past relationships, then he would have told me himself.' I lift my head to look her straight in the eye.

Silence follows while she stares right back. And there's no way I'm breaking the eye contact. Sam's right, I am good enough. More than good enough.

And then she laughs.

Throws her head back and does a proper big belly laugh.

Oh my God. What the hell is going on?

'Perfect!' she says, leaning across the table towards me. 'My dear, why don't we eat and really get to know each other and I'll explain why I thought you needed the trip to New York.' *Hmmm, curious!* She gestures grandly over the food mountain in front of us, before lifting a pair of silver tongs and selecting a seeded bread roll which she places on the side plate to my left. 'Tuck in!' And the way she says it, adopting a plummy Home Counties accent, makes me want to laugh – though I don't, of course.

'Oh, um, sure . . . OK,' I say, figuring it best to go along with her because, to be honest, what else can I do? This whole scenario feels a bit surreal, a bit parallel universe. She's definitely a control freak. She might even be a bit cuckoo. I break off a piece of the roll and push it into my mouth.

'Here's to us. And Georgie, don't look so petrified, I don't bite.' She laughs, but I'm not so sure. Eek! I manage a feeble grin, and she smiles, a proper smile, before pressing a button on the panelled wall beside us. A few seconds later, the guy in the navy polo shirt and shorts combo appears. 'Let's have fun. A bottle of champagne.' And the guy is duly dispatched to the temperature-controlled cellar, or wherever it is the good stuff is kept on board a yacht. 'So, was the trip truly amazing?' she asks, eagerly.

'It was pretty exciting. The apartment I stayed in was awesome; it had its own concierge and a bed so enormous I had to do a running jump to . . .' My voice trails off when I realise that she probably thinks I'm a looper – I'm sure a swanky Manhattan mansion is the norm for her.

'I'm so pleased you liked it. I thought you might.'

'Have you been there before then?' And she does a gracious giggle.

'My dear, the apartment belongs to the family. And you can stay there whenever you want to – a long weekend with Tom, perhaps,' she says, pleasantly. *Hmm, maybe, if Tom forgives me* . . . The waiter re-appears with a bottle of champagne in an ice bucket, which he sets down beside the table. Silence follows as he fills a flute for each of us.

'Um, yes, that would be lovely,' I say politely, thinking, blooming hell, I had no idea – how on earth did she manage to organise it all without Tom knowing? And then it dawns on me, maybe Tom was in on it – he was quite keen for me to go to New York! And the basket of flowers he had delivered to me on arrival! How did he know where I was staying? I can't even remember if I had given him the address. On second thoughts, I don't think I did, and I'm not entirely sure how I feel about that. But before I can dwell on it further, she continues.

'Did you manage to see all of the tourist spots?'

'Yes, we visited all those places that I've only ever seen on TV before in, you know, shows like *Sex and the City* and more recently, *Girls*,' I say, trying to find common ground, but then I bet she never watches television – this is a woman who has a Nobel prize for her pioneering work in global economics. I bet she much prefers watching TED lectures or whatever in her leisure time.

'Oh yes, wasn't *Girls* a hoot? Rather good, I thought, although *Gossip Girl* has to be my favourite.' And I'm flabbergasted. Well I never. Maybe we have more in common than I ever imagined.

We sip champagne and help ourselves to more food – gravlax with dill, quail eggs; I even try a tiny forkful of caviar and instantly wish that I hadn't when I have to discreetly swill the salty little balls down my throat with a big swig of champagne – until, eventually, I pluck up the courage to ask why she engineered the trip to New York in the first place.

She places her flute on the table and dabs at the corners of her mouth as if deep in thought before she replies.

'You remind me so much of myself.'

'Really?' I say, creasing my forehead.

'Oh yes. Don't be taken in by all this . . .' She gestures around the deck. 'My dear, it hasn't always been this way. How is your father, by the way?'

'Err, he's recovering well, the surgeon reckons he'll be up to travelling home soon,' I say, feeling flummoxed by her sudden change of topic, and noting that she's deftly managed to avoid answering my actual question.

'Oh gosh, is he ill?' She clasps at her neck dramatically.

'Yes, I, um . . . I thought that's what you meant.' I swallow hard.

'I'm sorry, no. I meant his . . . misfortune. Prison. Something like that takes a long time to get over.' I glance away, wondering exactly what else Tom has kept from me – like having told his mother about Dad going to prison. No wonder she was frosty at that dinner in the private dining suite and then at the soirée – probably horrified that her son had hooked up with the daughter of an ex-con. So I wonder what's changed. Why is she being quite nice to me now? Surely it can't just be because she heard good things about me on her trip to Carrington's?

I decide to brave it out. Gone are the days when I would have been mortified. I made Dad my guilty secret for far too many years and it just made me an easy target for people to judge and bully, especially at school. But I'm older and wiser now. I take a deep breath and look her in the eye again.

'Yes, it does take a long time to deal with. And he's coped remarkably well – turned his life around. I'm very proud of him.' I pause. 'But I'm intrigued to know how you knew about it. Did Tom tell you?'

'Oh gosh no. Tom is a gentleman – you know that.

And so he should be, given his expensive education. Tom would never gossip about something personal, not even to me. He's very loyal. No, Gaspard mentioned it . . . He and I also go way back. We dated for a while at university, before he came out and admitted that he preferred boys, that is – only to the inner circle, of course, the group of friends that he trusted.' She smiles as if reminiscing a whole lifetime ago. 'Times were different then – it was the Sixties and still illegal to be gay.'

'Illegal?' I say, thinking how ridiculous that was, as if it was some kind of lifestyle choice. Or a crime even. Hardly.

'Yes, seems preposterous now, doesn't it?'

I shake my head in disbelief and think of Eddie and Ciaran, and wonder how they would have coped if they had been born just a few decades earlier.

'Anyway, as I said – I see so much of myself in you. I was just the same when I first met Vaughan's family – the wealthy Carrington dynasty, or so it seemed. I was in awe, having come from a far more modest background back home in Italy. My stepfather worked in an olive grove and my mother was a cleaner. You know, my father went to prison too . . .' *Blimey!* I'm speechless. It takes me a few seconds to respond.

'I'm sorry.'

'Don't be. He was a nasty drunk and got into a bar brawl where a man died. I was a toddler at the time. My mother kept up the monthly prison visits for a while, but then she met my stepfather, and well . . . that was that,' she says, pragmatically.

'Wow! But I just assumed you were . . .' I stop talking, unsure of what it is I really want to say, but rapidly realising what Marco meant now with his 'not that they always had it, mind you' line.

'Everyone does,' she says, quietly. 'But no, I did well for myself, I was smart, I learnt languages at school, figuring they'd be most useful, and I was right – I got a special scholarship to a school in England and then a place at Cambridge University. I was very ambitious and had already embarked on a successful career in business and economics when I met Vaughan. That's the difference between us – he's not at all ambitious. No, I'm the one who built our empire.' She casts an eye over the deck, glorious in the midday sun, while I surreptitiously glance at the wooden maritime clock embedded in the Maplewood-panelled wall. It's 2.30 p.m., so there's still time for me to make it to the music festival, and Dan isn't on stage until 5 p.m.

'But then, I was the one who knew what it was like to struggle, to have to go without. I guess it spurred me on . . . made me more determined.' Isabella laughs.

And I know exactly what she means. I left the care system with my whole world stuffed inside a couple of black sacks and a jaded social worker to guide me. I was on my own, eking out a junior sales assistant's salary as best I could. 'No, what Vaughan and I had in common was wanderlust! I had a yearning to travel, so did he. It's how we met, actually – on safari in Zanzibar.'

'Yes, Tom told me. It sounds so romantic.'

'Did he? Well I never. Funny isn't it, what we remember? I used to tell him that story when he was a child – embellish it a bit, of course. Each time there were more lions and tigers, and elephants so close you could touch their trunks.' She shakes her head in amusement.

'Ah, that's nice,' I say, trying to imagine Tom as a little boy – I bet he was really cute; all curly black hair and big, velvety-brown eyes.

'It was, but that yearning to see the world has never really left me – I guess it's why we move around so much now. Remember, I had spent my whole life, until I came to England, in a primitive little village in a remote part of Sicily, where they all presumed I would be a good Catholic girl – marry and settle down to have lots of babies at the first opportunity. But I wanted more.' I chew my lip. She's right – we do have stuff in common. And I'm still not sure I want to have babies, even if I have satisfied my yearning to see a world outside of Mulberry-On-Sea. 'And I saw that wanderlust in you.' She enjoys another oyster followed by a sip of champagne. 'That's why I arranged for you to satisfy your desire to see something more, before . . . Well, let's just say that I did it to protect Tom too.'

'To protect him? I don't understand . . .'

'My dear, he's so in love with you, anyone can see that. You'd have to be blind not to. And it's only natural to want to see the world. You're young, I was just the same . . . but I couldn't risk him getting hurt all over again, undo everything he's achieved since he turned Carrington's around – not when he's on the brink of expanding the empire, as it were. Not if you weren't ready.'

'Ready? I am ready, I love him too.'

'I know you do, my dear. I can see that now, and please forgive me if I was a . . . um,' she hesitates momentarily, 'a little distant with you at first. Lots of girls can appear quite charming at first, only to then show their true colours. I think you met Zara, my dear friend Kelly's daughter?' Isabella closes her eyes briefly and lets out a long sigh.

'Err, yes, I did have that pleasure,' I say, remembering how awful Zara was.

'So I do hope you can understand why I was wary.' She reaches a hand across the table and pats my arm.

'I can. We both love him very much,' I smile, placing my hand on top of hers and giving it a gentle squeeze.

'Marvellous. I think you and I are going to be the greatest of friends.' She beams. 'But I'm curious . . . Tell me, why aren't you wearing the ring?'

'The ring?' I squeak, the smile freezing on my face. What is she going on about? And, just when we were getting on so well, maybe she is crackers after all. Oh well, I guess it's not the end of the world. It could be quite fun, in a fabulously eccentrically bonkers kind of way. She'll be like the Dowager Countess of Grantham in *Downton*, making me laugh with her hilarious one-liners.

'That's right. Ahh, I get it, you're a modern girl, have you got it locked away for safekeeping? I don't blame you. It's a beauty. I gasped when Tom showed it to me. And I was so delighted – I knew you were the one for him and I couldn't be happier. Between you and me, I never liked that other girl – the one who broke his heart. Last I heard she had run off to Tinsel Town to try her hand at adult movies.' Isabella pulls a face.

'Err, I'm sorry, the ring? I have no idea what you're talking about.'

'The engagement ring. Oh gosh, you did say yes, didn't you?' She makes big eyes and leans forwards towards me. 'He was so excited planning the weekend – the helicopter ride, the picnic, the breathtaking view. Just perfect.' She beams and claps her hands together.

Oh my actual God.

Nooooo. No. No. No.

Not only did I ruin my thirtieth birthday surprise, I ruined my own ring moment. Tom was going to propose!

The deck sways. My hands are trembling. My mouth drains of saliva. What have I done?

'I have to go. I'm so sorry Isabella. I've really enjoyed our lunch, but I err, I'm expected at the music festival right now, I forgot the time,' I babble before standing up, placing the napkin on the table and lifting my bag off the seat beside me.

'Yes, yes of course. I totally understand. You must go; I mustn't keep you from making the regatta a success. Goodbye, my dear. Perhaps we can do this again, another time.' And she smiles, kindly. A proper smile. I stop moving.

'I'd like that very much.' And I would, I really would. But right now, I have to find Tom. I've got to see him. Go all out to apologise. No wonder he was too annoyed to talk to me when I phoned him from Vegas

Airport. And who can blame him? I know I would be mightily irked if I had gone to all that trouble to arrange a brilliant birthday surprise and proposal bonanza weekend only for it to crash and burn at the last minute. It might not be so bad if he had actually seen me at the airport, at least then he would have known I had tried, that I was there after all. . . . No, I need to find him and make it up to him. And *fast*.

24

Five minutes later and I'm at the entrance to the marina, next to the Hook, Line and Sinker pub, and the music festival is just about to start. Marco's van is in place, maybe he's seen Tom – I head there on the off-chance, figuring it has to be worth a shot.

'Sorry, love, not seen him around, but then there are so many people here, I could easily have missed him. Maybe he's in hiding, you know, to escape the crowds,' Marco laughs.

'OK. Thank you. And for what you said to Isabella – that was very kind.'

'Ah, don't be daft.' Marco bats the air with his hand.

And then I have an idea. A brilliant one. Well, two in fact. One that might just make things all right between Tom and me, if I can pull it off. It would be even better if I could do it today, but there's no way – I have something else in mind for that.

'Can I ask you a favour?'

'Sure. Hop in and tell me what it is . . .'

*

The Mulberry Mittens, a glamorous all-girl Golden-Era vocal group are singing a big-band-style number when I make it to the music festival – all crimson movie-star red lipstick and Forties pin-curl roll hairdos – they look sensational. They finish their last number and the huge crowd cheers and claps as they head off stage. I look around, chuffed to see so many people, girls mainly; trillions of girls in Dan Kilby T-shirts – chanting his name and shouting out declarations of their love for him as they hold their mobiles up in the air to take Snapchat pics of the stage. Some even have DK stencilled on their faces with makeup; others have photos of him, presumably on the off-chance of getting close enough for an autograph opportunity, and lots of them have flowers, pink carnations – I'm guessing in tribute to his new album, which has a pink carnation on the cover. The atmosphere is amazing, buzzy and charged, just how I imagine a One Direction concert to be, or like a proper festival, a mini-Glastonbury, or a Party in the Park, only much better because this is on an actual beach. And the sun is gloriously hot, making the mood happy and summery; everyone is smiling and laughing and having a wonderful time. I love it. I just need to keep my fingers crossed that my plan will come together with Tom and everything will be perfect.

I whizz around to the side of the stage and duck into the VIP area at the back.

'Hey lady, how are you?' It's Annie, and she looks radiant.

'Not as good as you by the looks of it. You look sensational. Wow!' I smile, taking in her white halter-neck playsuit and long chestnut curls loose around her shoulders.

'Thank you. Oh G, I'm going to burst if I don't tell you.' She does a little squeal and claps her hands together.

'Go on,' I say, suddenly desperate to know her news right away.

'Dan has asked me to have a drink with him tonight, just the two of us . . . When he comes off stage, he asked me to meet him here and then we're going to his boat.'

'Oh my God. Annie, that's amazing. But tell me, when did this all happen?'

'Well, we kind of got chatting while you were away; obviously I had to talk to him quite a lot. To, um, you know, make sure I got everything organised properly for the green room – his favourite fruit, snacks, drinks, relaxation methods, favourite shower gel, Cher let us have one of the en-suite bedrooms upstairs in the pub, that kind of thing . . .' She grins, counting off Dan's perceived requirements, one by one, on her fingers.

'Obviously. In fact, I would have been extremely disappointed if you hadn't bothered; it was a vital part of your role as team manager.' I grin, going along with her enthusiasm.

'Anyway, we kind of got close, and then he called me last night, on my mobile . . .'

'I'm so happy for you. And good luck, Annie, I truly hope he's your one.'

'Thank you. I hope so too.' And she heads over to the refreshments marquee that Cher has set up especially for the performers.

Jared, from Mulberry FM, is standing near me with a young boy of about sixteen who looks familiar. I think he might have been on last year's *X Factor* and asked to leave at judges' houses and, by the glimmer of terror in his eyes, I'd say he'd rather be anywhere but here. A rotund woman hovering nearby grabs his face and gives it a big squelchy kiss before wiping her fluoro pink lipstick stain off with a tissue.

'That's my boy. You show 'em son, you're ready

now. You really are! Whoop whoop.' And she practically drags him towards the steps leading up to the stage.

'Hey, Georgie. You made it. How's it going?' Jared beckons me over once the poor boy and his awful stage-mum are out of earshot.

'Good thanks, no disasters today, thank God,' I say, scanning the backstage area just in case Tom is here somewhere.

'What do you mean?' Jared creases his eyebrows.

'Oh just, you know, the stuff that went on yesterday . . .'

'I wouldn't worry about that. I heard from our news team that the local constabulary want to shake your hand – apparently they had been after that guy at the carousel for some time, so they're delighted that you effectively handed him to them on a plate as it were.'

'Really? Well, um, that's nice,' I grin, thinking how things have a funny way of turning out. Today sure has been full of surprises – who would have thought that Isabella and I would now be the best of friends?

'Yep, sure is. And the festival is going really well. I'm surprised Dan isn't here, though. His security blokes are, and his manager said he has a routine he likes to go through before going on stage – get a feel for the crowd, that kind of thing. He's cutting it very fine.

Perhaps you could give him a call and chivvy him along; the crowd are starting to get impatient.'

'Oh, sure. I'll get onto it right away.' I'm just about to call when my phone rings. Lawson's 'Juliet' blares out. Jared, who's still standing nearby, looks up from his clipboard, rolls his eyes and shakes his head. He's not a Lawson fan obviously.

'Babe, it's Cher.'

'Oh hi Cher. How are you?'

'It's Dan, he's been taken hostage!' she cuts straight to the point.

'What do you mean?' I ask, thinking this must be some kind of joke.

'Exactly that! Hostage. Handcuffs. Locked to the bed. He was here in the green room one minute, tuning his guitar and chanting – I never knew he was a Buddhist: so cool,' she pauses to catch her breath. 'Anyway, some groupies turned up, ran in, body-slammed him and cuffed him to the bed. And now his manager is going mental. He only stepped out of the room for a second to get some drinks and they were in! Like athletes on the racket they were. And now they've barricaded the room, so we can't even kick the door in.' She inhales sharply.

'Oh my God. But he's due on stage any minute now – the crowd will go berserk if he doesn't turn up.

Shouldn't we call the police?' I ask, racking my brains for the fastest solution.

'That's the first thing I said, but his manager said not to. Not until we have, and I quote, "exhausted all the options", I think he's worried about the media getting wind of it and blowing it all out of proportion.'

'I see, OK, I'm on my way. See you in a minute.' I end the call before turning to Jared who, after over-hearing me mention the police, is now standing right next to me with a concerned look on his face.

'What's going on?'

'That was Cher! Apparently Dan is being held hostage by some crazeee groupies in a bedroom at the pub.'

'Bloody hell.' He runs a hand through his hair. 'You're joking, it's a wind-up, right?'

'I wish it was.' I toss my phone into my bag and go to leave.

'Hold on.' Jared puts a hand on my shoulder and I turn back to face him. 'I'm coming too.' He looks frazzled.

'But you can't, what about the music festival? Aren't you in charge of it?'

'Yep, but if Dan isn't here to go on stage, then what's the bloody point? He's the headline act, the one all these people have come to see. And he's supposed to

be on stage in ten minutes! He can be a bit fashion-
ably late – the crowd will wear a short wait – but not
a no-show.'

Jared races over to a guy wearing big headphones
and thrusts the clipboard into his hands while simultaneously motioning for The Mulberry Mittens to get
back on stage pronto. The guy nods back at Jared and
gives him a man-hug. Jared is back beside me. We run
as fast as we can out of the backstage area, across the
pebbles and into the Hook, Line and Sinker pub.

Cher, looking totally stressed, comes bombing over
to us.

'What a nightmare!' she puffs, chewing her gum
frantically. 'I'm so sorry—'

'It's not your fault,' Jared says, standing next to Cher.

'If it's anyone's fault, then it's mine.' A guy steps
forward, running a hand through his hair. 'I'm Dan's
manager by the way.'

'Pleased to meet you,' Jared and I say.

'I really think we should call the police,' I suggest
again, thinking it could take ages to talk the fangirls
round and we just don't have the time. 'They'll probably panic if the actual police turn up, and open the
door in any case.'

'But Dan won't thank me if this turns into a media
frenzy, and that's exactly what will happen if we call

the police in. There are already paps hanging around on the beach hoping to get the money shot before he goes on stage.' He shakes his head.

'OK, but we have to do something, because I'm sure as hell not telling the crowd that their idol, who they've been waiting months for, and now all day to see, here in their hometown of Mulberry, isn't turning up,' Jared says. 'And what if they want a ransom? Or have set traps and stuff up there that get triggered when the door goes in? Do you know how to diffuse a bomb, because I sure as hell don't!' We all stare at Jared, goggle-eyed and speechless.

'Look, why are we hesitating? This is ridiculous. I vote for calling the police and getting them to kick the door in. Done. We can chase away the paps or something,' I say, knowing if we don't sort this out soon and get Dan on the stage then that massive crowd will hate Carrington's for promising their idol and then letting them all down. That's hardly going to foster good relations in the local community – those girls, the DKers or whatever they call themselves, are definitely a force to be reckoned with. Plus, they're customers, their families too. Mr Dunwoody will be raging when he has them all beating a path to his constituency office to complain.

'Please, no police! Jared, you've obviously been

playing too many games on your Xbox or whatever. They're teenage girls, they don't have bombs or traps or anything,' Dan's manager says, trying to laugh it off, but there's a dart of fear in his eye. A short silence follows while we all stare at each other.

'Look, if you're adamant about no police involvement, then I have another idea,' I say, pulling out my notebook. I thumb through until I find my list of contact numbers.

'Go on,' Jared says.

'You'll see.' I rush to punch out the number and luckily he answers right away.

A few minutes later, and commando man – the owner of the Mulberry Sound and Vision TV shop is running full pelt towards us like he's auditioning for *The Hunger Games* – he's wearing full-body black neoprene with a padded section to protect his vital organs, has a coil of thick rope in one hand and a proper bow and arrow in a holster slung over his left shoulder. He comes to a halt in front of me.

'You rang!' And for some ludicrous reason I have to stifle a laugh. I don't know if it's the bizarre circumstances I'm in, or that he looks totally ridiculous, but I cover my mouth with my hand and will myself to get a grip, truly hoping he does actually have some combat experience and doesn't just like dressing up.

'So what's the MO?' he asks in a deadly serious voice, his face set like concrete.

'Um, MO?' I ask, baffled.

'Modus operandi?' commando man explains.

'Dan is being held hostage in one of the bedrooms upstairs and we have no idea what ammo they have in there.' Jared offers a brief summary, throwing Dan's manager a pointed look.

'And we need to get him out and back to the concert in like . . .' Dan's manager pauses to check his watch. '*Now!*' He paces up and down. 'Jesus, the fans will go mental if we don't get him there. But we must do it with the minimum fuss possible. If the media get wind of this, those fans will implode. I'm telling you now, they live for Dan, and I sure as hell don't want a mass suicide on my hands.' He stops pacing.

'Which room is it?' commando man asks Cher.

'Follow me.' And she goes to show him the way, but he swiftly places a hand on her arm to stop her.

'Just tell me.' Cher points to the room above us.

'Right. I'm going in.' And commando man strides off upstairs. We follow close behind. He stops on the landing and puts a finger to his lips, presumably so as not to alert the groupies who are singing 'Sweet

Sugar' at the tops of their voices from the room at the end of the corridor. 'Stand back,' he whispers, lifting his right foot up as if to boot the door in.

'Hang on. What are you doing?' Dan's manager hisses, his face creased with concern.

'Have you got a better idea?' commando man mouths.

'Um, no, but what if they have set up a trap on the door?' Dan's manager whispers back.

'Hmm. OK, I'll find another entry point.' And he runs back downstairs with us all following close behind.

We're in Cher's private garden at the back of the pub now, and commando man has lassoed a length of rope up and over the roof. And, oh my God, he's shinning up a drainpipe, just like Spider-Man, he's that fast; because, within seconds, he's smashed through the bedroom window. And all hell breaks loose. Teenage girls are everywhere after fleeing the room and racing out of the pub – screaming and shrieking, jumping up and down and flapping their arms around. There must be at least ten of them in the garden now, blaming each other and saying stuff like 'grow some tits' and 'bore off and die'. Commando man appears at the window gripping Dan's arm up in the air like a trophy and the screaming intensifies to near hysteria with them surging forward and shouting, 'Ohmigod he's sooooo quiche!'

'Now you can call the police!' Dan's manager bellows to me, before bombing back into the pub to get Dan and race him to the stage.

25

What a day! And it's a welcome relief to see the regatta drawing to a close. The still-warm sun is sinking slowly when I make it to Carrington's, and the last of the regatta visitors are dawdling on their way home – eating ice creams and candy floss, the children being carried, sleepy but still clutching their helium banana balloons.

'It's all ready for you, my dear.' It's Mrs Grace, and she gives me a conspiratorial wink. And I gasp. It's so much better than I ever imagined. I rang Mrs Grace from inside Marco's ice-cream van and asked if she would mind leaving the beautiful twinkling lights in place for a very special last event – a surprise for Tom! And, right on cue, my phone buzzes with a text message reply from him.

OK. See you at 9 x

And my hands tremble with relief. Relief that he actually got the last message I sent, also from Marco's van, asking if he could join me for a very special 'apology picnic' here inside the Carrington's tunnels, where it all began, where we first met. I was going to come up with some pretext to lure him here, seeing as it's pretty obvious by his silence that he's still cross with me, but I figured it best to be honest about my intentions, something I should also have been months ago, instead of dithering when he asked me to move in with him.

'You'd better hurry; he'll be here soon. Come on, I'll give you a hand – best be organised before he gets here.' Mrs Grace grabs the blanket and the cushions from my arms and leads me further into the tunnel. 'There's a brilliant spot just around this corner.' And she shows me a glorious little opening where the four tunnels come together in a circular junction; it even has an old-fashioned lamp on one wall and carved low wooden benches running around the sides. 'I thought you could put the cushions on the benches and lay the picnic out on the blanket in the middle – like in a Bedouin tent. My Stan's niece did exactly that for her wedding breakfast and it was wonderful. We all sat around on the floor, very bohemian.' She smiles, getting into the romance of it all. 'Mind you, my Stan is still moaning about his stiff knees, and it was months ago now.' She shakes her head with a look of sheer exasperation on her face.

'It's perfect, and you didn't have to go to all this trouble . . .' I lean in to plant a kiss on her bony cheek.

'Oh, it's no bother, I'm just pleased to see you two lovebirds so happy. And here,' she hands me an old-fashioned cassette player. 'I've put a lovely romantic Frank Sinatra tape inside. Play it so Tom can follow the music to find you.'

'Thanks so much.' I busy myself by scattering the cushions – I don't have the heart to tell her the truth, which is that I have a lot of making up to do, if Tom and I are to be 'lovebirds' again.

'Did you bring the champagne and the picnic food?' she says, her eyes lighting up.

'I sure did,' I point to the two carrier bags on the floor beside the blanket, thanking my lucky stars for the new bakery. After the fangirls dispersed, eager to see their crush on stage, I raced over to the food marquee and managed to get the last of the ready-made sandwiches, some cakes from Sam and a box of strawberries, bags of crisps and a chilled bottle of champagne from the One Stop Shop opposite the pier.

'Here, we can put it all in this.' Mrs Grace lifts out an original Fifties picnic hamper from under one of the benches. 'Far nicer than carrier bags. I "borrowed" it from the summer display instore – nipped up there just after you rang me – and got these too . . .' She flings open the hamper to show me a selection of those gorgeous melamine Orla Kiely plates and bowls. 'And there are two champagne glasses – I swiped them from Homeware; we'll just put them back in the morning and nobody will be any the wiser,' she chuckles as we start unwrapping the food and loading it onto the plates. I tip the Twiglets into a bowl – Tom's favourite – and glance at my watch. It's almost time!

'Right, I'd better be off. Have fun.' Mrs Grace gives me a hug before disappearing off into the dark of the tunnels.

I sit on a bench to wait for Tom. Ahh, I can hear footsteps, it must be him. I smile and plump up the cushion next to me, but he doesn't appear. Maybe it was Mrs Grace making her way outside instead . . .

I pop a big strawberry into my mouth, unable to resist, and immediately regret it when Tom arrives. My tummy flips and my heart soars. He looks incredible as always, in jeans and a white polo shirt that shows off his glorious tan – like warm caramel – and he smells amazing, of chocolate and spice.

'Oh, um . . . I wasn't expecting you to come from that direction,' I squelch through a mouthful of strawberry, jumping up and flinging my hand over my face to cover the truly unromantic mess I'm making. I duck down to grab a napkin from the blanket and quickly wipe my lips.

'Sorry, did I startle you? I know these tunnels like the back of my hand. I came via the Mulberry Grand Hotel, the tunnel we ran along at Christmas time when we went up to the ice rink on the roof. Do you remember?' he says, pushing his hands into his pockets. And how could I forget, it was the most romantic night of my life? But that's a whole other story.

'Yes, I do. It was amazing . . .' There's a short silence. 'And no, you didn't startle me, I was, err, just expecting you to arrive from . . .' My voice trails off as I wave a hand nervously before stepping closer to him. But he takes a small step back and away from me. So he's definitely still annoyed with me, then.

'I followed the music. Shall we sit down?' He gestures to the blanket.

'Um, sure, would you like a sandwich?' I ask, sitting down too and offering him the plate. He shakes his head.

'No, thanks. How's your dad?' He lies on his side, propped up on one elbow.

'Oh, yes, he's much better thank you.' God, I hate this. It's like we're strangers. Not lovebirds, as Mrs Grace called us, at all.

'Good.' He pushes his dark curls back from his face. 'So when did you get back?' he asks.

'Oh, not until yesterday morning, can you believe it?' I start speaking, too fast, and he frowns. 'But it wasn't my fault, it really wasn't, there was a strike at the airport in Toulouse and I had to get a train and . . .' I stop talking.

'So is that why you didn't call me on Friday? I was expecting to hear from you . . . when we last spoke, you said you'd call when you got home. I was . . .' He pauses as if deliberating on what words to use, '. . . surprised not to hear from you.' He looks me straight in the eye.

'I'm sorry,' I say quietly. 'Tom, I truly am. And not just for not calling on Friday – it was chaos at the airport and then my battery died somewhere near Bordeaux and then by the time I had charged it up, I had to get to the regatta. Then I called you as soon as I could, but you . . .' Silence follows.

'Georgie, I was devastated when you didn't turn up in Vegas.' He gets straight to the point.

'I know, and I was too,' I say. 'Tom, I really am so sorry for ruining your surprise. I did try to make it right, but you didn't see me.'

'What do you mean?'

'I came to Vegas, I made it to the airport as you were leaving.'

'Oh God, did you?'

'Yes, but it doesn't matter now.'

'Well, it's a shame I missed you, but it's not just that . . .' He picks at a loose thread on the blanket.

'Oh. What is it then?' I fiddle with the hem of my dress, rolling it up tightly over my knee before letting it go and starting all over again.

'Look, Georgie,' he clears his throat. 'There's no easy way to say this . . .' Oh my God! No. Seriously, noooooo, surely not . . . Him being angry that I ruined his surprise proposal is one thing, but surely he isn't about to dump me over it? I will myself to keep quiet, having made the mistake in the past of jumping in and making it all a million times worse. I inhale sharply and hold my breath. 'But I'm just not sure how committed you are to this relationship. I guess what I'm saying is that, if you want out, then, well . . . then I'll understand.' He looks away and a shiver trickles down my spine. He'll understand? But I don't want him to understand. I want him to want me. And then I remember what Isabella told me – he's been hurt too. I can't blame him for wanting to put on a brave face, not after I've let him down too.

'But Tom, that isn't what I want at all. It isn't, please, please believe me.' I move closer to him and place my hand on his arm. 'Tom, I love you. I really do. You're

351

my one. Why would you think I want out?' I look up into his eyes.

'Because . . .' He pauses, 'Can I have some of that champagne?'

'Um, sure. Here.' I lift the bottle and flip open the cork in one swift movement; it bounces off the wall and lands on my head before plopping into my lap, but neither of us says a word, whereas usually we'd laugh. Tom picks up a glass and I pour. He takes a mouthful.

'Why don't you want us to live together?'

'But I do,' I say, trying to keep my voice even as I place the bottle on the bench.

'Do you? Because it seems to me it's the last thing you want. You were too preoccupied to remember my surprise for your birthday, which kind of tells me I was far from your mind while you were in New York, not to mention whenever I've mentioned you moving in with me, you've laughed it off or—'

'Oh Tom, that's not it at all. I want us to live together, I really do, I just thought we should talk about it first, you know, sensibly like adults, because it's not just a case of me packing a bag and coming to your place. But there never seemed like a right time or indeed *enough* time. It's what I want more than anything, and being away from you has just made me want us to live together even more. And I truly, truly am sorry for messing up Vegas.'

Tom takes my hand in his and his shoulders soften. He finishes the champagne and places the glass on the blanket before moving in closer to me. I tilt my face to his. 'And I know you made loads of effort to make the weekend special, the prop—'

There's a noise. There's someone here.

What's going on?

'Meredith?' She's standing behind Tom.

'Shut up,' she hisses. And, oh my God, she's got a knife in her right hand. And now she's crouched over Tom with her arm around his neck. Instinctively, I lunge forward, but Tom somehow manages to struggle to his knees.

'Georgie, stay there!' he shouts in a deadly serious voice, before lifting his palms up into a 'surrender' position. He tries to turn his head to face Meredith, but she tightens her grip.

'Meredith, what the hell are you doing?' I say, my voice trembling. Her eyes are massive, manic almost.

'Doing what I should have done years ago.'

'OK. Let's just calm everything down,' Tom says slowly. 'I'm sure we can sort this out. Tell me, tell us . . . what happened years ago?' Tom's voice is shaky and it scares me.

353

'Oh, you think you're smart,' Meredith spits, the knife glinting in the light from the lamp. 'Well, you won't fob me off that easily. I won't be fooled for a second time by you Carringtons. You think you can do whatever you like. And *you!*' She quickly flicks the knife in my direction before catapulting it back into place at Tom's neck. 'You think you have it all. With your Mr Carrington. Walter, he was my Mr Carrington.' Oh God! A trickle of sweat snakes a path down my spine. Betty was right. Meredith still bears a grudge. But it happened years ago . . . 'But you won't take him again. You won't steal him away from me.' Oh, sweet Jesus, she thinks Tom is Walter, aka the Heff. 'Oh no you won't.' She shakes her head vigorously. 'Because I won't let you. I won't. I won't. I tell you I won't. If I can't have him, then nobody will.' She babbles, almost incoherently now, and I'm *really* scared. And a part of me feels sorry for her. She's obviously not well – having some kind of mental breakdown. In my peripheral vision I spy the champagne bottle on the bench. I could do it, I'm sure. If I'm quick. I could grab the bottle and hit her. Throw her off balance so Tom can sit on her or whatever. My heart clambers inside my chest. I have to do something. What if she plunges the knife into Tom's neck? He's scared too – I can see it in his eyes. And he's spotted the bottle as well. He flicks his eyes to it, and then straight back to me. But it's no use, as Meredith cottons on to what we're up to and drags Tom towards the bench, just close enough so she can swipe the bottle onto the ground and out of my reach. All the while keeping the blade of the knife dangerously close to Tom's windpipe. Champagne fizzes and swirls across the blanket, drenching my legs, but I can't move, I'm frozen to the spot.

'Meredith, I'm not going anywhere,' Tom says. 'I'm here, right here with you.' Ah, Tom has worked it out too and is going along to appease her. Meredith looks confused for a moment and her face softens, only to crumple into a hideous grimace before she tightens her grip once more. And then a sudden movement catches my eye, followed by an almighty screech.

'Aggggggghhhhhhhhhh.'

It's Mrs Grace! Back in the tunnel and right behind Tom, with her granny bag held up high in the air with both hands. And in one swift movement she crashes the bag against the side of Meredith's head, propelling her prostrate on the blanket. Tom seizes the moment, leaps up and snatches the knife still clutched in her hand, and stabs it into the solid wood bench. Mrs Grace pounces, ninja-style, straddling her spindly legs across Meredith's back, whacking her again with her granny bag. Meredith lets out a whimper before her body sags in defeat.

*

It turned out that Meredith actually had a full-on breakdown all those years ago, when Walter, aka the Heff, had told her he was going to leave his wife Camille and marry her. Meredith had seen through her part of their pact and left her husband, told him everything about the affair, only to have it thrown back in her face the following day when Walter back-tracked, leaving her high and dry, destitute and alone. The saddest part of it all is that Meredith was pregnant with Walter's babies, twin girls that she later had to give up for adoption because she couldn't cope on her own – it was the Sixties and she was a young single mother without a job or a place to live after her husband refused to take her back.

Mrs Grace, being an old softy at heart, had sneaked back down to the tunnels to make sure my plan went without a hitch, which is how she came to be there when Meredith pounced. Mrs Grace recognised her right away, remembering what had happened and how unstable Meredith had been at the time – but had been under the impression that Meredith had rebuilt her life, working in local government. Anyway, it turns out that when Meredith had to come back to Mulberry to work on the regatta for Mr Dunwoody's office, being in such close proximity to the Carrington family set her back and, well, she relapsed, but is now getting treatment. After hearing all about Meredith's sad tale, Tom was happy to leave it at that, and not involve the police.

26

One week later . . .

The glorious smell of creamy-sweet loveliness fills the hazy afternoon air as Tom and I leap out of the taxi and practically run, hand-in-hand, to meet Marco. He's waiting at the main door to the factory. Once inside, and gowned up in white coats and not-so-fetching hairnets, my heart does an actual leap. It's just how I imagined. It's just like Willy Wonka's chocolate factory but, instead of chocolate, there are huge vats of sugary, milky mixtures churning away. Tom squeezes my hand.

'It's exactly how I remember. Come on, let's get involved,' he shouts over the hum of ice cream being made, his face beaming, and it makes him look instantly younger. And I'm so pleased. I wanted to bring him here, to see him have some fun, just like he did as a child, on those rare occasions away from his private tutors.

'Have fun, you guys. And Georgie . . .' Marco moves closer to me. 'It's all here for you.' He winks and I give him a covert grin before grabbing Tom's hand and leading the way.

We see waffle cones being made and one of the factory workers hands me a giant scoop.

'Give it ten big ones,' he instructs, and points to a sack of brown sugar on a workbench beside a giant chrome blender. Laughing, Tom and I take it in turns to add the divine-smelling granules – all warm and cosy and reminiscent of my baking days as a child with Mum. Wonderful. We're then handed jugs of caramel flavouring to tip in too. Next, dollops of waffle mixture plop from chrome pipes to be cooked on hot plates and then scooped up and swivelled into cone shapes before being conveyor-belted over a cooling mechanism and into boxes all ready for distribution. It's amazing how a sequence of metal machines can make something so delicious.

We move on to the actual ice-cream section and, oh my God, I don't know where to start first. There are massive containers everywhere with all kinds of scrumptious ingredients in – strawberries, blueberries, raisins, cherries, jelly beans, Smarties, peanut butter cups, it's all here. We're like kids let loose in a giant sweet shop.

'Go on, get stuck in.' Marco reappears carrying a big bowl of hot cookie dough. 'Here, tip it in Tom.' And he does. We both stand transfixed as the dough hardens inside the cold creamy mixture before being chunked up by a big blender. We move on to the next vat, chocolate this time, and Marco gestures for me to pour in the hot chocolate sauce. It smells incredible. Rich and velvety. And the same thing happens: the smooth, creamy dark mixture hardens before being broken up and blended into the ice cream. So that's how chocolate chip ice cream is made! I always wondered how the chocolate chunks stayed hard even when the ice cream is soft. It's like magic, much like this place. And to my left are a dozen plastic tubes, each with a different coloured liquid flowing through, all ready to be dispensed into individual sections. Lollies. Oh wow! But the best bit of all is the giant Perspex tube right in front of me – rainbow sprinkles are whizzing all around before cascading out onto the lollies. It's amazing.

We move on to the next part of the process and Marco gestures to the picture on the giant sheets of wrapping paper to be cut and sealed around each lolly. Fab. Oh my God! A real blast from the past. I haven't had one of these in years.

'Wanna try one?' Marco takes two lollies from a

packing box at the end of the conveyor belt and hands one each to Tom and me. Delicious. Strawberry, vanilla and chocolate layers with a truly scrumptious rainbow sprinkle top tier. Treble mm-mmm!

'Georgie, this is brilliant. Thanks for organising such a wonderful surprise,' Tom says, in between licks of his lolly. We got the early train this morning from London to Scarborough, which gave us loads of time to finally have the talk that I had hoped for – just me and him and no distractions. In other words, no secret visits and meetings about the new store, no impromptu trips to New York, no bungled surprises, or crazed women with knives at his throat – none of those shenanigans: just two ordinary people enjoying a day trip in the glorious sunshine. So lovely. And I've never ventured this far north before. The lush rolling green countryside from the train window was spectacular; easily as good as the Grand Canyon, I reckon – although I have yet to watch *Thelma and Louise* as per Eddie's suggestion. That was followed by grassy cliffs overlooking the electric blue hue of the sea. There's even a castle. It took my breath away. I know I can see the sea every day, but the beach up here is different – wild and evocative and in total contrast to Mulberry, where it's calmer. Tranquil, and then touristy in season.

'Well, you know me . . . I'm really good at surprises!' I tease. Tom shakes his head.

'Hmm, that's debatable! You ruined mine, remember, and then your "apology picnic" in the tunnels turned into a disaster.' And with a cheeky look on his face, he swiftly leans away when I go to play-punch his arm. We both grin.

'Well, that was hardly my fault. How was I to know she had a personal vendetta against the Carrington family?'

'And my neck still aches . . . .' He grins, tilting his head from side to side as if to emphasise the fact.

We had a proper heart to heart after the regatta, and Tom admitted that he'd been angry at first – furious, in fact, which is why he'd avoided talking to me for a bit in case he said something he might later regret. But he was devastated and hurt too, just as Dad had predicted he might be. But, interestingly, he hasn't mentioned his planned proposal in Vegas.

'Come on, there's more.' I take his hand to distract him from his neck issues. Tom doesn't know that Isabella inadvertently told me about the engagement ring; I called her when Tom was showering after Meredith's knife attack, and explained everything to her. She totally got it and agreed to keep it just between us, as I really didn't want him to feel even more angry or hurt about the whole ruined-surprise thing than was necessary. I had spoiled his moment, yes, inadvertently, but still, I imagine your own girlfriend not turning up to your planned wedding proposal is a massive thing for a man. Or a woman. And then to find out that your mother had let on about it all by mistake – well, I guarantee that I would still be reeling if the situation had been reversed and my plans had fallen so flat. But, hopefully, today will go some way in making it up to him. Bring back a cherished childhood memory too.

'Gosh it's warm in here,' I say, making big eyes at Marco, and he knows what I mean right away. He leads us through a door into a changing area.

'Why don't you two get those hairnets off and pop outside to cool down?' Marco gestures towards double doors while surreptitiously giving me a look when Tom isn't watching.

'Cool down? But it's sweltering outside; even hotter than Italy is at this time of year.' Tom laughs as he pulls off his hairnet and hands it back to Marco. I do the same.

'Follow me.' Taking Tom's hand, I push through the double doors and out into the sunshine at the back of the factory, and there, just as I had planned with Marco on that day at the regatta, is a bona fide, proper vintage ice-cream van. It's painted a glorious sky-blue colour and has Rossi Ice Creams stencilled down the side in baby pink lettering.

I run towards it, keeping hold of Tom's hand so that he has to follow too, until we're standing right outside the open serving hatch.

'Wait there!' I run around to the other side and jump in the van and quickly find the box marked Harvin – it's exactly where Marco said it would be, on the dashboard. And, right on cue, 'Greensleeves' chimes out of the Tannoy. I pop my head out through the hatch to see Tom grinning and shaking his head in amazement.

'What can I get you, sir?' I laugh as I pretend to serve him.

'Um, I don't suppose you have a Screwball by any chance?' Tom plays along, and I could kiss him right now. So I do. I had banked on him going for a Screwball; it was his childhood favourite, after all.

I fling open the freezer cabinet lid, and there, where Marco said it would be, is the Screwball. I bounce out of the van and whizz back around to stand opposite Tom.

'Here you are.' After ripping the plastic top off, I hand it to him with a little pink plastic spoon. 'But you must eat it really quickly,' I say, barely able to contain my excitement. He looks so thrilled with his Screwball. 'I'll help you.' I push my spoon into the raspberry split ice cream too.

'Hey, what's the rush?' Tom laughs, gently nudging my spoon out of the way so he can get more ice cream for himself.

'You'll see.' And then, 'Ta da!'

'What's this? Where's the bubble gum? I was going to let you have it, seeing as you were never allowed it as a child.' Tom frowns.

'Aw, you're just too kind and thoughtful.' I grin. 'But this is *my* surprise, remember?' I take the Haribo sweet ring and push it onto the tip of his little finger. 'Tom, can I ask you a question? Well, two questions really,' I say, trying to sound casual, but my heart feels as if it's about to burst right out of my chest, it's clamouring that fast. Tom tilts his head to one side.

'Sure,' he says tenderly, with a quizzical look on his face. I take a deep breath and go for it, remembering Dad's sage advice about being 'so busy trying to avoid getting hurt that we forget to enjoy the good bits'. After everything that's happened recently, I'm going to concentrate on enjoying the good bits from now on.

'Good. Um, err. Right, here goes . . . question one – can Mr Cheeks and I please move in with you now?

Like tonight, if you'll still have us, of course, because you may have changed your mind after, you know, well, what with everything that's gone on . . . With me spoiling your Vegas surprise and then you being held at knife-point . . . well, I wouldn't blame you, it's OK, really—'

'Stop talking.' Tom gently lifts my chin to look me straight in the eye. His eyes search mine momentarily. And then his face creases into a massive smile. 'At last.' He laughs. 'Georgie Hart . . . she say yeeeesssss. She will move in with me. It's a miracle. Hal-le-lu-jah!' And, after lifting me up, Tom twirls me around and around. I feel as if I'm flying on top of the world as the warm summer air mingled with the delicious aroma of ice cream flows through my hair.

After everything that's happened, it's made me realise just what really counts when it comes down to it. What's important to me – Tom, my friends, my family; that's what it's all about.

Eventually, we pull apart and, still holding hands, Tom gently bumps my arm with his.

'So, what else did you want to ask me?' And I can see that he's trying really hard to keep a serious face.

'Um . . .' I will my cheeks to stop flushing and my heart to stop pounding; even my palms are tingling, which only ever happens when I'm *really REALLY* nervous. But it's now or never – I've spent the whole

366

week rehearsing this inside my head. I may even have practised out loud in my bathroom mirror. And besides, it's not just me who has experienced heartbreak in the past, and who worries sometimes about it happening again – Isabella told me Tom has been there too. And I never even considered that, I just presumed he had lived a privileged, sparkly kind of life where nothing bad ever happens, but I know now, that perception is a weird thing and, underneath it all, we're actually just the same. Plus maybe it explains why he was a little cool about asking me to move in with him, citing it as the 'practical' solution; I guess he was just being cautious too. Besides, I'm a grown woman; I can take whatever life puts in my path, I know I can – not that I'm anticipating Tom will let me down, I don't think he will, and I'm excited about finding out what the future holds, together, if he'll still have me. And for some bizarre reason, the conversation with Eddie over that silly bet pops into my head – I wonder if the terms still stand, if I'm the one asking Tom to marry me? Eek! OK. Deep breaths, lots and lots of them. On second thoughts, maybe not, I'm starting to feel a bit dizzy. Right, I can do this. I open my mouth. I close it when Tom speaks instead.

'Actually, I have a question of my own,' he says, casually.

'You do?' I swallow hard, wondering if this is a good or a bad thing. I was going to do it, I really was . . . I open my mouth again, but he gently puts a finger to my lips.

'Shhhussshh. Ooops, oh hold on.' And he bends down. 'I've dropped the Haribo ring.' But he doesn't get back up; he stays down on one knee.

And oh my actual God.

I cup my hands up under my chin. I shiver.

Is this what I think it is?

'Georgie. Please will you marry me?'

It is! I freeze. *Scream.* And instead of retrieving the Haribo ring, Tom stands up and pulls a small red velvet box from his pocket, and winces.

'Tom! Are you OK?' Instinctively, I dart forward to help him as he bends over in obvious discomfort.

'God, I'm so sorry, I'm still getting twinges in my neck.' He stands up straight and pulls me in close. And then he laughs. A proper big belly laugh. 'Only joking.'

'Whaaaat? But I don't understand.' My forehead creases and my voice wobbles. Tom lifts my chin.

'Oh God, no, sorry. Oh Georgie. No, I didn't mean it . . . I wasn't joking about that. My neck is fine, honestly, look.' And he shakes his head around. 'Jesus. No, I've never been more serious in my life. I can't believe I've bodged it all up for a second time. You know I had it all planned – helicopter ride, champagne picnic, romantic moment with the Grand Canyon for a backdrop.'

'Oh my God. Really? Oh no! No wonder you were so cross with me. But in that case, I think you'll find it was me who bodged it up the first time around for forgetting to open the envelope.'

'None of that matters now,' Tom smiles tenderly, and my heart flips over and over, and I now know beyond a shadow of a doubt that this is what I want. I love him. I always have, right from the first moment I clapped eyes on him, standing by the help-yourself salad bar in the staff canteen, with my jaw practically on the floor. And I know I can't guarantee that we'll live happily ever after forever and ever, but something I do know is that one day I'll be old and have lived a life worth living. And that will be a truly awesome thing.

'So what do you say? Marry me!' And he flips open the box. I gasp. Inside is the most beautiful diamond ring I think I've ever seen. And not at all the style I thought he would choose. I imagined something modern and huge. A statement. A rock. Oh God, I'm doing it again – perception. I vow to make a concerted effort to relax, to wait and see in future, instead of trying to second-guess all the time. This ring is exquisite. And the box is worn, the gold lettering on the inside of the lid is all faded, and I instantly imagine a sophisticated flapper lady graciously accepting it from her beau. 'Is it OK? It's old – well, they call it antique. But I know that you like stuff with a bit of history . . .' Tom shrugs and grins, a little nervously.

'It's more than OK. It's breathtaking. Perfect.' And it is. It's an Art Deco diamond cluster tablet ring, already with a lifetime of memories attached. I tiptoe up to kiss his cheek, thinking he knows me so well. He lifts the ring from the box.

'So how about it, Georgie Hart. Me and you, what do you say?'

'Yes! Yes please. A trillion times . . . I'd love to marry you!' Tom slips the ring onto my finger and pulls me in close. I can feel his heart pounding right next to mine.

'It's going to be amazing,' he murmurs, nuzzling into the side of my neck, then tracing a path with his lips to my mouth.

'And I can't think of anywhere I'd rather be than with you, at home in Mulberry-On-Sea.'

'Ah, about that . . .' Tom pulls back to look me in the eye and I'm sure there's a hint of apprehension.

'What is it?' I smile tentatively, looking straight into his gorgeous velvety-brown eyes.

'Ah, you'll see.' He grins and gently lifts a stray tendril of hair away from my face.

'Oh, you're such a tease.' I bat his arm.

'It's a surprise!' he says, cheekily. And his beautiful face breaks into an enormous smile. It sure is. And one I'll definitely, definitely not be messing up this time around . . .

Epilogue

One year later . . .

The warm morning sun rises on the horizon as we stand back to get a better view.

'It's fantastic,' Tom says, taking my hand. 'I knew you'd make it perfect.'

'Wait until you see inside,' I beam.

'Hang on, there's something I must show you first.' Tom squeezes my hand and, after lifting his free hand, he points towards the main display window, which is concealed by an enormous white sheet. 'Any minute now . . .' He flings his arm around my shoulders and pulls me in close, treating me to a burst of his delicious chocolatey scent. And the sheet is whipped away by Winifred from the window display team; she does a quick thumbs-up to Tom before tapping her watch as if to say, 'right on cue, just as we planned'. Tom waves to thank her before she disappears back behind the scenes. And I gasp.

Oh my God! It's the Georgie Bag. The collection is right there in the display window of the new boutique Carrington's store, and it looks sensational. The satchels, top handles, coin purses and crossbody bags in a variety of rainbow brights and fluoro colours gleaming under the spotlights on a selection of little podiums, simple and understated, but perfect for summer and for the 'everywoman', as Gaspard likes to call us. There are even some bags in warm berry hues to take us into autumn/winter. I clap my hands together. Above the bags is a huge display sign hanging on lengths of crystal-covered wire under twinkling spotlights, with the words *GET YOUR GEORGIE BAG HERE* in swirly silver lettering. But best of all are the pencil drawings of me in Central Park – well, you can't tell exactly that it's me; they're in profile, they really could be any woman strolling in a park in cherry-red satin pedal pushers. But I guess that's the whole point – the normality, the 'everywoman' appeal of Gaspard's collection.

'It's brilliant.'

'So you approve then?' Tom grins, kissing the top of my head.

'I sure do. I absolutely do. I love it.'

We're in London. Well, Chelsea to be precise, and the ideal location for the new Carrington's boutique department store, designed to whet the appetite of well-heeled customers and entice them to come and see where it all began, over a hundred years ago, in the real Carrington's flagship store in Mulberry-On-Sea. After months of planning, meetings, persuasion and negotiation, Tom eventually managed to secure the leasehold for the building that had housed the old department store Mum and Dad used to bring me to for a treat as a child. Tom kept his promise, and told me as soon as he could, the very next day after I asked to move in with him, and he proposed beside that ice-cream van. He had wanted it to be a surprise, knowing how special this place was to me. And I can confirm that this is one surprise that has gone meticulously to plan.

Tom then promptly asked me if I'd consider coming back to Carrington's on a full-time basis – the board had all agreed that I was the best woman for the job: project manager to oversee the refurbishment of the glorious old Georgian building. Tom was suitably impressed by my organising of the regatta, especially my varied collection of notepads and highlighter pens and Pinterest pages, which he still teases me about, although he and the rest of the board never did find out about the punch-up over the carousel, or the ice-cream van turf war, or the queue for the tunnel tours, or indeed Dan being held hostage and very nearly missing his guest appearance. Isabella knows, Mr Dunwoody complained to her, citing something about going straight to the top. So patronising, especially when Tom is the one in charge of Carrington's, not Isabella. But after putting a call in right away to another old friend from her university days, who luckily now owns the *Mulberry Gazette*, in addition to a number of other newspapers in his portfolio, Isabella was able to make sure the planned 'carousel crunch time' story, complete with up-close and gory pictures of the fight, was instantly shelved. *Sky News* never did show footage of the regatta, either; something big happened in Toronto that day, which took precedence, luckily for Carrington's and the quaint little seaside town of Mulberry-On-Sea. And Isabella agreed with me that there was nothing to be gained from Tom and the board being told. Besides, the deal had already been done for the new store, far away from Mulberry-On-Sea where Mr Dunwoody had no real influence over planning or building regulations in any case. And he didn't get re-elected to Westminster – rumour had it that he had been fiddling his expenses, so he was very keen to keep a low profile and not make a fuss.

Of course, I jumped at the chance to get involved

in Carrington's new adventure, and bought some shares too, enough to give me a seat on the board. So, after today, I'm going to be the new Carrington's operations director, dividing my time between both stores – London and Mulberry. Making sure the staff are all happy and serving our customers with a smile. It's what I love best, and I'm looking forward to passing on everything I learnt from Mrs Grace, who's busy penning her second autobiography and enjoying a well-earned retirement.

And Annie was delighted when I asked her to take over my column for *Closer* magazine. She said it was the cherry on the proverbial cake, especially as she's all loved up again. That's right, she and Dan are in a proper relationship now. Luckily, the DKers fully embraced Annie; things could have got very tricky indeed if they hadn't, although Mel, Carrington's number one store detective, has been hacked off on occasion after having to herd them away from the Women's Accessories section – they like to gather at Annie's till to do Snapchat selfies with her while she's trying to serve proper customers.

As for our actual wedding, Tom and I haven't managed to organise it yet. We've been far too busy getting the new store ready for today's grand opening, but it's next on the calendar – probably a year from now. We just need to agree on the location. Isabella is keen on having it in Sicily, in the church on the hillside overlooking the village where she grew up, but Dad has hinted he wants it to be at Mulberry-On-Sea, in the little chapel overlooking the wild-flower field where Mum's grave is. Nancy is delighted too and is still holding out for a grandchild, and who knows what the future may hold. And I guess we'll eventually decide on the wedding too. You never know, it may even be a dual-location do, and why not? I know it'll be perfect, wherever it is.

Dad is full of health these days. I think what happened in Andorra gave him a bit of a scare, so he's taken up cycling now with Dusty on a special long lead; they go all over Mulberry and beyond. He says he needs to be fighting fit and ready to do the honours when it comes to my wedding. They made it back from Andorra, just about; Daisy conked out two streets away from the retirement complex and is now in a specialist VW restoration garage getting a new engine. Nancy has said that Daisy will make the perfect little runaround to take her to bingo, or maybe a jaunt along the south coast of England next summer . . . Certainly no hairpin bends on mountain roads, thank God!

We step inside the staff lift, a brand new gilt cage

replica – I was keen to keep the character of the original building, but figured we could really do without the staff getting trapped between floors.

'You're here!' It's Sam and she's glowing. She grabs my hand and almost pulls my arm out of the socket as she runs me into her new patisserie. Tom makes a more leisurely entrance and wanders off to take a look at the state-of-the-art professional kitchen. 'Ta-da! What do you think?' And I'm stunned. The last few times I've been here, Sam hadn't let me in, and even the glass doors had been covered over so I couldn't get a sneaky peek inside.

'Oh Sam, it's incredible.' And it is. It's just how I imagine a chic Parisian patisserie to be – all smoky brown walls with marble pillars and low lighting. Opulent flower arrangements cascade down china stands and sultry lounge music plays melodically in the background. And in the middle is a table piled high with cakes that customers can help themselves to – all kinds: enormous strawberry cream gateaux, delicate pastel-coloured macaroons, chocolate muffins, giant swirly patterned meringues and, of course, my favourite in the centre, a three-tiered cake stand bulging with magnificent red velvet cupcakes with buttercream icing. Mm-mmm!

'Have one if you like.' Sam takes a cupcake and a

napkin and hands them to me. 'I know you can't resist.' She laughs and I kiss her cheek.

'Thank you.' I tuck in right away, making a mental note to make sure we have loads of red velvet cupcakes at the wedding. I glance around. At one end of the patisserie, Sam has created another café – through an arch, complete with custom-built safety gate, there are lots of little tables and chairs. There's a soft play area too, and a juice bar. There's even a converted ice-cream van, which children can climb inside. Wow!

'Now I have the best of both worlds, I get to bake and spend time with Holly and Ivy,' Sam says. 'To be fair, it was Ben's idea.' Hearing his name, Ben looks up from the box of Lego that he's unpacking and waves over. Sam and I do little waves back before she nudges me. I nudge her back. We hastily turn around and go to leave – Sam sniggering and me desperately wiping buttercream icing from my face, which I wish would stop blooming flaming.

'Stop it. He'll notice,' I whisper, trying not to giggle as Sam loops her arm through mine as we walk away really fast like a pair of silly schoolgirls.

'I think there's a high chance he may already know that the pair of you have crushes on him.' Nathan appears behind Sam and, after wrapping his arms around her, he plants a big kiss on the side of her neck.

'Honestly, you two are incorrigible. Leave the poor guy alone.' We are all grinning as we head back to the lift.

'You wait until you see the brasserie,' Sam says, pressing the button to take us up. 'It's my dream come true. Who would have thought, all those years ago when Dad made me do that culinary course instead of the round-the-world cruise?' She's full of happiness as the lift whizzes us to the rooftop.

'I bet he'd be so chuffed, Sam.' I give her hand a squeeze as we step out of the lift.

And it's breathtaking, with panoramic views across the city; we can even see the Thames, shimmering in the sun. Christy, being an interior designer, has helped Sam to create something truly remarkable here. In addition to spending lots of time getting to know Sam and her family (Christy lives in Mulberry-On-Sea now – she decided against the flat in Brighton, wanting to be closer to Sam), she has gone to great lengths to make their reunion work. It's a joy seeing Sam so happy, and now that I've got to know Christy too, I can see that she and Sam are so alike. We get on well, too, especially after Christy apologised for being such a diva, throwing her pashmina my way that time. She explained that she was just so nervous after all those years apart from Sam, that the reunion moment she had played out inside her head a trillion times hadn't had a stranger in it, so when I answered the door she panicked and went all aloof. But she's really not like that at all. In fact, she's funny and down-to-earth and kind and caring . . . just like Sam.

I look around. There are real palm trees lining the route to the maître d's desk. There's even a giant fish tank embedded into the walls either side. Nathan and Tom head straight to the open chrome kitchen set right in the centre of the brasserie.

'It's like being in LA,' I say, weaving through the tables and stepping out onto the terrace. 'Eddie would be sooooo impressed.'

'Why don't you ask him what he thinks?' Sam laughs.

'*No!* Oh my God, is he here?' I yell, not having seen him since New York. We've FaceTimed and spoken on the phone, of course, but it's really not the same.

'I sure am, honeypie.' And he is too. Eddie walks out onto the terrace to join us. 'I wouldn't miss this for the world.'

'Group hug!' Sam flings her arms out and the three of us, BFFs, have a massive cuddle. We've been through so much together, a proper rollercoaster of good times and bad, but we've always been here for each other and long may it continue. My two best friends. They mean the world to me.

'Oh God, I'm getting emosh,' I laugh, wiping away happy tears as we break apart.

'Maybe this will cheer you up,' Eddie says, pressing something into my right hand.

'What is it?' I ask, opening the white envelope; inside is a wad of twenty-pound notes. 'Oh Eddie, you looper!' I grin on realising. 'But you didn't need to.'

'Well, a bet is a bet. And you did propose first, well, sort of . . . you put the Haribo ring on his finger.' He shrugs. 'But, honestly darling, please can you hurry up and book a venue already? At this rate, even the draughty village hall will be taken.' He pulls a face and I can't help laughing. I shake my head – he never changes. 'Oh, sweet pea, I'm so happy for you. Come here,' and he pulls me in close for another hug, followed by, 'right, that's your lot,' a few seconds later. He smirks and drops his arms to straighten his exquisitely cut Tom Ford suit.

Sam darts off and then reappears a few minutes later with a tray of drinks – flutes of pink champagne. She hands one to me and one to Eddie before taking a glass for herself.

'I propose a toast,' she says. 'To Carrington's!' We lift our glasses in the air and chorus.

'*To Carrington's.*'

Tom is here now, Isabella and Vaughan too, followed

382

by Nathan with little Holly holding his left hand and Ivy holding his right. They look so cute in navy polka-dot dresses. Christy is here too, looking far less LA and more proud mother and grandmother in a smart linen trouser suit with chiffon scarf. Ciaran arrives carrying Pussy in his arms – she's wearing a tiny pinstripe suit complete with bowler hat. Dad and Nancy are right behind them with Dusty, her black fur coat all shiny; she gives Pussy a superior look of disdain as she saunters past her. I quickly glance at Sam in case we're breaching a health and safety law.

'It's fine.' She shrugs, unfazed. 'Dogs are allowed in my brasserie!' And we all laugh.

Ah, I feel so happy having them all here. Tom moves in close to me and lifts my hair to whisper into my ear.

'I love you, Georgie Hart.' And my stomach flips over and over, just like it did that very first time he kissed me, in the moonlight on the pier with the waves lapping gently below us, and the shoreline twinkling in the distance.

'I love you too, Mr Carrington.'

I turn to the group and see that everyone has a drink now.

'I propose another toast.'

They all stop talking and gather around me. Dusty

nuzzles my hand and I stroke her velvety-soft ear. This glorious new store may signal the end of one part of my life – my time in Women's Accessories selling luxury handbags before moving onto the personal shopping suite in the pretty seaside town of Mulberry-On-Sea – but this, right here and now, with my friends and my family, well, it's also the start of something fresh and exciting.

'To new beginnings!' I lift my glass up high in the air.

And we all cheer.

'*To new beginnings!*'

Sam's
Recipes

Marco's delicious recipe for
homemade vanilla ice cream

Ingredients

4 free-range eggs, yolks only
100g (3½ oz) golden caster sugar

1 tsp cornflour, optional
300 ml (½ pint) double cream
300 ml (½ pint) full-fat milk
1 vanilla pod

Method

Before you begin, make sure that you have plenty of room spare in the freezer.

- To make the custard, separate the eggs, placing the yolks in a large bowl. (You will not need the whites for this recipe. You can use them to make meringues.)

- Add the sugar to the egg yolks and whisk until pale and thick. Add the cornflour (if using), and whisk well to incorporate into the egg yolks.

- Put the cream and milk into a medium saucepan. Cut the vanilla pod open lengthways and scrape out the seeds with the back of a knife, then add to the cream and milk. Heat the mixture until just below boiling. Slowly pour the hot cream and milk onto the eggs and sugar, whisking as you go.

- Sieve the custard into a clean pan, and set it over a very low heat. Stir the custard constantly with a wooden spoon, paying special attention to the corners of the pan, until it is steaming and has thickened slightly. The custard is ready when it coats the back of the wooden spoon and you can draw a clear line through it. This can take up to 10 minutes.

- Tip the custard into a large, shallow, freezer-proof container, and allow to cool to room temperature (you can speed this up by sitting the tub of custard in a large bowl of iced water).

- Once at room temperature, place a lid on the container and chill in the fridge overnight. Once chilled, transfer the custard to the freezer and take it out every hour, for three hours, to whisk it with an electric handheld whisk. This will disperse the ice crystals and keep it smooth.

- Then leave the ice cream in the freezer until it is solid.

- Remove the ice cream from the freezer ten minutes before serving, so that it's easy to scoop.

Make your own

strawberry and custard lollies

Ingredients

400g (14oz) hulled strawberries

150g (5oz) tub ready-made custard

Method

- Puree the hulled strawberries in a food processor or liquidiser then sieve into a bowl.

- Stir in the ready made custard and mix until smooth.

- Pour into six standard lolly moulds, add lollysticks and freeze overnight.

- To serve, dip moulds briefly in warm water then lift out of the moulds.

Kirsty
@LoveOfAGoodBook
interviews Sam

Q. Cupcakes at Carrington's is famous for its Red Velvet Cupcake. If you could create a cupcake that sums up your life, what would it be and why?

A. Ooh, such a brilliant question, it would have to be a chocolate cupcake with a swirly whipped cream peak smothered in a trillion red heart sprinkles, because I'm such a romantic and love playing Cupid.

Q. We know that Georgie loves her handbags and red velvet cupcakes, what are a few of your favourite things?

A. Baking – I love everything about it, I find it cathartic and cosy and delicious and... I could go on and on about how wonderful it makes me feel. Nathan – he's definitely my favourite man, and the memory of marrying him on that picturesque Italian hillside with the scent from the lemon grove in the warm breeze, is something I shall treasure forever.

Q. I am going to give you 4 names and I would like you to tell me what cakes springs to mind and why?

A. Georgie: Red Velvet cupcake, because I know it's her favourite.
Eddie: Lemon curd Queen of Hearts Tart, because he's wickedly acerbic with a heart of gold and very loyal... if he likes you!

Nathan: Triple-tiered Victoria sponge cake, because he's solid and traditional.
Mrs Grace: A lavender cupcake, because she reminds me of my granny who always smelt of lavender.

Q. Who inspires you in life?

A. Mary Berry! I love her, no... I actually want to be her!

Q. You are a great friend to Georgie and always there with helpful advice. If you could give one bit of advice to live your life by, what would it be?

A. Be happy, smile, eat cake and have sex if you want to!

Q. What are you hoping the future holds for you, Georgie and Eddie?

A. Lots of love, laughter and happiness. Oh, and plenty of delicious creamy-peaked cupcakes with gold glitter sprinkles.

Thanks for the questions Kirsty, do pop in and see me some time - we can share a cupcake or three xxx